BOOK OF SHAI

ALL HALLOWS EVE

A Novel

MICHAEL PENNING

ALL HALLOWS EVE

First edition. May, 2020
ISBN: 978-1-7771812-1-5 (paperback)
ISBN: 978-1-7771812-5-3 (hardcover)

www.michaelpenning.com

For my mother,
who helped me write before I could spell.

Chapter 1

Alice Jacobs stood at the edge of the wharf and stared at the sea in horror. Thousands of bones were washing ashore. They flooded the great expanse of Salem Sound with skulls and spines and fragments of skeleton that rolled and tumbled in the surf. An eerie clattering filled the salty air as wave after wave heaped bones of all shapes and sizes upon the rocky coastline. Sheltered in the calmer waters of Salem Harbor, a floating mass of skeletal remains swept in with the tide and inundated the merchant fleet. Their horrifying numbers swelled by the minute as they bobbed and collected between the timber hulls of the ships.

Alice's young daughter, Abigail, sidled up to her side and slipped her tiny hand into Alice's palm. "Where are they all coming from?" Her voice was small and uneasy.

"I can't say that I know, Abigail." A flutter crept into Alice's stomach as she gazed at the macabre panorama. Not for the first time since they had left Boston, she wished her husband was there with her. Samuel would know what to say; his were the words that comforted their little girl, not Alice's.

A bitter gust tore from the ocean. A shiver ran over Alice as the salty sea air landed on her skin. The pale orb of the afternoon sun was barely visible behind a thick veil of clouds. The cheerless October light did nothing to warm the dismal atmosphere. To the east, the long horizon where sea met sky was the dull grey of a frozen lake. Somewhere out over the open ocean, a storm was approaching.

Alice and Abigail weren't alone as they surveyed the unending swath of bones washing ashore. The long stretch of Derby Wharf was overrun with men and women of all social standings. It was a sight that was seldom seen in the prosperous decades since the War of Independence. Wealthy merchants and ship-owners pressed shoulder-to-shoulder with the very deckhands and dockworkers they employed. Humble seamstresses and housekeepers mingled with rich housewives from the Derby Street mansions. The weather-beaten planks of Salem's longest wharf flexed and groaned as they all huddled together to witness the dreadful phenomenon happening at sea.

With the crowd growing larger and more agitated by the minute, Alice drew Abigail into the folds of her cream-colored skirts. She tightened her own overcoat around her shoulders against the chill wind and straightened her bodice. Anyone who noticed her would have considered Alice to be a stunning woman. She had honey-blond hair that fell to her shoulders in ringlets. Her large eyes were the clear blue of glacial meltwater, and her skin had the softness of powdered sugar. She had a small nose that rounded slightly downward, like a tiny raindrop suspended above her full mouth. Her beauty was interrupted only by the white cleft of a small scar that curved across her plump bottom lip.

"What bones are they?" Abigail wondered aloud. The seven-year-old was a perfect miniature of her young mother, sharing the same striking eyes and flawless symmetry of features. Beneath her white overcoat, she wore a rose-colored frock with long sleeves and a round neck. A wooden doll dangled from her hand as she huddled against Alice's hip.

"Whale, missus," rasped a salty fisherman who had jostled his way through the mob. His weathered face was grim. "Those be whale bones. And dolphin and seal—the bones of all the sea's great beasts. The very oceans have turned to poison!"

Alice wrapped a comforting arm around Abigail's shoulders and gave the man a frown. Something in his voice had sent a prickle up her spine. The old salt wasn't merely unsettled by what he was witnessing. He was *afraid*.

A young boy's voice pealed from the multitude of onlookers. "Make way! Make way for Magistrate Holm!"

The crowd parted for an imposing man with massive shoulders and a barrel chest. Hamilton Holm was no longer a young man, but he still cut an intimidating image of physical prowess and strength. Only the barest trappings identified him as the town magistrate. He had the wide collar of his heavy greatcoat pulled up to his solid jawline, and he bore no wig to conceal a mass of hair that was only beginning to go gray. His head was square and compact like a bulldog's and his neck was thick with muscle and tendon. His face bore an unfortunate assortment of scars as souvenirs from his soldiering days.

An elderly gentleman trailed behind Holm with a wrinkled

hand clamped on the magistrate's sleeve to keep from being separated in the crowd. The man was tall and lanky, his shoulders wide and square like a doorframe while his back betrayed the slightest hint of a stoop. He had a long, thin face that was still handsome despite its age-worn creases. He wore no wig and the snowy white of his hair matched his well-trimmed moustache. As he struggled to keep up with Holm, he peered through the throng of onlookers from behind a pair of wire-rimmed spectacles.

The last of the crowd parted before him and the old man saw the terrible scene that had provoked such widespread distress. "God in heaven…"

"'Tis the work of the witch!" a voice cried from the crowd.

"She'll come for the children now!" another shouted.

"The coming of the prophecy is nigh!"

There was fear in their voices. Its poison scent hung thick in the air.

Magistrate Holm swung around. "We'll have no more such talk!" His pale eyes blazed as he glowered and waited for the crowd to fall silent, challenging someone to say another word. None did.

Nervous murmurs rippled among the townsfolk in the hush that followed. The news had spread to every corner of Salem and there was a rising tension among them, a constricting sense of dread mounting like pressure in a steam engine.

Holm strode to the brink of the wharf and motioned for his elderly companion to join him for a better view. "What do you make of this?"

The old man remained silent. His face was grey and pensive

as he tried to make sense of the ghastly event he was witnessing. His voice was low and brittle when he spoke. "'Tis the final omen."

Holm stiffened and gave the old man a sideways glance. "You haven't any other explanation?"

"No, sir."

"Nothing at all?"

The old man shook his head. "For seventy-eight years I have lived here in Salem—born here, as was my father, in the house built by *his* father. For seventy-eight years, I have witnessed the history of this town unfold." He looked the magistrate in the eye. "But never have I witnessed a sight such as this."

Holm frowned and drew a breath of salty air into his chest before letting it out. "Thank you, Mr. Emmons."

Emmons!

The old man's name rang like a ship's bell in Alice's ears as she strained to catch their conversation. Benjamin Emmons was the very man she had made the long journey from Boston to see, the man upon whom so many of her desperate hopes now hung.

Magistrate Holm swivelled to the young, straw-haired boy who had cleared the way through the crowd. "You, boy! Run to the chapel! Fetch Reverend Warwick!"

The boy spun on his heels. He was about to race off when Emmons laid a gentle hand on his shoulder. "Save your breath, Duncan. God had no hand in this."

With a lingering glance at the nightmarish coastline, Emmons turned his back on the ocean and let the boy lead him away, leaving the magistrate to his thoughts.

Alice gathered Abigail and plunged into the crowd after them. "Mr. Emmons!" She called over the simmering uproar. "Mr. Emmons, may I have a word? My name is Alice Jacobs!"

The old man slid to an abrupt halt and pivoted. His eyes squinted through his spectacles as he searched the multitude for the voice calling his name. His gaze found Alice and her daughter squeezing their way through the throng toward him.

"Jacobs?" He scrutinized her with a mingling of confusion and curiosity.

"Yes," Alice panted. "Mr. Emmons, I have come to—"

Emmons held up a wrinkled hand. "I believe I know why you are here, Mrs. Jacobs. You have no doubt come to find your husband… and I am the last man to have seen him alive."

Chapter 2

Benjamin Emmons set a brisk pace as he led Alice and Abigail northeast along the wide expanse of Derby Street and left the chaos of Derby Wharf behind. "Have you just arrived in Salem?"

"From Boston this afternoon." Alice took in her surroundings. Salem had gone from a hardscrabble village to a bustling seaport in the decades since the infamous witch hysteria of 1692. Some of the town's wealthiest families had made fortunes from cod fishing, privateering, and trade with the Orient. Alice could see evidence of the town's newfound prosperity all around her.

Derby Street was the commercial and residential heart of Salem, running for almost half a mile along the harbor-front. To Alice's right, wharves of various lengths pointed out from the harbor like skinny grey fingers. They hummed with activity. Throngs of sailors and longshoremen swarmed the docks, shouting to each other and gawking at the bones amassing between the hulls. Cargo holds brimming with exotic teas, spices, silks, porcelains, and countless other treasures imported from the Far East now lay open and ignored. A long line of horse-drawn carts stood unattended in front of the counting houses, waiting to be emptied or filled with freight. The strong odor of horsehair and manure mingled with the pungent smell of drying seaweed and brine.

The magnificent homes of Salem's richest merchants stood facing the ocean from across the street. The stately grandeur of these Georgian manors far exceeded any of Alice's expectations and even rivaled those in Boston.

"That one looks just like a dollhouse," Abigail marveled. Her clear blue eyes twinkled as she cradled her wooden doll and strolled at her mother's side.

"Perhaps one day you'll live in a dollhouse of your own." Alice winked as they went past the row of majestic mansions. The modest cottages of Salem's less affluent residents peeked from behind their larger neighbors like spectators in a standing-room theatre.

"I trust your journey was agreeable?" Benjamin asked.

"Quite pleasant," Alice lied. The long ride from Boston had been anything but pleasant. The hired coach had smelled of cheap perfume and stale tobacco. Every jostling bump and rut had sent jolts up her spine and she was now thankful to be stretching her cramped legs after the long and torturous journey. Despite the chilly autumn winds sweeping from the ocean, Alice enjoyed the fresh sea air and the freedom. At twenty-seven, she had never travelled without an escort before. It was exhilarating and intimidating at the same time.

"Duncan!" Benjamin called to the straw-haired boy, who now ambled several yards ahead of them. "Run ahead and lay a fire."

"Aye, Grandfather!"

Benjamin's eyes crinkled with a smile as he watched his grandson race several blocks ahead.

The old man carried himself with a gentle dignity that Abigail found charming. He possessed a youthful vitality in his gaze that seemed to belie his age.

"Has your grandson any siblings?" Abigail asked.

Benjamin lowered his eyes and swallowed thickly. "That charming young man is my second grandchild. His elder sister died nine years ago."

"Oh, I—I am so sorry…" Alice stammered.

"'Tis quite alright." Benjamin made an attempt at a thin smile, but his eyes betrayed a long-buried sorrow.

Alice sensed his discomfort and looked for a delicate way to change the subject. "Correct me if I am mistaken, Mr. Emmons, but might that have been the town magistrate in your company at the wharf?"

Benjamin's expression seemed to darken. "Aye. Magistrate Holm desired my counsel on the matter of the bones."

"An unsettling sight, to be sure."

"Indeed. The entire town is in an uproar."

"Surely there must be some rational explanation? Perhaps the natural result of the storm brewing at sea?"

Benjamin slowed for a moment. His Adam's apple bobbed in his long neck as he swallowed hard, cast a glance at Abigail, and lowered his voice. "'Tis best we not speak of it in front of the little one." He moved along without a further word and soon drew to a halt before a rickety fence separating Salem's East India Museum from Derby Street. "Here we are."

The museum was a relic of a building standing on a

forgotten parcel of land on the oldest stretch of the harbor-front. Its newer Georgian neighbors stood far away, as if ashamed of their ancient ancestor. The building was short and rectangular, its brown clapboard cracked and weathered by the salty sea air. There were visible gaps in its gambrel roof where some powerful Nor'easter had ripped away the wood shingles. Five square windows faced the sidewalk, revealing nothing of the museum's dusky interior.

Benjamin led his guests through the open gate and up the creaking planks of the steps to a pair of heavy doors inlaid with small, stained-glass windows. A faded sign hanging above the lintel advertised the museum in black copperplate script. It featured a painting of a schooner flying the red and white stripes of a merchant ship from its mainmast.

Benjamin pushed the doors open and ushered them into a hall so large it seemed impossible it could fit within the structure presented to the outside world. Dark timber walls vaulted twenty feet to a high, coffered ceiling. Three massive iron chandeliers flooded the hall with a warm, yellow glow. A series of horizontal display cases standing waist-high in the centre of the museum stretched away to the far recesses of the hall. Parallel rows of walnut cabinets rose on either side of the centre aisle and marched back toward the rear wall. Each was polished to a gleaming shine. Large glass doors exhibited some of the museum's eclectic collection of natural history. An astonishing variety of taxidermy animals stared at Alice from all corners of the room. The sweet hint of embalming spices lingered beneath the musty smell of dust and wood wax.

"Mother! Look at *that*!" Abigail marvelled at an enormous

clamshell sitting beneath a glass dome on a walnut pedestal. "Have you ever seen anything like it?"

Alice read the identifying label aloud. "Man-Eating Clam from the Cook Islands, generously donated by Captain Walter P. Sayer of the merchant ship *Actaeon*."

Abigail's eyes widened and she stood back from the dome. "Do you believe it could eat a man?"

"I find it doubtful." Alice smiled and led Abigail away, following Benjamin to where his grandson now waited by an open door at the rear of the hall.

"Your study is ready for visitors, Grandfather," Duncan announced.

"Thank you, Duncan." Benjamin ruffled the boy's unruly mess of hair. "Mrs. Jacobs, please come in and be seated. You must be exhausted."

"Thank you." Alice glanced at Abigail. "If it is all the same to you, Mr. Emmons, I would prefer to keep our conversation private. Perhaps Master Duncan might give my daughter a tour of your museum?"

Duncan looked up and grinned, revealing a large front tooth he hadn't quite grown into yet. "Gladly! We'll begin with the gastropod mollusks. Follow me please…" He whirled and disappeared around a cabinet.

Abigail's eyes trailed after him. "Mother, I don't want to go with him. He's… odd."

"Mind what you say of people," Alice chided. "I'll be speaking with Mr. Emmons alone for a few moments, but I won't be long. Besides, it's not every day that a young girl is fortunate enough to be treated to a private tour of such curious wonders."

Abigail nodded, her cheeks dimpling with a reluctant smile as she turned and went after Duncan.

The boy's keen voice rose from somewhere among the cabinets. "This particular species is terrestrial, however, there are a great many that thrive in marine environments. If you look here, you will see…"

Alice silently wished little Duncan Emmons luck as he went on with his lesson. He would have to do better than the common snail to sustain her daughter's interest.

Chapter 3

Benjamin waited for Alice to settle into a tufted leather chair before setting a delicate porcelain teacup on the heavy writing desk before her. Twirling wisps of fragrant steam wafted from within. "A delightful variety from the Bay of Bengal," he explained, pleased at Alice's reaction to the exotic aroma. "A gift from an old friend who still works the docks."

The modest study Benjamin kept in his East India Museum was a warm and comfortable change from the stiff winds sweeping off the harbor. A fire crackling on the hearth sent shadows dancing around the room. The heartening scent of burning cedar mingled with the musty smell of book-leather and parchment. Shelves crammed with pamphlets and manuscripts of all sizes and ages crowded the dark timber walls. Miniature ships, old paintings, and nautical maps occupied the remaining spaces. A beam of pallid sunlight filtered through a square window, catching thousands of lazy dust motes drifting through the air.

Benjamin eased into a worn leather wingback behind the desk and gazed at Alice. "Tell me, Mrs. Jacobs, what news have you of your husband?"

Alice sighed between sips of tea. "Very little. His colleagues at Harvard remain at a loss and the inspectors in Boston have begun to pursue other matters. Their official conclusion is that Samuel was set upon by Indians or waylaid by highwaymen and left for dead."

"But you don't believe that is what happened?"

"I believe there is little evidence to support either assumption. Truth be told, Mr. Emmons, it is this very lack of progress that brings me to you today. Samuel has been missing for three months and I can no longer afford the luxury of patience. If I do not continue the search on my own, no one else will. Regardless of how unlikely it may seem, there remains a chance that Samuel is alive, lost or stranded in the wilderness, perhaps. The investigation has yielded nothing to prove otherwise, and I have no intention of informing my daughter that her father is dead until every logical piece of evidence convinces me I am being truthful."

Benjamin cocked an eyebrow. "Your daughter does not yet know her father is missing?"

"I have led Abigail to believe that Samuel has been continuing his research for the university and that we have made this trip to Salem to visit your museum."

The crinkled lines around Benjamin's eyes deepened with sympathy as he sipped his tea. "How may I help you, Mrs. Jacobs?"

"While the authorities in Boston pursued their investigation, I took to examining the research Samuel had compiled in preparation for his journey here. I had hoped to find something that might be of aid, some clue that was overlooked. I learned much of the dreadful witch trials that took place here a century ago."

Benjamin gave a grim nod. "Nineteen townspeople hanged for witchcraft. Another pressed to death when he refused to render a plea on the charges laid against him. Twenty souls lost on nothing more than the wild accusations of a gaggle of wayward village girls. For one hundred years, we in Salem have borne the weight of our guilt. I suppose 'tis the amends we must pay for the innocent lives we sacrificed during those dark times."

Alice waited, but Benjamin said no more. "Mr. Emmons, I understand my husband was lodging with you and your wife at the time that he went missing. Have you any thoughts about what may have taken place?"

Benjamin drained the last of his tea and spread his hands. "Your husband wrote to me regarding his work on local folklore at Harvard. He desired my assistance with his research, and I was happy to oblige. You see, while I spent much of my youth as a mariner, local history has forever been a passion of mine." The old man's face grew grave. "Samuel was particularly interested in Sarah Bridges."

Alice blinked. Here was a name she hadn't come across in Samuel's notes. "Who is Sarah Bridges?"

"A century may have passed since the dark days of the witch trials, Mrs. Jacobs. But despite this modern age, Salem is still not without its witches. Sarah Bridges is the last of a family of outcasts, banished from Salem decades ago for their pagan practices."

"What sorts of practices might those be?"

"Black magic, sacrifice, conjuring. For years, they lived

alone, taking refuge somewhere deep in the Northern Woods. No one knew what they were doing out there or what became of them. Most preferred to believe they were dead. Over time, they were nearly forgotten until one night a year ago when Sarah returned to Salem, foretelling a terrible curse. Come All Hallows' Eve—when the veil between this world and the next is at its thinnest and the souls of the dead are free to mingle with the living—the spirit of Rebecca Hale would return to have her revenge."

"Rebecca Hale?" Alice interjected. "The woman hanged for witchcraft?"

"Aye. Not all of Salem's accused witches were innocent, Mrs. Jacobs. In the black pit of Salem's dungeon, Hale signed her name to Satan's black book and sold herself to him, body and soul. One hundred years of torment in his inferno for one night of vengeance in his name, such were the terms of her bargain with the devil." Benjamin shuddered almost imperceptibly. "A century has now passed and Hale has repaid her debt. Sarah Bridges vowed we'd know her prophesy to be true by the coming of four omens: afflictions of the eyes, blood, flesh, and bone."

"Ah, yes," said Alice. "It was word of a string of dire incidents that had befallen Salem that had drawn Samuel here from Boston. What can you tell me of them?"

Benjamin noticed the fire burning low and eased himself from his chair with a mild grunt. He crossed the room to the hearth, where he stooped before the fireplace to turn the log with a pair of iron tongs. The fresh side of the cedar caught and burst into flames. Each of Benjamin's knees cracked as he eased himself back into his chair. His brow creased and his brown eyes seemed to cool as he studied Alice.

"The first omen came to pass just before Christmas. On that bitter day in December, not a single fire would light."

"None?" Alice did her best to keep her skepticism hidden.

Benjamin shook his head once. "I know how this must sound to such an urbane woman. But I swear to you we couldn't strike even a single spark. No candles, no lamps, no fires—nothing. For one whole day in the dead of winter, we shivered in our unlit homes as if… as if our very eyes were stricken by darkness."

Alice waited a moment. "What of the second omen?"

Benjamin swallowed and squeezed his eyes shut, as if still trying to clear an unwanted vision from his memory. "Months went by before it came to pass. One morning in May, the town awoke to find the grave markers of the Burying Point drenched with blood. It was a ghastly sight. They couldn't be wiped clean. 'Twas as if the headstones themselves were *bleeding*."

Alice nodded. "It was this incident that had caught Samuel's attention in Boston. Part of his work at Harvard seeks to reconcile superstition with science. He had a theory that what had been interpreted as blood running from the grave markers had been the oxidization of iron caught in the rock."

Benjamin gave a deferential shrug. "Before long, your husband had identified a pattern. Each of the omens had manifested on an ancient pagan day of power. The first had been on the celebration of Yule; the second on the feast known as Beltane. Samuel predicted the third affliction would happen after midsummer, on the next pagan day of power."

"Lammas Day, the Festival of the Wheat Harvest," said Alice.

"You are familiar with the folk customs of the Old World?" Benjamin remarked with some surprise. "You are an uncommon woman, Mrs. Jacobs. Independent *and* educated."

"My husband is missing and I may soon be a widow. A woman in my position cannot indulge antiquated traditions —nor have I ever had much use for them." She paused a moment. "Was Samuel correct?" Alice knew her husband had disappeared on the third of August, after the celebration of Lammas. Was there a connection?

Benjamin bowed his head and spoke in a somber whisper. "Every baby delivered that day was stillborn."

Alice breathed a quiet gasp despite herself.

"Two lambs, a foal, a litter of dogs and… and Charlotte Meade's poor little girl. All of God's creatures were born dead on a single day." Benjamin's tone was low and grim now. "As for the fourth omen, you have already witnessed it for yourself, Mrs. Jacobs."

"The bones," Alice murmured.

"Aye. Today is Samhain, the year's final pagan day of power. Sarah Bridges' prophecy has been fulfilled."

Alice swallowed her derision for the old man's quaint superstitions. "Has no one questioned this woman?"

"Aye. Only fear keeps the townsfolk from seizing her and bringing her to justice."

"Surely this town's superstitions cannot outmatch their love for their own children. Is love not a more powerful force than fear?"

"If it were fear of ghosts alone, it might very well be. But the woods of Gallows Hill are cursed lands, poisoned by the blood spilled upon them a century ago. Since the afflictions began, some of Salem's bravest men—strong and hale one and all—have attempted its threshold, only to be seized by a paralyzing fear and sent fleeing." Benjamin let out a bitter sigh. "Unfortunately, the supernatural cares very little for love."

Alice squeezed her bottom lip between her teeth and ran the tip of her tongue across her scar, keeping her opinions to herself. Samuel had been eager to explore Gallows Hill and the Northern Woods for his research, yet it was the one place that the local constables hadn't searched. Despite their excuses, Alice had long suspected their reluctance was because of the very superstitions Benjamin was speaking of now. She resolved that Gallows Hill would be the first place she visited in the morning. Surely she could find a guide willing to relinquish his fears for some hard currency. Alice had little to spare, but she had no choice. The search for clues had to begin with an exploration of the mysterious woods.

The shrill chime of a small clock rang through the study, announcing that it was now four o'clock.

"Oh, my." Benjamin rose from his seat with a sudden sense of urgency. "My apologies, but I'm afraid I must take my leave. My daughter is infirm and expects me before dusk. I dare not keep her waiting, on this night, least of all."

Alice stood as well. "Please, Mr. Emmons. What more can you tell me of Gallows Hill? If you could—"

"I am sorry to leave you so hastily, but I have already tarried too long as it is." Benjamin gathered his overcoat from a spindle rack in a corner. "With the witch's curse upon us, I have arranged for Duncan and the children from the orphanage to spend the night in the stockade at Fort Pickering on Winter Island, where they will be guarded until sunrise."

Alice waited while the old man turned to a tidy bookshelf behind his desk. Unlike the jumbled mess of the adjacent shelves, this one held only a handful of arranged volumes.

Benjamin plucked a small, leather-bound book from its neighbors and presented it to Alice. The day Samuel disappeared, he left this diary behind. I have kept it here for safekeeping. Everything you wish to know about your husband's discoveries is recorded within."

Alice's breath caught in her throat as her eyes fell on her husband's notebook. "Did you share this with the investigators?"

Benjamin nodded. "They found nothing significant within."

Still, Alice thought it strange that the investigators had never mentioned the diary's existence. Had they simply been neglectful? Alice often felt they had been rather inattentive in their investigation, despite their assurances. Even more troubling was the possibility that they had been willfully hiding the journal from her. If so, for what purpose?

The unexpected appearance of Samuel's personal notebook brought on a flood of emotions. Determined not to let them get the best of her, Alice tucked the slim volume under her arm and swallowed hard. "Thank you, Mr. Emmons. You have been too kind with your time."

Benjamin's white brows creased at the slight flutter in her

voice. "Mrs. Jacobs, if 'tis not too bold of me to say, your husband was very devoted to his work, but I believe you were always his one true passion. He loved telling stories, but his eyes would never sparkle as bright as when they were stories of you."

Alice felt a tightness in her chest, like a dead man's hand clutching at her heart. A crack appeared in her cultivated poise as she struggled against her tears and spun for the door.

"Mrs. Jacobs…"

Alice stopped at the door and willed away the lump in her throat.

Benjamin's expression had grown somber as he stood gazing at her from across the room. "Mrs. Jacobs, you and your daughter are welcome to spend the night at the fort with us."

Alice opened her mouth to decline, but Benjamin held up a hand. "Please… I do not expect you to understand or accept all that is transpiring in this town. But for the sake of your daughter, I would urge you to join us."

Alice groaned inwardly. She wished she could tell the grandfatherly old man that All Hallows' Eve was merely a night like any other. "I appreciate your concern, Mr. Emmons, but the inn will be a crowded public place. We will be safe enough."

"I pray you are right, Mrs. Jacobs," said Benjamin. "But if there is any truth to Sarah Bridges' prophecy, I fear none of us will be safe enough this night."

Chapter 4

Magistrate Holm remained at Derby Wharf long after the townspeople dispersed. His face was a mask of composure, an illusion that took all of his considerable will to maintain. His gray eyes revealed nothing of the turmoil sweeping his mind. He watched as the rolling swell of a wave surged toward him and sent a load of bones crashing against the barnacle-encrusted pilings of the wharf beneath his feet.

Holm dragged a hand across the sandpaper stubble of his chin. His troubled thoughts barely registered the salty foam spraying onto his boots. As a colonel during the War of Independence, he had fought bravely at the Battle of Bunker Hill. He had witnessed the hideous consequences of war while weathering the British assault—men skewered and disemboweled by bayonets; blown apart by musket-fire; obliterated by cannon balls.

None had chilled him as much as what he was witnessing now.

The afternoon was growing late by the time Holm turned his back on the grim scene at sea. He locked his hands together behind his back, spun on his heels, and marched the long stretch of the wharf. He heard the anxious murmuring of the few onlookers who still lingered on the pier, gaping at the bone-strewn coastline reaching northeast toward Cat Cove and the small hump of Winter Island. Holm felt their eyes falling on him as he strode by, the weight of their stares on his back as they looked to him for answers.

Holm's reputation as a fearless patriot during the war had earned him a powerful standing among the town's selectmen. Despite Salem's rising prosperity, it had not yet been granted a city charter and was still being administered by the town government. The town had no official mayor, but the citizens still looked to Holm for leadership. He considered it an honor. The freedom of the people to determine their own representatives was a right he had fought and bled for. He was determined to reward their confidence in him.

But after today's ghastly spectacle, how could he possibly ease their fears? How could anyone?

Holm crossed Derby Street and left the wharves behind as he made his way north toward Salem Common. With the salty reek of the harbor receding into the distance, his heavy boot-heels clicked against the cobblestones and echoed off the squat walls of the neighboring buildings. The crooked street was deserted except for the occasional dockworker hustling to or from the wharves. Salem was a more intimate place here, one more connected to its ancient roots. Holm would have enjoyed a stroll through this old neighborhood, but his mood was now as grey as the bruised sky overhead.

On the battlefield, Holm had seen what happened when men gave in to fear. The consequences were brutal and unforgiving. Fear led to panic and hysteria—and when a mob became hysterical, people died. Since that terrible night when Sarah Bridges had returned to Salem, the townspeople had been on edge, dreading what All Hallows' Eve would bring. Holm had heard the talk spreading like a plague through his town: *'Tis a sign of an evil hand upon us… The ghost of the witch is coming… God hasn't forgotten what Salem did to those poor wretches a century ago…*

When Holm arrived at the sprawling expanse of Salem Common, he found his horse, Eclipse, still tethered to the post where he had left her hours ago. It had been early afternoon and Holm had been letting Eclipse graze on the Common when Benjamin Emmons' grandson fetched him with news of the bones washing ashore. The streets were already crowding with people rushing to the wharves, and they had forced Holm to leave Eclipse behind to join them.

Now, Holm was glad to get back to the venerable charger that had carried him through so many battles. Everyone in town knew and recognized the magistrate's prized Arabian by her chestnut hide and flaxen mane. Some even snickered the mare was the closest Holm had come to female companionship. Eclipse neighed affectionately and offered her muzzle at Holm's approach, eager for the attention of her master's hands. Holm stroked her neck and swept his gaze across the grand houses that surrounded the outskirts of the Common.

Shutters were closed. Curtains pulled. Lights extinguished.

The entire town was bracing for nightfall.

Holm grimaced with dismay when an explosive *craaack!* erupted nearby. Downhill from where he stood, a troop of militiamen was engaging in a series of military maneuvers. A billowing cloud of bluish smoke rose above them and the acrid tang of their musket-fire filled the air. Holm recognized the rakish profile of Ollie Dennard as the captain giving the orders.

Dennard noticed the magistrate observing them from atop the rise. He peeled away from his men and hurried across the open ground to meet him. The captain was a wiry man with unusually round eyes and a pointed face like the result of an eagle mating with an owl.

"Is it true?" Dennard asked, huffing for breath. "What they say about the bones? Is it true?"

Holm frowned and nodded.

"Dear God." Dennard shook his head. "What did Old Man Emmons say?"

Holm's frown tugged heavier at the corners of his mouth. He had hoped Emmons could offer some sort of rational theory to explain the sudden flood of bones. The magistrate liked the old historian. Emmons had been a brave friend of the patriots and had even served as a privateer, capturing and seizing British warships during the early months of the war. Instead of squandering his share of the plunder on useless luxuries, Emmons had used it to care for his widowed daughter and her son. What little remained, he had spent on opening his quaint museum of natural curiosities. Such selfless devotion to family and community had earned Holm's respect. Emmons had spent the better part of his life at sea, and the magistrate trusted his opinion. Surely the bones had to be some sort of natural phenomenon? Something the veteran sea captain must have seen before?

In the end, Emmons was as frightened as everyone else.

"'Tis like nothing Emmons has ever seen," Holm replied.

"'Tis the last sign of the prophecy!" Dennard blurted. "Rebecca Hale rises tonight!"

Holm couldn't contain a scowl. Among his fellow selectmen, his was the only vote against Dennard's plan to deploy the militiamen from Fort Pickering. Convinced that the people of Salem would be in danger once the sun set on All Hallows' Eve, Dennard had now emptied his garrison to patrol the streets. Only his lieutenant and a few young privates manned the fort on Winter Island. To Holm's mind, leaving the garrison empty was a reckless idea. Fort Pickering was the only protection Salem Harbor had. The threat of a British assault was no longer a concern, but there were still pirates and Indian raids to be considered. *These* were Holm's most immediate worry, not some foolish ghost story.

Holms drew the musket from the holster strapped to Eclipse's saddle, cocked the hammer, and inspected the weapon. The .75-caliber Brown Bess flintlock was a thing of beauty that he had trained himself to reload at an astonishing speed of ten seconds. The musket hadn't killed a person since the end of the war, but last August he had picked off two whitetail deer from a hundred yards on horseback.

Dennard watched the magistrate inspect the contents of his gunpowder pouch. "What do you intend to do?"

"What we should have done months ago. I will go to the Northern Woods myself and drag that horrid woman from whatever pit she calls home."

Dennard paled. "You go to seek—" A name caught in his throat, as if speaking it aloud would conjure something deadly and demonic. "You go to seek… *her?*"

The muscles in Holm's temples bulged as he clenched his jaw tight. "You disagree with this course of action?"

"No sir, of course not." Dennard swallowed. "It's just that you've only a few hours of daylight left and, well… you know the stories about the woods that surround Gallows Hill. They're *haunted.*"

Holm scoffed as he mounted his horse's saddle. "Captain, there are no vengeful spirits. I find it exasperating that you would choose to believe in the ghost of a dead witch rather than a flesh and blood suspect. For all of this town's talk of ancient curses, 'tis clear to me that a mortal woman is to blame for the horrors that have befallen us. I know not how she has done it, but when I return from the Northern Woods, we will see that Sarah Bridges pays for the crimes she has wrought upon this town."

"Shall I have some of my men accompany you?" Dennard offered grudgingly.

"No, I will go alone. If you insist that they patrol the streets, your men may at least provide some comfort to the townspeople until my return." Holm spun Eclipse around and was off with a snap of the reins, leaving a maelstrom of dead leaves swirling in his wake.

An unsettling possibility occurred to Dennard as he watched the magistrate go: he may soon be the last person to have seen Holm alive.

Chapter 5

Alice and Abigail stood outside the rusted gates of the Burying Point as the children of Salem gathered in the cemetery. All of them wore disguises. Most were simple burlap masks, but others hid their faces behind crude and misshapen papier mâché. Some even had rough impressions of skeleton bones painted on threadbare outfits that were no longer wearable. Each child cradled a jack-o'-lantern lit from within by the melted stub of a flickering candle.

An orange slash hung in the sky to the west, where the sun was making its final descent toward the horizon. The afternoon was fading like the lights of a stage, and dusk was waiting in the wings.

Alice stood beyond the limits of the crooked fence, clutching Samuel's journal in one hand and her daughter's palm in her other while the gathering of children roaming the graves began placing their jack-o'-lanterns on the crumbling headstones.

"'Tis a custom of the Old World," Alice explained to Abigail. The eerie beauty of the jack-o'-lanterns glowing in the dusky evening light riveted the girl's attention. "The children leave jack-o'-lanterns as offerings to the dead, lighting the way for wandering spirits to return to their graves on All Hallows' Eve."

For over a century, the people of Salem laid their dead to rest at the Burying Point. On a slope overlooking the South River, tombstones of all shapes and sizes crowded the cemetery. Some were ancient and covered with green lichen, the epitaphs barely legible. Others were newer, straight and upright, etched with winged skulls and grim *memento mori*.

The children's parents milled in the lane on the periphery of the cemetery. They exchanged vague and nervous greetings while they waited but said little else, preferring to keep to themselves. There was nothing social about this gathering.

A gust of wind broke loose from the approaching storm and rattled the skeletal limbs of the elms. Stripped from their branches, the desiccated leaves swirled and swept across the graves, scratching like nails against the ancient limestone and granite. The change in the air was palpable, as if it were alive and gathering strength.

Alice pulled her collar tighter around her neck as her gaze settled on a young boy kneeling before the jagged tooth of a headstone. He brushed away the dead leaves, laid his jack-o'-lantern on the ground, and bowed his head in silent reverence, as if taking part in some solemn ritual.

Instead of bearing a mask, white flour dusted the boy's face. Someone had smudged dark rings of charcoal around his eyes so that his blue irises peered out from hollow sockets. More charcoal smeared below his cheekbones turned his likeness skeletal and ghostly.

Alice couldn't help a discreet frown as the boy rose and returned to his waiting mother. How could anyone fill their child's head with such absurdity when the unexplained was crumbling under the weight of scientific discovery with each passing day? Even if Sarah Bridges' prophecy was taken seriously, these symbolic offerings would do nothing to appease the vengeful spirits of those executed for witchcraft. The Burying Point was the last resting place of many bones, but those of Salem's accused witches weren't among them. They were denied a proper Christian burial, their bodies left in unmarked graves somewhere near Gallows Hill.

Alice turned her back on the Burying Point and led Abigail away without a second glance.

"Can't we remain just a while longer?" Abigail protested.

"We have witnessed more than enough for one day," Alice replied. "'Tis growing late and we are expected at the inn."

The street grew darker and more deserted as they left the graveyard behind. According to Benjamin's directions, Charter Street and the inn would be just around the next corner. The old man had offered to arrange a carriage for Alice, but she had declined. She wanted time to clear her thoughts after the chilling scene at the harbor. The haunting sight of all those awful bones washing ashore had affected her more than she liked to admit. She could still see them when she closed her eyes: spilling onto the shoreline, amassing in grisly heaps, clattering against each other with the ebb and flow of the tide.

Alice pushed the images from her mind and tried to focus on the day's discoveries. Her first afternoon in Salem had given her much to think about, and her mind teemed with questions. Had her husband discovered some rational explanation for the strange and terrible afflictions that had befallen Salem? And what had he made of Sarah Bridges' prophecy? He would have found the idea of vengeful spirits rising from Hell to be curiously quaint but foolish. Were his thoughts recorded in the diary Alice now carried tucked beneath her arm?

Eager to study Samuel's notes, Alice quickened her pace until she glanced at Abigail and noticed something missing. "Abigail, where is your poppet?"

Abigail looked up at her. "I left it at the museum."

Alice heaved an exasperated sigh. "You must be more careful. Now we will have to return for it in the morning. Honestly Abigail, until your father returns, we cannot afford to have you being careless with your toys."

"But I wasn't careless, Mother. I left it there on purpose."

Alice halted in the middle of the cobblestone street and stared at her daughter. "Why would you do such a thing?"

"Because of what the boy said."

"What boy? Duncan?"

Abigail dropped her eyes to the brass buckles of her shoes and nodded sheepishly. "He said that girls who played with poppets were called witches." Her voice was so low and meek it was almost a whisper. "I don't want to be a called a witch."

Alice stifled the flicker of impatience that had risen within her. Samuel had given Abigail the wooden doll as a gift before he had left for Salem. It had become her prized possession; a memory of a father she hadn't seen in months. Alice could only guess how frightened her daughter was to have parted with it. Not for the first time, she wondered if it had been a mistake to bring Abigail on this journey. Perhaps she should have accepted her parents' offer and left her daughter in their care? Perhaps Alice shouldn't have come at all?

No. She had no choice but to take up the search for her husband. Despite the generosity of her family—taking her in and providing for her and Abigail in Samuel's absence—they couldn't support her forever. Her father would soon expect her to find another husband to care for her. And *that* was something Alice couldn't bear to consider. She was desperate to find an alternative to the repugnant idea of being with another man. It was in this desperation that she had compromised with her father: if she found no evidence Samuel was still alive after two weeks in Salem, she would return to Boston and marry a man of her father's choosing.

With her bargain made, Alice had brought Abigail along on her journey to Salem. Alice couldn't part from her daughter, not now. The poor girl had already been through too much. Samuel had been gone for months, and Abigail missed him terribly. She asked about him daily and Alice experienced a fresh stab of grief every time she lied to her. How could she tell her daughter that no one knew where her father was? That he had simply vanished?

Alice kept these thoughts in mind as she rested her hands on Abigail's small shoulders. "Abigail, you know there are no witches. When people tell you such things, remember it is only meant to frighten you. It wasn't kind of Duncan to frighten you. He will apologize when we return to the museum."

"But he showed me a book that said it was true." Abigail screwed the leather toe of her shoe into the ground.

"Simply because 'tis written in a book, does not mean it is true, Abigail. Think about your bedtime story about the princess and the fairy. Is that a true story?"

Abigail shrugged and shook her head.

"And what about the explorers who once believed the world was flat? For centuries, they wrote books claiming that if they sailed too close to the edge of the world, they would fall right off. But now we know the world is actually round. We can say the same about witches. A century ago, people believed they were real. They even wrote about them in books. But they were wrong. There is no such thing as witches."

Abigail nodded once in quiet understanding but kept her eyes averted, not entirely convinced.

Alice placed a gentle finger beneath her daughter's small chin and raised it up to look her in the eyes. "Fear is a failing, Abigail. Only by struggling with it can we acquire experience and knowledge. And in this struggle, our reason is our greatest virtue. When we have reason, we have nothing to fear. Do you understand?"

Abigail thought it over for a moment. Her cheeks conceded a dimpled smile as her blue eyes met Alice's. "Yes, Mother."

Chapter 6

Lieutenant Henry Maddock inspected the cells of the stockade and prayed that Fort Pickering's defenses would hold for one more night. He brandished a torch as he pushed further into the gloom of the corridor and ducked under a dusty lantern hanging from the timber ceiling. The lieutenant was a big man, so tall he stood a head above the rest of the fort's garrison. If there was one thing he hated, it was a tight space. He grunted with chagrin as he opened the sooty glass of the lantern dangling overhead and lit the old candles. The wicks were still good after years of being inactive. A tawny glow flared to light. Maddock wrinkled his nose as the foul stink of burning tallow mingled with the damp odor of stale air and mildew. It smelled like a moldy tomb that hadn't been opened in years.

Fort Pickering was buried in a strip of high ground at the southeastern tip of Winter Island, guarding the north entrance to Salem Harbor. Many had tried to breach the stone walls, but none had been successful. During the war, the fort's twenty-four-pound cannons had protected privateers fleeing British warships. The heavy guns had ensured Salem remained one of the few New England ports that weren't seized by the British, despite the redcoats' repeated attempts. The fort itself comprised five subterranean bunkers that burrowed from the central bastion like a star. Each of the tunnels was gouged into the hill, framed with timber and masonry, and covered with sods to absorb the impact of enemy cannon fire. From the sea, the bunkers presented virtually no target, appearing as little more than low mounds of turf, shrubs, and beach grass. The blockhouse housing the garrison and the prisoner stockade stood in a shallow depression at the center of the star.

It was here, deep in the dank, cold bowels of the stronghold, that Maddock now assessed cells that hadn't been occupied since the war and readied them for Salem's orphans.

The tiny corridor disappeared into murky darkness beyond the flickering glow of the lantern. There were no windows down here. Two more lanterns hung at intervals behind Maddock, illuminating the thirty yards of stone floor that stood between him and the door he had left open at the top of the wooden staircase. This unremarkable door was the only access to the stockade. Its location was a security precaution, making it impossible for prisoners to overtake the blockhouse from within in the event of an escape.

Maddock moved to the next cell, jammed a skeleton key into the lock, and heard the *clunk* of the tumblers releasing. He gave the bars a shove. The iron door swung inward with a squeal of rusty hinges that reverberated off the thick walls. This was one of the larger cells—about ten feet by twenty— wide enough to house half the children. They would keep the others in the neighbouring cells, furthest from the staircase to the world outside.

Maddock shook his head as he searched the space for rats. He couldn't understand why anyone would ask to be locked in here overnight. The cells were dank and unpleasant even in summer; in the winter, they were downright cruel. Tonight, they would be miserable at best.

Dampness was already seeping through Maddock's wool coat, and he made a mental note to fetch warm blankets from the fort's supply room. Whether he liked it or not, caring for Benjamin Emmons and the old man's band of orphans would be his duty for the next twelve hours. As much as he resented this assignment, there was no need to be mean about it.

Maddock shook his head again and sighed. He had opposed the idea of emptying the fort's garrison for the night and had voiced his concerns to Captain Dennard—in private, of course. As a result, they had assigned Maddock this menial duty. Ostensibly, he had been left in charge of the fort because he was the highest-ranking commissioned officer beneath Dennard himself. But Maddock suspected the assignment was an implicit reminder of his proper place in the chain of command.

After closing and locking the cell door once more, Maddock gripped the bars and hauled on them with all his might, shaking them furiously. They groaned and shuddered and a sprinkling of rust shook loose, but the bars held. Satisfied, Maddock held his torch high and waded further into the darkness. His broad shoulders wiped a patina of limescale from the wall as he squeezed toward the last cell of the corridor.

He lingered here for a while.

It was in this very cell that British Major Worthington T. Leslie had been imprisoned. Captured leading a commando troop in a stealthy attempt to sabotage a rebel ammunition warehouse, Leslie was held behind these bars for almost a year at the height of the war. An important prisoner like Leslie gave the Americans a significant bargaining chip in their efforts to negotiate the release of their own captives from the awful prison ships in New York harbor. The fort had repelled no less than three rescue attempts during the time of Leslie's imprisonment. The last of these ended in the annihilation of the entire British raiding party.

It also resulted in the death of Maddock's older brother Elijah, a British Loyalist.

Maddock sometimes wondered if it had been his own shot that had ended his brother's life. It was certainly possible. Maddock was in the northeast bunker the night of the British assault. He was a scared teenager, firing his musket madly through a murder hole at anything that moved in the darkness. What if one of those dark shapes beyond the walls had been Elijah? What if he had killed his own brother? Maddock would never forget when he had rolled over the stiffening corpse in the attack's aftermath and seen Elijah's familiar but lifeless eyes staring up at him.

Maddock pushed the memory from his mind as he gazed at the shadowy cell. It had now sat empty for almost a decade. He doubted he would ever make his peace with what had happened that night, but he'd sealed his fate when he had thrown in with the rebels. His family had called him a traitor; his own father had threatened to see him hanged for treason.

He had turned his back on them, and although he would like to say he had never looked back, that would be a lie.

"Lieutenant Maddock!"

The muffled call of a young man from somewhere outside brought Maddock back to himself. He hurried through his inspection and lit the last overhead lantern as a slim figure appeared in the doorframe and cast a long shadow down the steps. It was Tad Howell, one of the young privates assigned to help guard the children. The two other privates—Dunbury and Keith—walked the perimeter on the last patrol of the night.

"Lieutenant Maddock?" Howell called again. "I've sighted them, sir. They're crossing the Neck."

"Thank you, Private Howell." Maddock's boots echoed off the walls as he strode to the staircase and peered up at the figure in the doorway. Howell was so slight, he was barely a silhouette. It was a wonder he had even passed muster. Maddock himself had put on some pounds since the end of the war, but he still prided himself on his fitness. He maintained a disciplined exercise routine that he followed every day, rain or shine.

Maddock paused for a last glance around before dousing his torch into a bucket of water. He climbed the steps two at a time, glad to be leaving the cramped space behind. A blast of chilly wind instantly greeted him as he stepped into the fading afternoon light. Maddock was no mariner, but he had spent enough time in Salem to know a violent storm was brewing. To the east, far beyond the seaward bunkers, the horizon had grown shadowy and indistinct. The sky was gray like slate and growing darker by the minute.

Maddock locked the stockade and circled around to the blockhouse's main entrance, where he navigated his way through the labyrinthine corridors. He passed the mess hall and the bunk-rooms and ascended several creaking staircases on his way to the roof. Howell followed close behind, nipping at Maddock's heels. Moments later, they reached the top of one last tight set of stairs, passed through a heavy door, and stepped out into the swirling winds of the rooftop lookout. High above them, the stars and stripes of the fort's flag whipped and snapped in the steady gusts.

Maddock crossed the distance to the northwest corner, narrowed his eyes, and peered into the dirty orange sunset. For one fleeting moment, it bathed the treetops of the mainland in a fiery glow. They blazed in stark contrast to the pewter sky as if a hellish inferno was smoldering somewhere far in the distance. Then the radiance fell and was gone. An oppressive gloom descended like a shroud on the island.

Maddock made out a dark spot moving across the murky horizon. He retrieved a brass spyglass from its station, extended the lens, and squinted with one eye. Through the scope, he saw the magnified image of two worn-out mares drawing a wagon across the narrow causeway that connected Winter Island to the mainland of Salem Neck. The old historian, Benjamin Emmons, sat on the bench next to the grizzled driver. About a dozen small children crammed like sheep into the wagon behind them. Maddock squinted for a closer look. Many of them had white flour sprinkled on their faces and dark rings of charcoal smudged around their eyes.

"Oh Lord, look at this nonsense," he muttered, forgetting that Private Howell was still at his side.

"You don't believe in the curse, Lieutenant Maddock?" Howell asked with some surprise.

"I'm not from Salem," Maddock replied, as if the statement explained everything.

"Oh. I just… well, you've been here so long, I simply thought you were—"

"They posted me here near the end of the war," Maddock grumbled, painfully aware that the steel-grey streaks in his hair and whiskers made him look much older than thirty-one. "Prior to that, I was attached to the Fourteenth Continental."

"Colonel Glover's regiment?"

Maddock gave Howell a sideways glance and nodded. At least the chatty private seemed to know something about military history.

"And you've lived and served here ever since?" Howell asked.

Another nod. Maddock didn't bother telling him that when he had been posted at Fort Pickering, he welcomed the opportunity to venture as far away from his family in Connecticut as possible.

"I'm not from around here either," Howell went on. "My father fought in the war at Fort Ticonderoga. Must say, all this talk of ghosts and witches has got me somewhat spooked. I put little stock in it at first, but now, after the bones… After all your years of living here, you've seen nothing to make you believe the curse might be real?"

Maddock took a deep breath and turned. "Private Howell, in my life I've seen many dead—so many, my dreams are filled with corpses. But I've yet to see a single ghost."

Howell fell silent and followed Maddock's gaze back to the

wagon winding its way up the hill. It was visible without the spyglass now, a dull grey shape rumbling through the gloom along the rocky path.

Maddock caught a glimmer of movement from the corner of his eye. Howell's shoulders trembled in the bitter wind. "Private Howell, would you kindly proceed to the armoury and fetch my musket while I escort our guests to their quarters?"

"Certainly, sir." Howell swivelled on his heels.

"And Howell… When Dunbury and Keith return from patrol, have them bring some blankets and hot tea to the stockade before securing the powder magazine and assuming their posts for the night."

Howell saluted and was off. Minutes later, Maddock turned and followed him.

When he emerged from the blockhouse, the lieutenant crossed the empty courtyard to the fort's iron-strapped gate. He released the bolts and swung it open. The wagon drew to a halt in the open space beyond and the ragtag group of orphans spilled from its payload. Their threadbare clothes were patched with a rainbow of mismatched colors. Many were too thin for their ages. Maddock hadn't seen such a pitiful collection since the fort had taken in a boat of refugees from Newport during the war. Waiting at attention while Benjamin Emmons paid the driver, Maddock found his respect for the old man rising. He didn't know how Emmons had convinced Captain Dennard to indulge in this circus, but the old man did seem to have his heart in the right place.

"Are you going to protect us?"

Maddock looked down. A young boy gazed up at him with

bright, round eyes that were rimmed with soot. "That is my duty."

More chattering children gathered around him.

"Are you a soldier?" a girl asked.

"Yes, I am."

"Actually, you're a militiaman. Not a *real* soldier."

Maddock cocked an eyebrow as another boy jostled his way to the front of the group. He had hair so yellow and straight it seemed like a straw wig. A ragged burlap mask dangled from his small hand.

"They officially disbanded the Continental Army in 1783 after the Treaty of Paris ended the war," the boy explained to anyone who would listen. "Since then, the local militia have fortified Fort Pickering. They—"

"That will do, Duncan," said Benjamin while the wagon driver snapped his reins and rumbled away. "I'm sure this good sir is quite familiar with the military history of Fort Pickering."

Maddock gritted his teeth and forced a smile as he extended his hand to Emmons. He was surprised at how tall the old man was. Few people came close to looking the lieutenant in the eye. "Mr. Emmons, I am Lieutenant Henry Maddock. 'Tis my duty to ensure your protection this evening."

"Pleased to make your acquaintance, Lieutenant Maddock." Benjamin shook his hand with earnest. "Captain Dennard has praised you as a man of duty and honor. We cannot thank you enough for the compassion you've shown us this evening."

Maddock faltered for a moment, not quite knowing how to

respond. Compassion? He was about to lock these children in dismal jail cells reserved for criminals and prisoners of war. "I'm afraid the stockade will be quite chilly tonight. I have already arranged for tea and blankets. Is there anything more you require before I see you and the children to the cells?"

"Thank you, no. 'Tis already dusk and I feel it would be best if we secured the children without delay."

"Very well. Follow me, please."

Less than fifteen minutes later, Lieutenant Henry Maddock listened for the *thunk* of rusty tumblers as he locked Benjamin and the orphans into their cells. With his musket slung over his shoulder, he took his position in the dim corridor and waited for whatever the night would bring.

Chapter 7

The Ingersoll Inn was a large, multi-gabled house nestled among an ancient copse of maples. It stood on a lonely corner at the southeast end of town. A heavy wooden sign hung from a thick post at a corner of the lot swayed in the gusting winds of the approaching storm. Its squeaking chains welcomed Alice's arrival. Dusk was creeping through the streets like a thief, robbing the town of its colors and leaving only shadows behind.

Abigail insisted on carrying her father's diary. She clutched it to her chest as Alice led her up the path between the trees and pulled on the front door. The comforting smell of cinnamon, mulling spices, and hot apple cider greeted them.

Alice ushered Abigail into the warmth and followed her into a modest foyer. An unassuming chandelier filled the space with a cheery glow. Wide doorways on either side of the foyer opened to common rooms. Alice could hear the hum of voices in quiet conversation within. In front of them, a long staircase led up to the inn's second-floor guest-rooms. Next to the stairs stood a narrow door and a small desk decorated with dried Indian corn, pumpkins, and other harvest ornaments.

Alice was still recovering from the wind when the door beside the staircase flew open with a sharp *thump*. George Ingersoll appeared in the narrow frame. The innkeeper was a stout, middle-aged man with a balding head and cauliflower ears. He had a ruddy complexion that always made him seem jovial, even when harried and overworked. Puffing heavily as he emerged from the inn's kitchen, he wore a smeared apron and had the wooden handles of four mugs of ale wrapped in the paw of each hand.

"Mr. Ingersoll?" Alice inquired. "My name is Alice Jacobs. I believe you have rooms reserved in my name?"

"Mrs. Jacobs! Of course!" Ingersoll gave her a warm smile that even his crooked teeth couldn't ruin. "We was worrying about you, what with your baggage arriving this afternoon without you and all. If you'll allow us a moment, me wife will be right with you to see you to your rooms. Uncommonly busy tonight. Seems like everyone in town's looking for one last drink before hunkering down—though I can't rightly say I blame 'em. You're welcome to wait in our lounge if you'd be more comfortable, Mrs. Jacobs."

Alice returned the innkeeper's tired smile and trailed after him as he scuttled through the open doorway to her right. She hovered at the threshold and surveyed the room. The lounge was large and rectangular, its timber walls decorated with an assortment of bucolic landscapes. Men and women of various social standings filled the room. Such a mingling of the sexes wouldn't have ordinarily been acceptable. Evidently, this was no ordinary night.

Abigail sidled closer to her mother's side, intimidated by the room full of strangers. A fire crackling in the fireplace infused the room with its only warmth and merriment. Instead of the lively atmosphere Alice expected from such places, a dreadful foreboding choked the air from the room. Whether seated at one of the heavy tables or crammed standing around their perimeter, the patrons huddled close together, talking in hushed tones and casting furtive glances out the windows into the gathering darkness. The one exception to the suffocating sense of unease came from a round table in the centre of the room. Here, a rugged sailor elicited an outburst of laughter from a half-dozen of his shipmates.

"Here, I'll show you another!" Even seated, the sailor appeared tall and brawny. His eyes were deep and languid and he had thick, dark hair that he kept tied in a simple tail behind his neck. His tanned face bore a rough growth of roguish stubble over his heavy jaw and dimpled chin. "A voodoo chieftain showed this one to me on the island of Barbados." He gestured at an enormous bear of a man across the table. "Pike, lend me a coin."

"I'll do no such thing!" The burly man's salt-and-pepper beard bristled as he looked to his shipmates for support. "The last coin I lent Jonas here disappeared faster'n a whore's garters when I put ashore!"

The sailors burst into more laughter.

George Ingersoll's firm warning rang out from a distant corner of the room. "Mind your language in me inn, gentlemen! Or you'll be drinking naught but water! 'Twas good enough for Adam and 'twill be good enough for you if you don't mind your manners!"

With an absent glance, the handsome sailor named Jonas noticed Alice hovering in the doorway before he steered his dark eyes back to the beefy giant across the table. "Pike, please… there are ladies present. Now lend me a coin!"

Pike let out a sullen growl and jammed a massive fist into his pocket. He withdrew a gold coin and tossed it to his friend with obvious reluctance.

"Put out your hand," Jonas instructed. His shipmates leaned forward in their seats to get a closer look as the big man offered the calloused mitt of his hand. Jonas turned Pike's palm face-up, then covered it with his own. "Now watch as I push this coin through my hand and into your own."

An expectant hush fell over the table as the sailors came together. They huddled even closer as Jonas placed the coin on the back of his own hand. With a quick strike, he slapped the coin with his free palm.

The sailors let out a collective gasp.

The coin had vanished before their eyes.

"You did it again!" Pike's eyes blazed from the depths of his beard as he gaped at the empty spot on the back of Jonas's hand. "You slimy bastard! Gimme back my coin or I'll—" Pike's threat fell from his lips as Jonas slid his hand away, revealing the gold coin now sitting in Pike's own gnarled palm.

The sailors burst into applause as the big man gaped at the coin, dumbfounded.

"I'd be wary if I were you, Pike," Jonas warned. "That palm now carries a voodoo curse. The only way to rid yourself of it is to rid yourself of the coin. So be a gent and buy us a round of ale!" Jonas grinned as the sailors burst into another round of cheers and laughter. He stole a glance at Alice and gave her a brazen wink.

"Jonas Hobbes." A voice whispered into Alice's ear.

Startled, she whirled to find a middle-aged, matronly woman hovering by her side. "I beg your pardon?"

Martha Ingersoll was short and plump, bearing such a similarity to her husband that most would mistake her for his sister instead of his wife. She smiled and nodded toward the table. "Sailor's name's Jonas Hobbes. First mate of the *Peregrine* and widower these past six years. Poor man. Never remarried and rearing a daughter by himself ever since. A fine catch, if I daresay, Miss—"

"*Missus* Jacobs," Alice corrected.

Martha blushed, her round face growing an even deeper shade of cranberry. "Begging your pardon, Mrs. Jacobs. I didn't mean to cause offense."

Alice nodded and gave her a vague smile.

"Right… well then, let's get you settled." Martha led Alice back to the foyer, where she produced two iron latchkeys from a desk drawer. "Your rooms are ready for you on the second floor. We haven't any other guests this evening and I expect you'll find the second floor peaceful. Your baggage is waiting for you upstairs and our servant girl, Cassie, will be along shortly to see to your needs."

"Thank you, Mrs. Ingersoll." Alice gave a tired smile and was about to leave when George Ingersoll scurried back from the lounge.

"Hope all is to your liking, madam. Me apologies for the

comp'ny this evening." He gestured back toward Jonas and the other sailors.

Alice nodded while George caught his breath. It was then that he noticed Abigail for the first time. A troubled look seeped into the man's otherwise cheerful face.

"Mrs. Jacobs, are you certain you wouldn't prefer *one* room? You know, to keep an eye on your little one?"

"Thank you, but no. I will require my privacy."

George's candy-apple face lost some of its color. He reached for a pumpkin and slid it across the desk with a mirthless smile.

Alice eyed it. "I beg your pardon, but what am I to do with this?"

"For Jack-o'-the Lantern, Mrs. Jacobs."

"I'll not be needing it." Alice dismissed the pumpkin and turned to lead Abigail away, but Martha Ingersoll wouldn't let her go.

"Please, madam. You've picked a dreadful eve to visit Salem."

Alice resisted the urge to sigh. "Am I correct to presume you believe in Sarah Bridges' prophecy, Mrs. Ingersoll?"

"Seeing is believing," Martha replied gravely. "I was there a year ago at the Harvest Moon Ball, the night… the night *she* returned."

Alice's attention suddenly aroused. "What did you see that night?"

Martha drew a deep breath before diving into a tale she had recounted endless times before. "I was on the balcony overlooking the meeting hall, serving a rather expensive brandy to the cream of the town's genteel society. I remember admiring the decorations, the golden glow of the lamps warming the room. A quartet of the finest musicians in Salem played a gentle tune from their spot in the corner. By all accounts, Magistrate Holm's ball was an unrivaled success. But then, something wasn't quite right. It took a moment for me to realize what it was, but then it came to me: the quartet had stopped playing. A strange hush had descended on the hall. All at once, the screaming began."

Martha shuddered before going on. "I found myself gazing in horror at the scene unfolding below me. A cloaked woman was dragging the mutilated remains of a goat across the hall. When I close my eyes, I can still see the trail of blood streaking across the polished floor. I see the stain growing longer as the woman moved to the centre of the room. A heavy hood concealed her face in shadows. The cloak was grey and filthy and riddled with ragged holes, as if it had been buried deep in the ground for many years. Even from where I stood on the balcony, I could smell the reek of mold and rot rising to meet me. I saw the crowd scramble away in a panic, fanning out around the woman as she drew to a halt in their midst. Some were already streaming for the door as she released her grip on the goat. The carcass fell to the floor in a grisly heap, and I felt my blood run cold as a hollow voice issued from the black depths of the hood. Everyone in the room knew who stood before us."

"The witch of Gallows Hill," George intoned from Martha's side.

"Aye, she who haunts our nightmares on the blackest of nights." Martha shuddered again as her husband crossed himself and breathed a silent prayer. "It seemed to me the room was growing dimmer and colder the more the dreadful woman spoke. Even now, I can remember her prophecy as clearly as the Lord's Prayer."

"Did no one attempt to seize the woman?" Alice asked.

"I remember seeing the guards hesitating on the periphery of the room, rooted in place as if spellbound by fear. I wondered where Magistrate Holm could be and suddenly, there he was, at the entrance to the hall. His cry broke the spell, and the guards fell in behind him as he drew his pistol and charged for the woman. In that instant, the hall descended into chaos."

Martha lowered her eyes. "I'm ashamed to say I was overwhelmed by the tumult. The last thing I remember before fainting were the screams echoing through the hall."

George nudged the pumpkin toward Alice again. "Please, madam. For your little one…"

Alice saw the fearful concern in their kindly expressions and found her convictions too exhausted to protest any further. She swept the pumpkin into her arms and led Abigail up the long staircase to their rooms.

Chapter 8

Amos Abernathy helped himself to another swig and savored the heat of the rum as it washed down his throat. It wasn't the best bottle he'd ever had—nothing like the aged Jamaican jug he'd brought back from the islands years ago—but it did the trick.

The old lighthouse keeper stood huddled in his heaviest wool greatcoat by the jagged rocks on the seaward side of Winter Island. The indigo twilight was giving way to a black and starless night. A thick, unexpected fog had swept in just after dusk. Shrouded in the darkness and the swirling gray mists, Abernathy could hardly see the enormous base of Fort Pickering Lighthouse just a few dozen yards away.

British gunships had nearly destroyed the lighthouse that stood at the southeast tip of the island, about two hundred yards from Fort Pickering. It had taken almost two years to rebuild the whitewashed, rubble-stone walls. Since then, the beacon's giant oil lamps warned merchant ships and fishing vessels away from the treacherous rocks that threatened the approach to Salem's busy harbor.

But when a thick fog such as this descended, those lamps were practically useless. Smothered in the murky depths, their light was now a vague glow that was barely visible even to Abernathy, who stood only seventy feet below. On nights like this, with the beacon no longer reliable, the keeper remained by a six-pound cannon, waiting to return a warning signal to any ship that fired its gun as it probed the coastline for danger.

Now, with the last fiery notes of the rum fading from his palate, Abernathy lit the gun's fuse, watched the sizzling sparks disappear into the vent hole, and blasted a four-ounce charge into the fog. The mist flared a fiery orange as the muzzle-flash erupted from the cannon's mouth with a teeth-rattling roar.

Abernathy blinked to adjust his vision as the darkness rushed back over him. The damp air was crawling deeper into his skin and he contemplated indulging in another sip. He seldom drank anymore—not since his sailing days—but the heat of the rum still felt good in his gut. In the nine years he had now spent as the lighthouse keeper, he'd almost given up alcohol altogether.

Tonight, he couldn't help himself. He told himself he was only drinking to stay warm, but this strange fog had him spooked. He'd seen his share of soupy, sea-borne murk as a fisherman working the Grand Banks. But it seemed impossible such a fog could keep itself together with the winds so fierce in advance of the coming storm.

And yet, here it was.

A terrible sense of foreboding sat like rocks in Abernathy's gut as his thoughts drifted to the band of children huddled for safety in the fort's stockade. He shuddered and crossed himself. The fog was a sign of dreadful things to come. Abernathy could still hear the horrible clattering of bones raking across the rocky shore beyond the weak light of his storm lantern. Sarah Bridges' fourth omen had come to pass, and there was no doubt in Abernathy's mind that the witch's curse was upon them.

Abernathy shivered as he held up a hand and watched his palm vanish in the shifting veil of mist. He pulled off a glove and slipped a pocket-watch from his coat. His bony knuckles went white with cold as he checked the time: seven-twenty. It would be a long night if this fog held up. He ran his hand over the white whiskers of his grizzled chin before pulling his glove back on. He would wait another ten minutes before heading back inside to get warm.

Then he caught the voices.

Abernathy froze, not sure he had heard correctly. A minute passed—then two—as he stood listening, waiting.

There it was again.

Someone was whispering in the fog. It was faint, indistinct, too low to comprehend—but it was there.

Abernathy's mind raced until he realized the mysterious voice must belong to a deckhand aboard the ship he had just signaled. Sound could travel a great distance over open water. The man was less than a hundred yards from the shore to be heard in these winds.

A bolt of alarm shot through Abernathy. The vessel's crew must have misjudged the location of his cannon fire and sailed too close to the rocks.

"What ship is that?" he shouted. "Beware! Land here!"

He waited for long moments, but the voice had fallen silent.

"What ship is that?" Abernathy hollered again.

No answer.

Abernathy raised his lantern and squinted into the dense fog. The shifting gray mass stared back at him.

The whispering returned without warning.

Closer this time.

Abernathy's blood went cold. It wasn't the voice of a man.

It was a woman.

The light-keeper whirled around. A nervous knot tightened in his belly. The woman's eerie voice was joined by others—perhaps dozens—rising, whispering, falling over each other. They swirled around him from all directions like a breeze, tickling his ears with a song that was mournful and despairing. He opened his mouth to scream.

And then they were gone.

Abernathy waited, breathless, heart hammering in his chest.

Nothing.

After an eternity of howling wind and clattering bones floating in the surf, Abernathy swallowed and decided it was certainly time for another slug of rum. He reached into the folds of his coat and brought the spout of his bottle to his mouth with a trembling hand. It was inches from his lips, the amber liquid sloshing inside, when the ambient color of the surrounding fog changed abruptly.

Abernathy's eyes shot skyward. The bottle fell from his hand.

High above his head, the glow of the tower's beacon had

turned a ghostly shade of blue.

Abernathy stared up at the pale sphere that illuminated the murky haze with an otherworldly radiance. The blue glow wavered for a moment, as if the giant lamps weren't getting enough air to sustain their flames. Then they went dark, snuffed out altogether.

Abernathy's chest tightened. The only time he'd seen anything like it was that awful day in December. It was the day the town was visited by the first of the omens—the day none of the beacon's giant lanterns would light.

One minute became five as the frightened keeper stood rooted in the shadowy mist, wondering what to do. Everything about this was wrong. Abernathy wanted nothing more than to run for the safety of the nearby fort.

But there would be hell to pay if he didn't relight those lanterns. The town expected him to keep the beacon lit from dusk to dawn. In exchange, they paid him a handsome salary and gave him the use of the snug cottage next to the tower. Any dereliction of duty would cost him a hefty fine and possibly his posting as the lighthouse keeper. He would be out on his ear, an old man begging for a job on some fishing boat. At his age, Abernathy couldn't imagine going back to chasing cod across the frigid North Atlantic.

An anxious knot squeezed his insides as Abernathy collected his storm lantern from beside the cannon and crept through the fog to the tower. He paused before the door and noticed a strange clicking reverberating through his head. His teeth were chattering. Whether it was from cold or fear, he couldn't tell. When he pushed the creaking door open, Abernathy drew a sharp breath and stiffened.

Years ago, he had hung three lanterns at intervals along the spiral staircase. He lit them every night on his descent from the lantern room and kept them lit in case of emergencies.

Now, they had all gone dark.

Abernathy hovered in the doorway and stared into the gaping darkness that filled the tower. His mind cast about for an explanation. A powerful gust could have blown the door open and swirled up through the tower, snuffing out the lanterns along the way.

No. He had closed the door when he'd left the tower earlier that evening, just as he always did. He thought of the whispering he'd heard in the fog and came to terms with a chilling truth: the wind hadn't extinguished the lights—some *one* had.

Abernathy's hand trembled as he held his own lantern high. Its pale light spilled around him before dissolving into the yawning darkness of the lighthouse's upper reaches. The tower was empty, black, silent—*unnervingly* silent.

Abernathy lost his nerve. He thought about fetching a soldier from the fort. Whoever—or whatever—had doused the lanterns could still lurk in the tower's darkness.

But Lieutenant Maddock's current priority was to guard the orphans. If something happened to the little ones, Abernathy would never forgive himself.

The old light-keeper drew a deep breath and exhaled.

He was on his own.

Abernathy shuddered and stepped into the darkness. Ninety-two wooden steps spiraled up to the lamp room, groaning and creaking beneath his slow, wary tread. The wind howled and rattled the pane of the narrow window that marked the tower's halfway point. Abernathy stopped to catch his breath and listen. If someone was in the lamp room, he would now be able to hear their footfalls on the wooden platform overhead.

There was nothing.

Just to be certain, Abernathy waited a bit longer. Then he pressed on. As he neared the top of the staircase, the light of his lantern fell on the square trapdoor that accessed the lamp room. He halted and went rigid.

The trapdoor was closed.

Abernathy always—*always*—left it open.

The keeper's old heart pounded dangerously in his chest as he waited, scanning the cracks around the door for any signs of light, any signs of *life*.

There were none. Whoever was up there was lurking in absolute darkness.

Abernathy's courage failed, and he retreated a step. The beacon lamps were useless in this fog, anyway. He would check on them in the morning; it wasn't the night to be creeping around in the dark.

But what if the fog cleared? It would leave any ships depending on the lighthouse signal to wonder why the keeper hadn't kept the beacon lit. Abernathy had no choice, not if he wanted to keep this cozy job. He held his breath and reached for the trapdoor. His hand trembled as he eased the plank upward and raised his lamp to peek through the opening.

The lamp room was dark and still.

Abernathy climbed further through the tiny door and took his first tentative steps into the darkness.

The lamp room was an octagon, dominated on all sides by

immense windows. Beyond them was the narrow widow's walk, from which Abernathy kept the giant windowpanes clear of snow and ice in the winter. The lighthouse's four massive lamps stood clustered together on a solid brick pedestal at the center of the room. Each held a gallon of flammable whale oil, but they now sat in silent darkness. Their brass fittings ticked and popped as they cooled in the chilly air. Surrounding the lamp pedestal was the tight, round platform upon which Abernathy now stood. It spanned just over twenty feet from side to side and was interrupted only by the square hole of the open trapdoor.

Abernathy lingered at the threshold and glanced through a window.

The fog was gone.

Abernathy went to the glass, his heart hammering. He could see the yellow glow of a ship's lanterns, far below and perhaps a mile from shore. It drifted like a lonely ember in the endless darkness. Further out to sea, jagged streaks of purple lightning knifed across the horizon as the oncoming storm drew ever nearer.

Abernathy backed away from the window. It had only taken a few minutes to climb to the lamp room. How could such a fog have vanished in mere moments? Fear tightened its grip on his gut. Nothing about this felt right. Every instinct told him to flee, to go join the others in the fort. He just had to light the beacon and get out.

Turning to the giant lamps, Abernathy placed his own lantern on the pedestal and removed the first of the oversized glass chimneys. Then he reached for the tinderbox and struck the flint to the steel.

The bright spark illuminated a thick blanket of white gliding up the stairs.

Abernathy's mouth fell open as a swirling mist flowed up through the trapdoor, hugging the floor and spilling like water around the circular platform. His wonder turned to horror as the fog drew itself together into a solid shape. He shrank away, his old heart now thundering. A hot bolt shot up his left arm to his shoulder and stole the terrified scream from his tongue. He clutched at his chest as a searing wave spread to his heart like a spark sizzling along a cannon fuse. All that remained was for the charge to explode.

As he pitched forward across the platform, Abernathy's hand flew out for the pedestal and missed. His fingers clipped his storm lantern. It smashed on the floor, igniting immediately. Wild with fright, Abernathy recoiled and crashed into the lighthouse's giant lamps. The glass shattered beneath him, soaking him in gallons of oil. He burst into flames with a mighty *whoosh*, and then he *was* screaming, flailing his arms and tearing at his blazing greatcoat.

It was too late; Abernathy was engulfed within seconds. The flames burned through his clothes and withered his oil-soaked skin. His screams became shrieks, high and piercing and horrible to hear. With the roaring blaze devouring his flesh, he charged blindly toward the nearest window. The glass shattered as he crashed through, intent on flinging himself from the widow's walk, desperate for something—anything—to end the agony.

He never made it. Consumed by flames, he collapsed on the narrow perch. Countless shards of broken glass ripped through his blistered, blackened skin. In the last seconds of his life—before the blinding pain became too much to bear and a merciful white bliss overcame him—a single, horrifying thought kept him conscious.

There was a face in the fog! A woman's face!

Chapter 9

Night had fallen, moonless and dreary, as Abigail explored her bedroom and wondered if she really wanted to spend the night alone. Any other night, the prospect of such independence would have thrilled her. Now, after all she had seen and heard, she wasn't sure how much fun it would be.

Her room at the inn was small and snug, its plaster walls warmed by the light of a hurricane lamp perched on a cherry-wood nightstand. Alice had left Ingersoll's pumpkin on the nondescript dresser for Abigail's amusement. There was a slim closet in the far corner of the room. Two dusty paintings hung on either side of a square window set into the back wall. The leaded panes looked out over the inn's stables and the small cottage the Ingersolls kept as their private residence. The thin glass rattled and whistled under the wind's gathering fury.

You shouldn't be playing with poppets…

Duncan's warning echoed over and over in Abigail's memory. Could playing with dolls really be a sign of witchcraft? Try as she might, she couldn't stop reliving the scene at the museum in her head. Somewhere between the scarab beetles and the vial of squid ink, she had lost all interest in Duncan's tour. Her mother had promised a museum full of wonders, but all Abigail had seen was one collection of shriveled animal corpses after another. She couldn't recall having ever been more bored.

"Haven't you anything *interesting* to look at?" she had blurted.

Duncan had halted in mid-sentence. His round face scrunched with the most puzzled expression, as if he would never understand girls. He'd been in the middle of telling Abigail everything there was to know about *Echinus Melo*— commonly known as the sea urchin. A half-dozen of the spiky, desiccated globes were arranged in the glass display case beside him. They were the highlight of his tour of his grandfather's museum. Duncan had spent an entire July afternoon at the docks, hounding a grumpy deckhand to find out everything he could about the fascinating creatures.

"What is *that*?" Eager to change the subject, Abigail pointed to what looked like a burlap sack that Duncan had been carrying since their arrival. "What is that for?"

Duncan turned the burlap over in his hand and admired it, his eyes gleaming. "This was a gift from my mother. It's meant to protect me." He slipped the sack over his head and revealed it to be a crude mask adorned with colored patches stitched together to resemble a macabre scarecrow. Small slits were cut in the burlap so he could see.

"Protect you from what?" Abigail asked. She didn't like the look of the mask.

Instead of launching into another eager lecture, Duncan

removed the mask. His round face had become very grave. "From the things coming to hurt the children."

Abigail felt strands of hair rise on the back of her neck. Duncan's voice had fallen so low, she wondered if she had even heard it. It was as though even the words scared him, as if speaking them out loud would somehow conjure something terrible into existence.

A cold and unwanted sensation took root inside of Abigail when she saw the abrupt change come over the boy. It was the same uneasy feeling she got when her mother closed her door and the bedroom became dark and sinister.

That's when Duncan's gaze fell on the doll dangling from Abigail's hand. "You shouldn't be playing with poppets."

"Why shouldn't I?"

"They are the mark of a witch."

"Don't be silly," Abigail chided. "Mother says there are no such things as witches. Nor are there such things as ghosts, specters, or ap... appa... *apparitions*." She stumbled over the last word.

"There *are* such things as witches, and they've been known to make use of poppets when working their evil. I read it in a book." Duncan gestured toward the far side of the hall. "Come. I'll show you."

Still clutching her doll to her chest, Abigail fell in behind the boy as he led her through the maze of display cabinets.

"Since Grandfather Benjamin retired from sailing, he has collected more volumes on witchcraft than anyone else in New England," Duncan explained. "Except for Harvard's historical society, of course."

Abigail wasn't listening. Instead, she was thinking of a way to change the subject. All this talk of witches and things that hurt children was spooking her. She knew witches didn't exist —her mother had told her as much. But she couldn't forget the fear she had heard in Duncan's voice. It lingered in her mind, conjuring all kinds of unwanted images and stirring up a rising sense of fright.

Duncan skirted around an ornate pedestal and stopped before an enormous bookshelf built into the back wall. Abigail rounded the cabinet and gaped at the vast collection of books. Other than the occasional times she had accompanied her father to his offices at the university, she had never seen so many volumes in one place. Duncan ran his fingers along the leather spines, scanning the titles. A miserable feeling gnawed at Abigail's stomach while she waited for the boy to mount a stool and remove the heavy tome from its dusty neighbors. The faded yellow tooling of the book's title—*The Wonders of the Invisible World*—stood out from the brown leather binding.

The stool creaked as Duncan descended and sat on the floor. He crossed his legs and flipped the book open in his lap. Abigail crouched next to him as he riffled through the pages. She dreaded what she would see when he found what he was looking for. She had tried to tell herself it was a silly idea. This was just another superstition, the kind her mother so often warned her about.

But the boy seemed so convinced—so *scared*.

"There…" Duncan pointed to a paragraph and spun the book around for Abigail to see.

"I beg your pardon." She barely glanced at the page. "But I am *only* seven years-old."

Duncan rolled his eyes, shook his head, and began reading the passage out loud. "Upon inspection of the witch's premises, poppets fashioned of burlap and hay were found hidden in the walls of the woman's cellar. These poppets were missing heads or stuck with pins and thorns for the affliction of other people. Such hellish compositions were considered proof of the woman's guilt on the charge of witchcraft and on August 9, 1692, she was hanged by the neck until dead."

Duncan snapped the book shut with an explosion of dust.

For one speechless moment, Abigail's gaze had remained fixed on the worn leather of the book's cover, her eyes as wide as saucers. Her uneasy stare had crawled from the book to her doll. The rosy face of the tiny figure smiled back at her as usual.

Except that painted grin didn't seem quite so pleasant anymore.

Now, with her mother busy unpacking her valise and laying her clothes on the narrow bed in her room at the inn, Abigail bit her lip nervously. Maybe Mother would let her spend the night in her room? Just for tonight? Abigail knew Mother would think it ridiculous to be so afraid, but she just couldn't help it. If only the wind whistling through the windowpane wasn't so eerie.

Abigail's stomach twisted into knots at the thought of soon having to climb into bed. She had already slipped into her nightgown and brushed her hair. Through the floor, the voices from the ground-floor lounge were growing quieter as the patrons dispersed. The large, unfamiliar inn would soon become silent, frightening.

Abigail opened her mouth and was on the verge of voicing

her fears when an image of her father flew into her mind and stole her words. She saw him braving places so distant he couldn't write to her; so remote Mother couldn't even point to them on a map. When he returned, she wanted him to know how fearless she had been in his absence.

Abigail swallowed her anxiety and willed herself to think about something curious that lingered in her mind since their arrival at the inn. "Mother… that man downstairs. That was magic he did, wasn't it?"

Alice glanced up from the valise. "No, Abigail. It wasn't magic."

"But Mother, I *saw* it. He made that coin pass right through his own hand."

Alice stopped what she was doing and motioned for her daughter to sit on the mattress. "Abigail, let me see your hand."

Abigail did as she was told, peering at her mother as she offered her little palm.

With a quick flick of her wrist, a gold coin appeared in Alice's fingers, as if materializing from thin air.

Abigail's eyes flew wide. "Mother! How—"

"Shhh…" Alice grinned. "Just watch."

Abigail looked on, mystified, while Alice covered her tiny palm with her own. With the coin now resting on the back of her own right hand, Alice slapped it with her left as if she were swatting a mosquito.

Abigail gasped. The coin was gone.

Alice's cool eyes glimmered with amusement as she drew her hand away to reveal the coin now sitting in her daughter's palm.

Abigail's mouth fell open with speechless wonder. A moment passed while she remained motionless—not even blinking—too stunned to react. With a long and slow *gulp*, she leaned forward. The wooden bed frame squeaked beneath her as she brought her mouth to her mother's ear, as if to whisper the deepest and darkest of secrets. "Mother… you know magic too!"

"No, Abigail. Nothing as mysterious as magic." Alice turned over her left hand to reveal a second coin. "A simple trick. There are *two* coins. Instead of disappearing, my palm snatched the coin from the back of my hand when I slapped it. At the same time, I released a second coin into *your* palm." Alice held up both coins for her daughter to see, making sure the girl understood. "We live in the modern age, Abigail. Soon there will be a rational explanation for everything."

Alice dropped the coins into Abigail's hand and turned down the bed sheets. "It's now time for sleep."

Abigail heard the firm note in her mother's tone and knew better than to resist. As she crawled between the sheets, her eyes went to the pumpkin sitting on the dresser. "Mother, who is Jack-o'-the Lantern?" she asked, looking for something to get her thoughts off the eerie whine of the wind at her window.

A flicker of impatience crossed Alice's face as she fluffed the pillow beneath her daughter's head. "It's time for bed, Abby. But if you're a good girl and promise to go to sleep right away, I will tell you a story."

Abigail grinned. The blankets felt warm and snug around her body and she was already giving way to a swift and overwhelming sense of fatigue as Alice lay down next to her and began her tale.

"There is an old Irish myth that tells of a man named Stingy Jack who invited the devil to have a drink with him. True to his name, Stingy Jack didn't want to pay, so he convinced the devil to turn himself into a coin that Jack could use to buy their drinks. But Jack kept the money and put it into his pocket next to a silver cross that prevented the devil from changing back into his true form. Jack freed the devil under the condition that should Jack die, the devil would not claim his soul."

Abigail gave a small yawn and Alice paused for a moment before continuing her story. "Soon after that night, Jack did die. As the legend goes, God would not allow such an unsavory man into heaven. The devil—upset by the trick Jack had played on him and keeping his word not to claim his soul—would not allow Jack into Hell. He sent Jack off into the dark night with only a burning coal to light his way. Jack put the coal into a carved-out pumpkin and has been roaming the earth ever since."

Abigail yawned again, wider this time. The excitement of the day was taking its final toll. "Will we carve a jack-o'-lantern, Mother?" She eyed the pumpkin on the dresser across the room.

"'Tis just a story, Abby. Nothing more."

Abigail's eyelids had become heavy, but her furrowed brow told Alice there was something more on her mind. "Abby, what is it?"

Abigail blinked her eyes to keep them open as she peered up at her mother and whispered, "Are you certain you don't know magic?"

"Yes, I'm certain." Alice laid a gentle kiss on her daughter's blond curls. "*You* are all the magic I have ever known."

Abigail's smile faded as her sleepy blue eyes slid shut.

Chapter 10

Alice closed her bedroom door and took a deep, calming breath. With Abigail asleep in the neighboring room, she remained there for a few moments—eyes closed, just breathing—enjoying the silence, the heartening smell of the beeswax candles, the warmth of the rug beneath her feet.

When she opened her eyes, Alice took a candle from the nightstand and went to the window. The impending storm was whipping itself into a fury. She watched the wind lashing at the maples that loomed in the darkness before she pulled the heavy damask curtains together and turned from the window.

Alice's room was larger and better appointed than Abigail's. Besides the customary nightstand and dresser, there was a plush claw-foot armchair in a corner near the window. The pale green floral pattern of its wide cushions complimented the varnished timber of the room's elegant wainscoting. A full-length oval mirror stood in the opposite corner of the room. The journal Benjamin had given her now sat on a small writing desk stationed in front of the window. A hurricane lamp and a country basket of red apples sat on the desktop.

The luxury of the room was beyond what Alice could afford, but her father had insisted—and Alice had only disobeyed her father twice in her life. When she was twelve, she snuck his thoroughbred from the barn and took it for a ride without his permission. The horse had nearly killed her, throwing her and leaving her with a broken collarbone and the scar she still bore on her bottom lip.

The second time was when she had married Samuel.

Alice pressed her candle to the oil-soaked wick of the lamp and adjusted the size of the flame before replacing the chimney. A warm glow spilled across the room as she moved to her valise and unpacked. She was glad to slip out of the tight layers of her skirts and bodice and into the welcome comfort of her flannel nightgown. After taking a few minutes to brush her hair, it was time to examine Samuel's journal.

The comfortable cushions of the armchair enveloped Alice as she opened the worn leather cover. Her heart quivered at the sight of her husband's small, neat handwriting. How many nights had she watched him working away at notes such as these? The memories the book brought back were so strong she could swear she even smelled him, his scent lingering somewhere below the musty smell of the parchment.

Alice fought to keep her emotions under control and scanned the pages until she came across a brief recounting of the sad story of Rebecca Hale. According to Samuel's notes, she had been a widow and the owner of the Stag's Head, a somewhat scandalous tavern that once stood on the Beverly Road at the time of the witch trials. It was there that her rather unsavory reputation grew. With her husband dead, many roundly believed Rebecca had taken to prostitution. If the rumors were to be believed, the Stag's Head was founded on the gates of Hell and Rebecca herself held the devil's keys. She was a fiend who lured otherwise good people to drink and play wicked games until all hours. What happened next may have been inevitable, given the rampant fear and suspicion of the times.

When hunters found the remains of her husband's body eaten by wolves at the edge of the Northern Woods, they seized Rebecca and charged her with witchcraft. She spent months languishing in the squalor of Salem's witch dungeon until Judge Hathorne sentenced her to death. On a bleak morning in July, 1692, Sheriff Corwin led Rebecca to Gallows Hill and hanged her from an oak tree.

Yet, there remained the matter of her seven children. Many in Salem believed the devil himself was their father, that they were conceived during Rebecca's witch's Sabbaths in the hollow of the Northern Wood. In the weeks following her arrest, one of Rebecca's few remaining allies had gathered the children and fled to the wilds of Maine, well beyond the reach of the hysteria. They were never heard from again.

Alice looked up. What had become of Rebecca's family? Even children weren't safe from accusations of witchcraft at the height of the witch madness. The youngest to be jailed was five years-old. Did Rebecca's children hold fast to their mother's innocence while she suffered the horrors of Salem's jail? Or did they turn on her to save themselves, like so many others had? Perhaps some of her children would even have been glad to see Rebecca hang?

Alice returned her attention to the journal and walked her fingers through the pages of entries until there were no more. The last was a schedule of the interviews Samuel intended to conduct with local eccentrics. Alice smiled to herself. Samuel loved to make lists. She skimmed to the final few entries:

July 26: Ebenezer Barclay - Gloucester
July 27: Henry Caxton - Salem
July 29: Mrs. Mary Mastersmith - Andover
July 30: William Mallory - Revere
July 31: Timothy Higginson - Salem
August 2: Phineas Biggin - Marblehead

Alice turned the page and found it blank. She skipped ahead, leafing through the remaining pages and finding nothing there. The entries ended on August second.

There was nothing listed for the day her husband had disappeared.

Samuel kept meticulous notes and records. They filled the pages of his journals and his colleagues at Harvard expected nothing less. Yet, there was no mention of what he had planned for the third of August—or for the rest of his last week in Salem. The inspectors said Samuel had left to conduct an interview for his research and never returned. But who was he meeting? And why would he have neglected to record the appointment? Samuel was fastidious by nature and was obsessed with planning and organization. He was pressed for time in Salem, eager to gather his research and return home to Alice and Abigail. He didn't have the luxury of impromptu decisions, and would have accounted for each of his days.

Moments went by as Alice let her gaze wander over the empty page, pondering its significance. Was it at all relevant? She found it hard to believe she had already stumbled upon some sort of useful insight. Surely the investigators would have noticed this discrepancy. Wouldn't they have pursued it if it were at all important? Alice liked to think so, but she was no longer certain.

Then her gaze caught something peculiar.

Alice ran a finger down the gutter between the last page of entries and the next blank page. She leaned forward in her chair to inspect closer. Her finger was halfway down the sheet when a sharp sting flared from her fingertip. She flinched and snatched her hand away. A tiny bead of blood seeped from the razor-thin slice of a paper cut.

Alice blotted the drop in her palm, gripped the book covers, and bent them backward. The spine cracked wide open and revealed a sliver of parchment in the gutter. It was bound to the spine and hidden between the adjacent sheets, so thin it was almost invisible, as if someone had removed a page with an exacting cut.

Alice's pulse quickened. There *had* been an entry for the third of August.

But why would Samuel have removed it? The pages of the notebook were riddled with mistakes he had crossed-out. There was no reason to remove an entire page with such exacting precision. Not unless he was trying to hide something. But what? And from whom?

Another thought occurred to Alice: what if it wasn't Samuel who had removed the page? Benjamin Emmons could have shown the notebook to any number of people during the investigation. The man could have removed the entry himself. He would have had the opportunity. Did he have a motive?

Alice sat for a moment. She was now certain she had discovered something significant, something the authorities had either overlooked or ignored. Whatever Samuel had written on that page was removed in such a way to avoid detection. Alice had to know what it was. What was her husband's plan on the day he vanished?

Squinting, Alice took a hard look at the blank page again. She raised the book to the lamp and craned her head. From this new angle, she noticed some small, almost imperceptible indentations on the page. They were so subtle she would have missed them if it wasn't for the light playing off the tiny ridges. Alice traced her fingers over the surface, detecting the minute but unmistakable grooves left by the pressure of her husband's pen strokes on the missing page. An idea came to her.

Alice rose from the armchair and brought the book to the writing desk, where she reached for the apple basket. She snapped a piece from its wicker frame, removed the glass chimney from the hurricane lamp, and held the stick to the flame. Within seconds, the wood smoked. Another few seconds and it began to char. Alice drew it back in time to keep it from catching fire. She then returned it to the flame, repeating the process again and again, charring the tip of the stick until it was nothing but a slim piece of charcoal. Returning to the page that bore the indentations, she then used the charred tip of wicker to create a rubbing, working carefully to avoid snapping the delicate sliver of charcoal.

Within seconds, the vague impression of a single line of handwriting emerged like a phantom rising from the shadows:

August 3: Giles Dicer

Alice laid the charred stick on the desk and stared at her husband's entry. She squeezed her bottom lip between her teeth, teasing her scar with her tongue and allowing herself to feel something she hadn't experienced in weeks: hope.

She now had the name of the person Samuel had intended to visit on the day he had gone missing, possibly the last person to have seen her husband alive.

But what Alice lacked was a destination.

Unlike the other names on Samuel's list, this one omitted where this Giles Dicer lived. She only had a name and date. Alice skimmed backward through the pages, studying Samuel's scribbled notes and sketches. She was searching for any reference to Giles Dicer when she came to an abrupt stop.

At the center of a page was the outline of an ink-drawn heart. Inside, the names *Samuel and Alice* were inscribed in her husband's neat, flowing script. It seemed like a childish thing, something a lovesick adolescent would draw while pining for his sweetheart. And yet, Alice felt warm tears springing to her eyes as she traced her fingertips across the ink.

Oh, how she missed him! Seeing Samuel's handwriting, his name—knowing his thoughts had been with her even across the miles between them—the dull ache that had made its home in her heart threatened to overwhelm her. The past few months without Samuel had been unbearable. There had been nights, in the quiet solitude of their bedroom, when she would have given anything to feel his arms encircling her, the musky scent of his skin, the touch of his lips against hers.

A tear fell from Alice's eye and landed on the page with a tiny splash, splotching the black ink. Confronted with this memento of the man she loved, the possibility entered her mind she might never see him again. It was a terrible thought, one that slipped like a shadow through her carefully arranged defenses. She pushed it away, but it still left an impression. What if she failed to find anything in her search for him? What if Samuel was gone forever?

Alice sensed she was about to crumble under the weight of a thousand repressed emotions and laid the journal aside. She went to the window where she cast the curtains wide, slid the pane open, and welcomed a chilly gust of air into the room. The night felt vibrant—*alive*. The winds tore at the trees, rocking the empty branches and sweeping leaves across the ground below. Flashes of pink and purple lightning streaked the sky like jagged scratches clawed across the darkness by an invisible hand.

Alice stood by the open window, taking deep gulps of the cool air and struggling to master her emotions. She closed her eyes, willing herself to think about anything other than her missing husband. Her thoughts went to Abigail, asleep in the neighboring room. She felt a rising need to *see* her daughter. It was a silly, irrational impulse, but it was one Alice suddenly couldn't resist.

Sliding the window closed, Alice collected her robe from

where it lay on the bed and shrugged it on. The soft flannel felt warm and snug against skin that had become goose bumped with the chilly air. The floor beneath her bare feet had grown cold, and she took a moment to step into the familiar comfort of her wool slippers. Then, retrieving her candle from the nightstand, she rounded the bed to the door, turned the key in the lock, and swung it open.

Alice's room was at the end of a long hallway running the length of the inn. A large window looked out into the darkness at the opposite end, its square panes throwing long shadows across the floor rugs with each blast of lightning. An oil lamp sat on a narrow side-table in the middle of the hallway, where the staircase descended to the ground floor. The closed door to Abigail's room stood to Alice's right.

Alice cinched the knot of her robe and was about to step into the hallway when the light of her bedroom suddenly dimmed behind her. She paused at the door and turned.

The flame of her oil lamp had gone entirely blue.

The sapphire flame immersed the room in a ghostly glow until it flickered and died with a flailing sputter.

Alice raised her candle and eyed the darkened lamp, wondering what could have extinguished it. A draft coming from the window? She was sure she had closed it. Even if she hadn't, the glass chimney would have protected the flame. Was the lamp out of oil? Alice crossed the room to where it sat on the desk and rocked it gently. She could hear the *swish* of liquid sloshing in the reservoir.

Alice removed the chimney and pressed her candle to the wick. The oil caught. Warm yellow light bathed the room before the flame turned blue and died once more.

Alice's candle went out too.

As did the lamp in the hallway.

Engulfed in the darkness, Alice went rigid. A tingle of fear crawled up the nape of her neck.

A draft hadn't doused the flames. An unseen breath had *snuffed* them out.

Alice stood motionless and waited for her eyes to adjust to the darkness. She could make out the indistinct outline of her bed, the dresser, the armchair.

Something creaked behind her.

Alice whirled and peered through her open door into the gaping darkness of the hallway. Was that a footstep? She waited, listening, her nerves curling together.

There it was again, the unmistakable creak of a floorboard.

"Who is there? Who are you?" Alice demanded, her heartbeat quickening.

There was no answer.

Alice's unease grew into genuine fear. The Ingersolls had retired to their cottage by now, and the inn was supposedly deserted. She was alone. Trapped. And so terrifyingly vulnerable.

"My husband will return in an instant!" Alice shouted into the darkness. She did her best to keep her voice from quaking, to sound strong and confident. "I can assure you he will not tolerate your intrusion!"

A cold sweat sprung in Alice's palms and her knees trembled as she waited for a response.

None came.

Alice waited a moment longer before slowly—very slowly —stepping from her room into the hallway. She kept her eyes fixed ahead on the darkened corridor, expecting the sound of pounding footsteps to come rushing at her from the shadows at any moment as she reached for Abigail's door. Her hand rested on the door-handle. She stood listening for a moment before easing the door open.

Her daughter's bedroom sat in quiet blackness.

It was startlingly cold, as if someone had left a window open.

Goosebumps rose on Alice's skin. Something was wrong. A tingling sensation crawled all over her flesh. The room was too quiet. It was the silence of a place with the life gone out of it.

"Abigail?" Alice whispered, her tone shrill with a rising sense of dread.

Just then, a violent blast of lightning shattered the darkness with a deafening *CRAAACK!*

Abigail's empty bed was illuminated in the blinding flash.

Alice gasped. Seized by a sudden, overwhelming panic, she burst into the room and tossed the blankets. "Abigail! Abigail, where are you?" she cried, searching the room, spinning in desperate circles in the darkness.

There was no sign of her daughter.

Abigail was gone.

Chapter 11

Alice spun and rushed for the bedroom door. "Help me! Someone help me, *please!*" She screamed as she tore into the darkness of the hallway.

She wasn't alone.

There was a woman there.

She stood silhouetted against the window at the far end of the hall, a tall and motionless figure looming in the gloom.

Alice skidded to a halt. Her mouth went dry and her cries for help died on her lips. The second floor had no other guests. This woman wasn't supposed to be here.

The shadowy figure moved. Dreadfully slow.

Another burst of lighting revealed a glimpse of the woman's old-fashioned dress. A black mourning veil concealed her face.

An overwhelming sense of malice engulfed Alice, a silent malevolence flowing from the shadowy woman like a freezing wind. There was something terribly wrong here. This stranger meant her harm. Alice's every instinct screamed *danger.* She felt the threat deep in her gut, the way prey can sometimes sense a lethal predator. The air rushed from her chest and her courage drained away in a flood. All thoughts left her except for one—that she must run. Overcome by terror, she could think of nothing else but escaping, of fleeing this baleful woman coming at her in the darkness.

Alice's instincts propelled her into action and she scrambled back to her own bedroom, where she slammed the door, turned the lock, and threw herself against the solid wood. She tried to shout, but fear had stolen the air from her lungs. Her mouth opened and closed in sputtering gasps until she found a voice.

"Where is my daughter?" she cried through the door. "What have you done with her?"

The only response was the relentless *thump* of approaching footsteps.

Alice's heart pounded in her chest as she cowered in the darkness. The footsteps beyond the door grew louder and more menacing. There was no urgency in the veiled woman's tread, only slow and steady footfalls that sent awful reverberations through the bedroom like nails being driven into a coffin lid.

Alice shrank back and scanned the room, desperate to find something to defend herself with. There was nothing—not a fireplace poker, not a letter opener—nothing. A ferocious thunderclap went off and Alice jumped. Her gaze fell on the oil lamp on the desk and she grabbed it, ready to hurl it if necessary. She whirled around, her blood running cold as a tremendous flash of lightning revealed a shadow spreading like spilled ink from the crack beneath the door. It grew longer and longer across her bedroom floor as the sinister woman in the hallway drew ever nearer.

The footsteps halted just beyond the door.

Alice held her breath, gripped the lamp, braced herself.

Nothing happened.

For long, shuddering moments, Alice listened for sounds in the hallway. Her eyes stayed fixed on the doorknob as she waited and waited, certain that at any moment the knob would squeak and slowly, slowly turn.

The room remained still. The only sounds were the howl of the wind, the crash of thunder, and the tense shudder of Alice's shallow breathing. She trembled in the darkness, consumed by visions of Abigail's empty bed. She couldn't stay in this bedroom. For the sake of her daughter, she had to confront the woman.

Another burst of lightning erupted. Alice's breath caught in her throat.

The shadow under the door had vanished.

Moments crawled by in silence. Where had the veiled woman gone? Alice's fear clashed with her urgent need to escape, to find Abigail. She crept to the door. The old floorboards creaked maddeningly with each wary step across the room. She pressed one hand to the door and gripped the oil lamp with the other. Alice turned her ear to the solid wood, leaned close, listened.

Nothing.

Alice's heart raced as she reached for the lock with an unsteady hand. She cringed when the key clicked much too loudly as it tripped the tumblers. She summoned all of her courage and reached for the doorknob. Her palm closed on the metal… and stopped.

Something was moving at her feet.

Alice's eyes fell to the floor and strained to adjust to the murky darkness.

Was that smoke?

Another blast of lightning illuminated a thick white mist streaming into the room underneath the door.

Alice gasped and retreated across the room. She watched, petrified but unable to look away, as the vapor thickened and swirled before her eyes. A scream was about to burst forth as the mist roiled and churned like smoke, changing color—first gray, then black—as it drew itself together, growing denser, taking shape.

The figure of a person.

A tattered dress.

A dreadful black veil.

And then Alice *did* scream—a piercing shriek of absolute horror—at the sight of the ghastly woman standing before her.

The useless lamp fell from Alice's shaking hands and shattered on the floor as the woman advanced, dreadfully slow, an abomination crossing the room with terrible purpose. Alice scrambled back against the wall. Her eyes darted for an escape, but the woman stood between her and the door. Desperate to get away, she spun to the window and flung it open. She wavered for only a second, the approaching figure now just beyond arm's reach. She snatched Samuel's journal, scurried over the desk, and climbed out onto the inn's gabled roof.

The wind whipped at Alice's face as she crouched low and inched her way down the shingled slope to the roof's ledge.

She struggled to keep her balance and staggered as she fought off a dizzying wave of vertigo. There was nothing but cold, hard ground two stories below her.

She was trapped.

A sudden gust rocked her. Alice reeled dangerously, nearly pitching over the edge. She wobbled and swayed, her knees buckling beneath her as she fought to keep from plummeting into the void. For one terrible instant, she imagined herself plunging to the ground, saw her bones breaking with the impact. When she recovered her balance, she glanced back over her shoulder, dreading what she would see.

Her window stood empty—a hollow square gaping in the darkness—until a ferocious bolt of lightning struck and illuminated the dark woman looming in the frame. She remained there a moment, watching Alice with unseen eyes buried somewhere deep behind her terrible veil. Then her figure came apart, disintegrating from the head down like a mound of fine black sand blown by the wind.

Alice teetered on the roof's edge and moved away from the window, traversing as fast as she could toward the rear of the inn. She didn't dare glance back for fear of glimpsing the unnatural mist swooping toward her. The old shingles creaked and shifted, threatening to slide away like an avalanche beneath her. At last, she reached the far brink of the roof. Alice steadied herself against the staggering wind, caught her balance, and looked down.

The inn's outdoor livery stable stood below her, empty except for some large bundles of hay stacked together.

Alice didn't need to look back to sense the dreadful mist drawing ever nearer.

Desperate to get away, she let Samuel's journal drop onto the hay before kneeling and swinging around at the roof's edge. She pressed herself flat against the splintered shingles and shimmied downward, letting her legs drop over the edge into space. The eaves groaned under her weight as she lowered herself further, as low to the ground as possible, her legs dangling in the air beneath her. She hung there for a second, arms stretched over her head, steeling her courage before letting go.

The ground rushed up to meet her.

Chapter 12

It wasn't the first time Jonas Hobbes had to help his old friend Pike from a tavern. Jonas had lost count of how many times he'd had the quartermaster's meaty arm wrapped around his neck as they staggered their way back to their ship. The worst had been that time in Port-au-Prince when Pike had taunted a big slave trader he'd whipped at arm wrestling. They had barely escaped with their lives that night.

Tonight, Jonas considered himself lucky—at least Pike could still walk on his own.

"Aw, c'mon... let's go back for jus' one more." The big man drawled as Jonas guided him down the windblown street.

Jonas grimaced. "I can't. Clara's home with Emily and I should've returned hours ago." He was already cursing himself for having stayed at the inn after nightfall. He knew he had taken an enormous risk leaving his sister alone with his six-year-old daughter on All Hallows' Eve.

"Why'd you join us if you were in such a rush?" Pike swayed as Jonas extricated himself from under his arm. Even in the chilly October wind, Pike's bulky limb was still sticky with sweat.

"I heard Enos Briggs might be at the inn tonight."

Pike snorted up a load of phlegm and spit it into the street. "The ship-builder?"

"Aye. There's a rumor on the docks he's putting together a building crew for his newest frigate, the *Essex*."

"Briggs here? In Salem? Who told you that?"

"Rye Chesley."

"Rye Chesley!" Pike's big belly shook with laughter. "That ol' manatee wouldn't know his ass from his blowhole!"

"Perhaps, but there's only one berth in all of New England with water deep enough to launch Briggs' new ship," Jonas shot back. "Our very own Winter Island."

Pike cocked a bleary eye. "So you're lookin' to get into the ship-building business now, are ya?"

Jonas nodded. "If I can get Briggs to hire me, I could leave the sailing life behind. No more squalls and hurricanes and Nor'easters. No more months at sea surrounded by naught but the likes of you. And no more nights away from Emily.

"Blow me down and pick me up!" Pike roared. "Listen to ya! I thought ya loved sailin'!"

"I do. But I love my daughter more."

"Aye, Emily's a cute one, she is. Good thing she takes after 'er mother." Pike's guffaw evolved into a rumbling belch that smelled of fish and onions.

With that, it was time to say goodbye. "You'll be fine getting back to the *Peregrine*?" Jonas asked. With all the strangeness going on, Pike was spending the night aboard the ship to keep an eye on things. Not that he'd be looking at anything but the inside of his eyelids now.

"Fine as swine." Pike smirked. "See ya in the mornin', Mister Shipbuilder."

While his friend disappeared into the gloom, Jonas turned and hurried along Charter Street toward the edge of town. He whistled a bawdy old tune as he turned left onto the dark and nameless lane he called home. The wind had intensified to a furious pitch, and he whistled the ditty as much to distract himself from its eerie howl as to pass the time. The seasoned sailor could feel the tingling current of the storm's electricity as it drew nearer.

Jonas doubled his pace and whistled louder, eager to get home to Emily. If it hadn't been for his sister's convincing reassurances, she wouldn't let the girl out of her sight, he never would have left his daughter in her care—not tonight. But Clara insisted Jonas take advantage of the opportunity for an introduction to the famous Enos Briggs.

Jonas's sister was one of the few in town who put little faith in the witch's curse. She was a widow whose husband died in the war fifteen years ago at the Battle of Oriskany. They had been married for just seven months. They had no children and Clara had never remarried. The death of her husband so soon after their wedding had hardened her against such capricious notions as curses. The only evils Clara believed in now were those of cannon-fire and war.

Jonas himself didn't know what to make of Sarah Bridges' prophecy. He had been out to sea for all but the first of the omens. He had to admit the stories had been unsettling, but he'd seen enough in his travels to know that being unsettling didn't make a thing supernatural or sinister. Yet this last omen —the sea awash with thousands of bones? He'd seen nothing like *that* before.

No one had.

A blast of thunder cracked the night somewhere to the east. Jonas pulled his collar up around his ears and looked skyward. It was promising to be a nasty storm. It wasn't too great a stretch to imagine the ghost of Rebecca Hale arriving with it, riding the midnight winds, waiting for the storm to unleash its fury—waiting to have her revenge.

Jonas's stride quickened as he neared the end of the lane. He could now make out the faint glow of candlelight flickering in the windows of his modest cottage. He let the old tune drop from his lips as he swung open the picket gate and hastened up the footpath to the front door. His sister didn't approve of his sailor songs, especially not around Emily.

Jonas stepped inside and shut the door on the wind. The comforting scent of Clara's tea greeted him as he hung his coat on its peg.

The house was silent.

A shiver stole up Jonas's spine as he stood in the vestibule. Why was it so quiet?

"Clara?" he called.

"We're up here." His sister's hushed response came from the second floor.

Jonas exhaled with relief and followed his sister's voice up the stairs. He turned into his daughter's candlelit bedroom and found Clara sitting in a Boston rocker next to Emily's bed. Jonas leaned against the doorjamb and watched them for a moment.

"How's she been?" he whispered.

"An angel, as usual." Clara's smile was tired but warm. Jonas's sister was six years his elder—tall and sturdy like he was—with long, dark hair that was only recently betraying some strands of gray. "I read to her until she fell asleep." Clara nodded at a worn book of fairy tales sitting on the nightstand. "Was he there?"

Jonas frowned and shook his head.

Clara read the disappointment on her brother's face and gave him the kind smile that had comforted him in the hard years since his wife's death. "I'm sure there will be plenty of other opportunities for your *chance* encounter with Mr. Briggs."

Jonas shrugged. "I just hope they'll come along before it's too late." He crossed the room to help his sister from her chair. "Thank you for looking after her. Go get some rest. I'll take over here."

Clara slowed and turned as she approached the door. "Can I bring you anything?"

Jonas smiled as he settled into the rocking chair. "Perhaps some tea?"

Left alone with his daughter, Jonas made himself comfortable and tried to relax. He soon discovered it was hopeless. All he could hear were the sounds of the house creaking and groaning as it rebuffed the weather; the howl of the wind gusting through the eaves; the jarring *BAM BAM BAM* of the loose shutter downstairs, the one he had never gotten around to fixing.

As the first mate of a prosperous merchant ship, Jonas could afford a larger home, one closer to the town center. But when he had bought the property a few years ago, it had come with something he desperately wanted: a stable. It had taken nearly two more years to save enough to buy the horse to go with it. To Jonas's mind, it had been worth every hard-earned penny.

Just three months ago, he had purchased a powerful young stallion. Emily had named it Midnight for its black hide. In Salem, a horse opened the door to a world of possibilities beyond sailing. It meant Jonas could make the three-mile journey to work on Enos Briggs' building crew and return home every night. It would be a dream come true, something he had promised himself six years ago on the day he learned his wife had died giving birth to Emily while he was away at sea.

Now, sitting in the rocking chair in his daughter's bedroom, listening to the sounds of the storm intensifying outside, every sound—every *thing*—felt threatening. Jonas looked at the window and steeled his nerves. It *w*ould be a long night.

Movement from the corner of his eye caught his attention. Emily was stirring in her bed. "Father?" she muttered, rubbing her hazel eyes and blinking herself awake.

"Hello, Butterfly," Jonas said. It was the nickname Emily had earned chasing monarchs in the meadow. "Aunt Clara said you've been an angel."

To Jonas's surprise, his little girl gave a glum frown. "There are no such things as angels."

Jonas cocked an eyebrow. "Why would you say such a thing?"

"Is it true that there are ghosts out tonight?"

Jonas considered his answer. He always told his daughter

the truth, no matter how hard it might be. But now, he didn't know what to believe. He shrugged. "Some people say there are."

"Then how can there be angels if we become ghosts when we die?"

"Emily…" Jonas slipped from his chair to sit on the featherbed next to her and ran his hand along the waves of her ginger hair. "There's no need to be frightened. As long as my eyes are upon you, nothing can harm you."

Emily swallowed and cast her gaze to the pattern on her wool blanket. "Will Mother be with them?"

Jonas felt a cold wound open in his heart. "No. Your mother won't be with them. She died a smiling woman. She's with the angels."

"How do you *know* she was happy?"

"Because she gave birth to you. And you were all she ever wanted."

"Am I anything like her?"

"You are *everything* like her," Jonas said, forcing himself to put on a show of good humor. "You have her eyes…"

Emily erupted in giggles as Jonas crossed his eyes and peered down at her stupidly.

"Her nose…"

More giggles as he reached for her face and drew his hand back with the tip of his thumb protruding between two fingers as if he had snatched away her tiny nose.

"And her ears…"

Jonas puffed out his cheeks and flapped his ears with his hands, looking like a blowfish. Emily's giggles swelled into genuine laughter. Jonas savored the warmth that always blossomed inside him at the sound of her childish delight. He reached for the book of fairy tales Clara had left on the nightstand. "Aunt Clara told me you dozed off when she was reading to you."

Emily's eyes brightened, and she nodded. "It was during the story about the goose and the—"

A tremendous *CRASH!* erupted from somewhere outside.

"Jonas!"

The sailor heard his sister's panicked cry from downstairs and leapt to his feet. Footsteps pounded up the stairs. Clara appeared in the doorway, flushed and out of breath.

"The horse…"

Jonas gazed at her for only a second before her words sank in. Seized by a sudden, terrible dread, he rushed across the room, realizing what had happened but not wanting to believe it—not even *able* to believe it. He dashed down the stairs, tore through the kitchen, and flung open the back door. The garden lay in windswept darkness as he raced for the stable.

The smashed ruins of the door lay in pieces at his feet.

His horse was nowhere to be seen.

Jonas spun in circles, searching his surroundings. How could the stallion have broken loose? And why so suddenly? It seemed impossible. He kept telling himself it couldn't have escaped, it couldn't be gone. Not now. Not—

A noise came from inside the stable.

Jonas's head swiveled toward it. He listened, but heard nothing over the howl of the wind. He stepped over the splintered planks of the door and crept to the gaping hole where it had stood. A moment passed in silence as he waited for his eyes to adjust to the darkness. Was that the faintest hint of movement somewhere in the murky shadows?

Was that a man?

Jonas put it together in his mind: someone was using the cover of All Hallows' Eve to steal his stallion. Judging from the damage to the door, there had to be at least two of them. They had likely tried to work the lock on the stable before breaking their way in. While one thief took the horse, the other was now cornered in the barn.

"Who goes there?" Jonas bellowed. "I've a pistol armed! Come out now!" It was a bluff, but one so full of fury it sounded convincing.

Jonas planted his feet at the entrance and waited for a response.

None came.

After a few silent moments, he took another wary step into the gloom, wishing he *had* brought some kind of weapon. Anyone brave enough to venture out on this night wouldn't fear violence, especially not when trapped like a dog with its back to the wall. Jonas considered going back for the pistol he kept in the top drawer of his dresser. Then he thought better of it. There was no way he was letting this thief sneak away.

From the corner of his eye, Jonas caught the vague curve of a rusty scythe hanging on a peg. He reached for it—slowly, silently. He lifted it free and gripped it with both hands. A familiar rush of adrenaline flooded his muscles as his body readied for a confrontation. It wouldn't be his first fight… and there weren't many he had lost.

Another step brought him further into the darkness. He was nearing the far end of the stable now. The scythe was ready in his grip as he stopped and narrowed his eyes, searching the shadows for any sign of movement.

Nothing.

"You've nowhere to go," Jonas growled. "You'll not get through me, so better you should give yourself up now."

A jagged streak of lightning exploded outside the barn.

Two enormous, wild eyes stared back at Jonas in the brilliant flash.

His horse was back there, huddled against the far wall, terrified.

Jonas's whole body tensed. An awful wave of panic washed over him as he realized the dangerous position he had walked into. There were no thieves. There was only his terrified and very volatile stallion. Something had frightened the animal so completely it hadn't fled the safety of the barn, even after smashing its way through the door. It was as if it would rather die in the corner of the stable than go outside.

Denied the option of flight, the animal would now look to fight—and Jonas had snuck right up to it. He could already hear the giant beast panting in the darkness. It clicked its teeth and snorted, stamping its hoof into the dirt just yards away.

Jonas stood his ground, fully aware that the stallion would charge if it sensed his fear.

"Shhh… It's okay now…" He kept his voice so calm and soft it barely carried a breath. His heart beat furiously at his ribs as he lowered his eyes to the dirt and kept them there, doing his best to adopt a non-threatening posture. Any movement at all could provoke the frightened animal into a charge.

Another bolt of lightning revealed the horse's ears pinned flat against its massive head, its eyes so wide and wild they seemed nothing but white. In that instant, Jonas knew his soothing words were useless; there was no calming the panicked beast. Its terror was overwhelming, absolute, permanent. Now Jonas was right in the horse's path, dangerously exposed with nowhere to hide. He had to get out of there now, *now!*

It was too late.

The horse charged with the next blast of lightning.

Jonas spun away and almost impaled himself on the curved blade of his scythe as the two-thousand-pound stallion roared toward him. He crashed into the side wall and flattened himself against it, narrowly avoiding being trampled. In the darkness, he smelled the musty scent of the horse's hide as it flew past him, just inches from his face. He whirled around and recovered in time to see the enormous beast rearing on its hind legs, silhouetted by a vicious streak of lightning. Then the stallion swung around and bolted away. It thundered past the cottage and crashed through the picket fence into the darkness of the lane.

Jonas shouted after it as an ugly feeling sank into his gut. *NO NO NO!* He couldn't let it escape! Not now, not after all he'd worked for! Not when he was so close!

Another jagged bolt cracked across the sky. Jonas counted the seconds, using the old mariner's trick to calculate the distance of the storm. Twenty seconds later, the thunder came with a long, ominous rumble. Jonas stopped counting. Twenty seconds: the storm was still about four miles away. There was enough time for him to make it. He could find the horse and return before the storm struck.

Jonas retrieved the scythe and rushed from the stable. Clara stood in the open door to the cottage. She held a small storm lantern in one hand, its yellow sphere repelling the darkness. Jonas's coat was draped across her other arm.

"The horse has run off." He took the lantern from her and pulled the coat over his shoulders.

"Go. I'll stay with Emily." Clara saw the hesitation on her brother's face and placed her hands on his shoulders. "Jonas, nothing is going to happen to her. That horse is worth too much to let it go over a silly wives-tale."

Jonas wavered a moment longer. "I'll return before the storm breaks. Don't take your eyes off her."

Clara nodded and Jonas raced off into the night.

Minutes later, the sailor was far down the lane—much too far to hear his sister's strangled scream when she returned upstairs and discovered Emily's bed was empty.

Chapter 13

Alice felt the wind blasted from her lungs as she landed with a heavy *thud* among the bales of hay. But there was no time to recover. She dragged herself to her feet, scooped up Samuel's journal, and scrambled from the haystack.

Wind lashed her face as she raced across the yard to the Ingersolls' cottage and pounded on the door. "Mr. Ingersoll! It's Alice Jacobs! You must admit me!"

A candle flickered to life in the darkness of an upstairs window.

Alice drew back, panting hard, waiting for someone to unlock the front door.

No one came.

Alice waited with her heart in her throat, looking up at the delicate glow flickering in the window above her. What was taking so long? What were the innkeepers waiting for?

Someone extinguished the candle. The window went dark.

Alice gasped and went hollow. With rising horror, she finally understood the true depths of the town's terror. The Ingersolls had heard her cries; they knew she was out there, alone and terrified. But they were too afraid to help.

"Mr. Ingersoll, please! You must admit me!" Alice threw herself at the door again, screaming now, on the verge of tears. It was no use. Despair wrapped around Alice's heart like a sharp piano wire as she realized the innkeepers were never, ever, going to open their door to her.

Alice spun from the cottage and raced through the deserted streets, screaming for help. Salem's narrow lanes lay cloaked in darkness, a crooked maze of gloomy cottages illuminated only by erratic flickers of lightning. With Samuel's journal pressed to her breast and her nightgown whipping in the wind, Alice flew from house to house, hammering on doors, pleading for someone to come to her aid.

No one did. Not a single window was lit. No candles, no lamps—nothing to suggest there was anyone alive inside. The entire population seemed to have fled, leaving behind nothing but the silent, looming husks of an abandoned ghost town.

And yet, beyond the locked doors, the darkened houses were filled with families gathered around their children. Many of them heard Alice's frantic cries echoing through the empty night as she rushed past their windows. Like the Ingersolls, none dared come to their door. They cowered in their closets and cellars and crawlspaces, shutting their ears to her pleas and hoping she would go away. In their hearts, some wished they could help the pitiful stranger screaming in the night. But fear paralyzed them. So they kept their doors locked, looked to their children, and prayed that by sunrise, the anguished cries echoing through the streets wouldn't be their own.

Alice fled from one lane to another, turning one corner, then another, zigzagging her way into the oldest part of town where the lanes mingled like a tangled network of scars. There were no cobblestones here, and hard-packed dirt still lined the streets. Rocks and pebbles jabbed into the thin leather soles of Alice's slippers, but she felt none of it. Her mind was thrown into chaos as her thoughts struggled to make sense of all she had witnessed. *It couldn't be possible! The woman was made of mist! She wasn't alive! The curse was real! It was all true, every terrible part of it! The ghost of Rebecca Hale was real!*

And she had taken Abigail.

Alice emerged from the gloom of a crooked lane and found herself at an intersection. She skidded to a halt, her lungs blazing in her chest. Her face and hair were moist with a fine layer of sweat, despite the chilly air. With Samuel's journal tucked under one arm, her free hand fell to her knee and she remained there, hunched over, chest heaving.

As she gasped for air, Alice's desperation gave birth to anger. She hated this town and its cowardly people. She hated herself for bringing Abigail here, for leaving her daughter unattended at the inn. She hated Samuel for coming here, for disappearing, for leaving them all alone.

A tremendous cascade of lightning erupted overhead, warning of a downpour at any moment. The thunder came only seconds later, a blast so loud and violent Alice felt its explosion in her stomach. As the dazzling flashes receded, she glimpsed a street sign standing at the corner of the intersection: *Lynn St.*

Alice couldn't believe her eyes. Over the past few months, she had written countless letters to an address on Lynn Street.

It was one she remembered well: the home of Benjamin Emmons.

She started north without thinking, her jog speeding up to a run as she sped by the rows of shadowy houses until she found the address she was looking for. Like so many of its neighbors, Benjamin's small cottage stood silent and dark.

Alice dashed across the tiny footpath and threw her fists against the heavy door. "Mr. Emmons! It is Alice Jacobs! Please, Mr. Emmons! My daughter has been taken!"

It was no use. Alice's cries dwindled, and her fists fell away as she understood no one was home. Benjamin was with the orphans at the fort and his wife would surely spend the night with their ailing daughter.

Alice backed away from the door, her anger crumbling under the weight of her despair. She was alone with no one to turn to, no one to help her find Abigail. Her tears were flowing freely now, but she didn't care. She just let them roll down her cheeks as she slumped back to the street.

A man stood in the darkness.

Alice screamed and recoiled with fright. Her feet skidded across the dirt as she backpedaled and she slipped, hitting the ground with a jarring *thump* that knocked the breath from her lungs. She panicked and scrambled away in the dust, her eyes wide and frightened as she gazed up at the figure towering above her. She was on the verge of screaming again when the figure raised a lantern and revealed the handsome face of Jonas Hobbes.

"I… I'm so sorry, madam," He stammered as he offered his hand to help Alice from the dust. "I didn't mean to startle you. I heard your cries and I… Forgive me, I'm sorry to have

—"

"'Tis quite alright, Mr. Hobbes," Alice snapped. She waved aside his help as she caught her breath and picked herself up.

Jonas gave her a curious look. "I'm sorry, but you have me at a disadvantage, madam. Have we met? You seem to know me, but I do not know your name."

"My name is Alice Jacobs," Alice said as she went to retrieve Samuel's journal from where it had skidded away from her. She attempted to brush the dirt from her white nightgown before giving up and wiping the tears from her cheeks instead.

"Ah, yes!" Jonas's face lit with recognition. "The woman from the inn! I remember you. But what are you doing out here? You must know that the streets are not safe tonight."

"Please, Mr. Hobbes, I need your help. I…" Alice's voice cracked and faltered. She choked back the lump rising in her throat and forced the rest of her words from her mouth. "My only daughter is missing, taken from her very bed. I must—"

"Your daughter missing?" Jonas's dark eyes flew wide. "Quickly, tell me what you have seen!"

"There was a woman," Alice began, struggling to put her experience into words. It all still seemed impossible, too insane to be true. "A terrible black veil hid her face, as if she were in mourning. She came from the darkness, an apparition made of mist and smoke. She wasn't of this world, Mr. Hobbes. She *couldn't* have been. Oh God, forgive me… I never thought it could be true! I can scarcely believe what I am saying now, but I *saw* her! As sure as I am standing here, I saw her *with my own eyes!*"

"The prophecy has come true," Jonas murmured. "Pardon

me, madam. I must go. My own daughter is home without me."

"No! Please! You must help me! I must find Sheriff Feake, Magistrate Holm, anyone who—"

"You'll find no one out on this night, Mrs. Jacobs." Jonas waved a hand skyward where the wind howled and the trees swayed against a backdrop of storm-blasted night. "The dead are upon us. Even Captain Dennard has withdrawn his troops to the fort."

"They are abandoning the town?"

Jonas nodded soberly. "The lighthouse has caught fire."

Alice drew a sharp breath. "And the fort? What of Benjamin Emmons? Are the orphans safe?"

"We have no way of knowing. No one has seen Magistrate Holm since late this afternoon. And as for Sheriff Feake, you'll have no luck prying him from his hiding spot tonight. Even *I* would not be about, were it not for Midnight."

"What is to happen at midnight?"

"Nay, madam. Midnight is my horse, a great black stallion that broke loose from my stable this very hour, driven mad with fright. His loss would ruin me."

Alice grew impatient. "Sir, you will understand that I have no time for discussions about horses. If there is no one in this wretched town who will help me, I must take it upon myself to find my daughter."

"I am sorry, Mrs. Jacobs, but I am afraid that will be quite impossible."

"No. I refuse to accept that. I *will not* accept it," Alice insisted, her anger returning. "There *is* something I can do, something no one in this town has had the courage to do."

"What do you intend?"

"I will go to Gallows Hill and find the woman named Sarah Bridges."

An abrupt change came over the sailor. His face grew very grave and his eyes narrowed to hard points. "What would you have with that devil?"

"From what I have gathered, I believe 'tis possible that Sarah Bridges herself is to blame for my daughter's abduction. Perhaps she didn't merely predict the return of Rebecca Hale. Perhaps she somehow conjured the woman's spirit to punish the town that banished her years ago."

Jonas frowned. "You seek a perilous path, Mrs. Jacobs."

"Perhaps, but it is one that I am resolved to follow," Alice replied, her voice now carrying a hard edge of determination.

"It may already be too late."

"Then I have nothing to lose and nothing to live for. My life began with my daughter and it will end with her as well. Heaven help me, I will stop at nothing until she is returned!" Alice looked at him, her clear blue eyes glassy with tears. "Please, Mr. Hobbes… can you direct me to Gallows Hill?"

Jonas shook his head. "No. I must leave you now, Mrs. Jacobs. My sister is—"

"Please! For the sake of my daughter, you must direct me to the home of Sarah Bridges!" Alice shivered with cold now, the bitter wind cooling the sweat clinging to her skin.

"I'm sorry, madam, but I will not," Jonas said. "Do not ask me to visit death upon you. I am truly sorry for your loss, but I will not have your blood on my hands. Stay away from Sarah Bridges."

Jonas turned away, but Alice seized him by the arm and

whirled him around. "If you will not direct me, then I hold you responsible for the death of my child! Either my blood or hers will stain your hands this night!"

Jonas stood looking at her, his thoughts confounded by indecision. Something Alice had said resonated with him. *My life began with my daughter and it will end with her as well.* He knew that if he told Alice what she wanted to know—if he sent her into the Northern Woods—it would end in her death. But what if it were possible? What if she *could* find Sarah Bridges? Wasn't it her decision to make? She had already lost her daughter; wasn't she entitled to at least attempt a rescue?

Jonas gazed at the desperate woman standing before him. He could think of nothing worse than losing his child. Nothing.

"Mrs. Jacobs, I cannot direct you to Gallows Hill. But—"

Alice's face fell. "Please…"

Jonas held up a hand to quiet her. "I cannot direct you because *nobody* can. No one knows exactly where Gallows Hill is. The evils committed upon its soil were so unspeakable, we have stricken its very memory from every man, woman, and child in Salem. You will not find its location in any book, nor is it on any map. Every sign of its very existence was destroyed years ago. But…" He paused and drew a deep, wavering breath. "We know the gallows were somewhere deep in the Northern Woods, and I can direct you *there*. Somewhere in the dark reaches of that cursed land is where Sarah Bridges makes her home."

"Thank you, Mr. Hobbes," Alice said, sighing with relief.

"I fear you may not be thanking me for long," Jonas

returned with an underpinning of remorse. "I've heard it said there is an old animal trail that leads into the haunted woods —though nothing living will venture there. You will find it at the crossroads where the old Boston Road meets an Indian trail at the northern limits of town. Be wary as you travel, Mrs. Jacobs. I've heard tell of a wolf pack roaming about."

Jonas paused and looked at Alice's thin nightgown. "Oh Lord, forgive me…" he grumbled, already regretting his decision. He handed her his lantern, shrugged out of his wool coat, and wrapped it around Alice's trembling shoulders. "Take these. But I beg you, use the lantern to light your way back to the inn. Stay away from Sarah Bridges, or you stand to lose your soul as well as your daughter."

With that, Jonas turned and hastened his way down the dark street.

Alice waited until he vanished from sight. Then, pulling the coat tighter around her body, she held the lantern high and started north, toward the edge of town and the haunted Northern Woods.

Chapter 14

Benjamin Emmons knew something had gone terribly wrong. He didn't know what it was—not yet—but he knew something was wrong the instant Private Howell rushed in from his post. Benjamin had watched him scramble down the stairs of the stockade to speak to Lieutenant Maddock in low, anxious tones. And then he had seen the look of distress bloom in Maddock's eyes.

Until just a few minutes ago, Benjamin had been sitting on a stool in his cell, chatting quietly with Maddock as the lieutenant stood guard in the narrow corridor of the stockade. Benjamin shared the largest cell with his grandson and many of the younger orphans. Duncan was crouched in a corner with his knees gathered to his chest and his nose pressed into a book on maritime cartography he had brought from the museum.

Many of the other children had already fallen asleep, wrapped in the warm blankets Maddock's men had brought with them. Benjamin watched the rise and fall of their slumbering breaths and prayed they would stay that way for the rest of the long night. The older orphans in the neighboring cells passed the time playing cards, jackstraws, or Nine Men Morris. Most were too nervous to sleep; they were old enough to know what evils lay in wait.

Benjamin found Maddock to be standoffish at first. But the lieutenant warmed up as the minutes crawled by. Benjamin soon discovered they shared an affinity for trapping. They had been discussing the merits of a deadfall trigger to snare grouse when they had heard the first concussive *BOOM!* of the lighthouse keeper's cannon sounding its warning to a passing ship. It was perhaps half an hour later when Private Howell had come rushing in, his eyes wide and frantic.

Now, Benjamin stood at the door of his cell, watching the two soldiers and straining to catch a hint of their quiet conversation. He saw Maddock give a grim nod before turning away. The lieutenant's eyes betrayed his stormy thoughts as he stared at the floor, as if pondering his next move. Howell stood by, fidgeting and waiting for orders.

"Lieutenant Maddock, what has happened?" Benjamin asked. He was careful not to draw the attention of the children. The last thing he wanted was to frighten them.

Maddock said nothing and remained lost in thought. A long moment passed before he looked up. "The lighthouse is on fire."

Benjamin gasped, his mind reeling with the implications. He knew what had happened. He felt it with a certainty as firm as the iron and stone of his cell. This was no coincidence; it couldn't be, not tonight. A terrible evil had descended on Salem with the strange and ominous fog. Sarah Bridges' prophecy was coming true.

Overcome by a spasm of fear, Benjamin forgot himself and reverted to the command he had wielded as a sea captain. "Private Howell!" He waved a hand at the young soldier standing by the stairs. "Fetch the others and have them join us in here!"

Maddock whirled and raked the old man with an astonished glare. "Mr. Emmons! Need you be reminded you are a guest in this fort? You are not to address the men in my command, nor will you presume to give them orders."

Benjamin stiffened and glanced around. The children had stopped playing their games and were now watching them. A few were stirring in their sleep, awakened by the sound of the men's raised voices. Not wanting to alarm them any further, Benjamin motioned for Maddock to step closer. "Lieutenant, the curse is upon us." His whisper trembled with urgency. "I apologize for my outburst, but you must call your men inside. They are in great peril!"

Maddock frowned. "We are soldiers, Mr. Emmons. Our lives are always in peril."

"And as soldiers, you will know how foolish it is to wage a battle you cannot possibly win. This fog, the lighthouse set ablaze… they are the work of the witch! You saw the fog with your own eyes. It moves with a life of its own, doesn't it? Ask yourself if you have ever seen anything like it. Well, have you?"

Maddock wavered, his face darkening. "No."

"Please, lieutenant. The spirits will stop at nothing this night. You must call your men inside. Bring them down here before it is too late."

Still, Maddock hesitated, making little effort to veil his

skepticism.

"Lieutenant Maddock, I fear tonight Salem will bear witness to horrors the likes of which this town has never seen!" Benjamin hissed. Remembering who was listening, he glimpsed the fear creeping into the children's eyes and lowered his voice again. "Lieutenant, *you* are a soldier. But those men out there, they are militiamen. They are *volunteers*. They may have families of their own. Please give them a chance."

Maddock's brow furrowed as he thought it over. If he called the troops inside—if he left the lookout unmanned—he would leave the fort vulnerable and prone. But could he live with the consequences if something happened to them? There was a time when the answer to that question was certain. But now, he wasn't sure. He wouldn't admit it even to himself, but the outbreak of the fire in the lighthouse had shaken him. There was something wicked about this fog. He could feel it in his gut and his war-tested bones.

Maddock's hard eyes searched Benjamin's and saw nothing but fear staring back at him. Another moment passed before the lieutenant spun on his heels. "Private Howell, proceed to the lookout and have Private Keith ride to town to apprise Captain Dennard of our situation. You and Private Dunbury are then to report here to the stockade."

"Aye, sir." Howell saluted and darted up the stairs, leaning into the biting wind and slamming the door behind him.

Benjamin breathed a sigh of relief. "Thank you, lieutenant."

Maddock leaned closer to whisper through the bars. "Mr. Emmons, if you are correct—if there *is* something evil at work here—what can we do to defend ourselves?"

"We must—"

A muffled shriek erupted from somewhere outside.

The cry was faint—almost imperceptible above the eerie howl of the wind—but Howell's tortured wail was unmistakable to everyone who listened.

Benjamin's blood turned to ice in his veins. "Lieutenant Maddock, was that—"

"Shhh..." Maddock silenced him with a raised hand. The lieutenant's fingers trembled ever so slightly in the dim light of the lanterns. With his musket ready, he listened, hearing nothing but the incessant wind.

Benjamin noticed a small boy whimpering now, somewhere in the nervous silence of the cell behind him. The old man turned just as the door at the head of the stairs whipped open.

A terrified outcry broke from the children.

In a flash, Maddock dropped to one knee and wedged the butt of his musket into his shoulder. He aimed for the stairs and assumed the instinctive posture he had honed through years of disciplined training. Wind swept through the gaping doorway and he braced himself against it. With an earsplitting *CRACK!*, the corridor flooded with a dazzling flare as a bolt of lightning exploded beyond the door.

More of the children were crying now. Benjamin did his best to calm them, moving from one to another, gathering them together in his arms.

Still crouched in the corridor, Maddock kept his eyes focused on the stairs. Oblivious to anything else, he kept his tense finger on his trigger, ready for anything that came through that door.

Then the voices began.

They were soft at first; fragmented, ethereal, beyond understanding—drifting from the air as if they were part of the wind itself. Slowly, they rose. Whispers swelled into haunting words, a multitude of voices spilling over each other, filling the air. One voice—a man's—rose above the others.

Traitor...

Maddock went rigid.

Your shot...

The lieutenant's eyes grew wide. His face drained of all color and the musket dropped from his shoulder.

"Lieutenant Maddock, what do you hear?" Benjamin asked. A terrible sense of dread swept over him as he witnessed the abrupt change overtaking the soldier.

Maddock's head swiveled toward him, his face hanging blank. He gaped at the old man, dumbfounded, his eyes vacant and confused.

"What is it, lieutenant? What do you hear?" Benjamin repeated.

Maddock answered with a voice so tortured it barely drew breath. "I hear my dead brother."

It was yours...

Your bullet...

Overcome, Maddock staggered and fell to both knees in the corridor. *It couldn't be! It wasn't possible! It had to be a trick. One of those damn privates was—*

But no, that wasn't possible either. No one knew what had happened to Elijah, what Maddock *knew* he had done to his brother. He had told no one, not even when he had rolled that corpse over and seen his brother's horrible, ruined face. Maddock had turned away and kept it to himself, too ashamed to speak of it, too afraid to admit what he feared to have done.

Blasted the jaw from my face...

Ruined me...

Benjamin's heart went cold as Maddock dragged himself to his feet and took a step toward the stairs and the open door. "Lieutenant Maddock, don't! You must not go out there!"

Maddock's response was soft and distant, like a man speaking in his sleep. "Elijah..."

"No!" Benjamin was no longer mindful of the crying children watching them, no longer caring if they heard. "You mustn't leave us!"

Maddock reached into one of the deep pockets of his coat and withdrew an iron key ring. Without looking, he passed it through the bars to Benjamin. "Take these, Mr. Emmons. If something happens to me, these will release you from your cells."

"Lieutenant Maddock, that is *not* your brother!" Benjamin pounded furiously on the iron bars now. "'Tis his spirit! The ghost of Rebecca Hale will not be the only one haunting us this night! On All Hallows' Eve, *all* manner of dead are free to slip through the Veil. You must not go out there, lieutenant! Please! You must not leave us!"

But Maddock heard nothing beyond Elijah's beckoning voice. He crept along the corridor, the sharp point of his musket's bayonet gleaming in the lamplights. At the foot of the stairs, he paused and peered up at the black rectangle of the open door. Beyond it, there was only fog and wind and lightning.

Maddock waited a moment longer, heedless of Benjamin's pleas, ears pricked for that haunting, familiar voice—a voice so much like his own.

Traitor...

Come...

Learn the truth of what you've done...

Helpless, Benjamin could only watch in utter horror as Maddock ascended the steps and vanished into the thick, swirling mist. There was nothing but silence outside. Benjamin stood frozen, oblivious to the crying children, his old heart thudding in his chest as he waited for Maddock's return.

Minutes passed like hours until the thundering blast of a musket split the silence, exploding from somewhere in the fog beyond the open door.

Benjamin jumped with a jolt.

That's when Maddock's screaming began.

Even across the distance, the lieutenant's shrieks were loud and piercing, filled with an agony so unbridled it was unbearable to hear. Benjamin cringed and stood away from the cell door.

All at once, the lanterns went dark.

The children's terrified cries erupted in unison and filled the darkness.

"Stay calm!" Benjamin shouted over the chaos breaking loose. "There is nothing to fear! Lieutenant Maddock will return shortly!" The old man knew he was lying. There was much, much to fear—and Maddock would never be returning. Benjamin could hear the lieutenant's wails echoing in his mind as if they were still reverberating off the stone walls. He and the children were trapped in the darkness like mice in a cage, while some terrible predator lurked beyond the open door.

Another jagged streak exploded outside.

A woman stood silhouetted in the darkened corridor at the foot of the stairs. Her face was shrouded behind the black lace of a long veil.

The children saw her and the cells exploded with hysterical screams. Their shrill voices amplified off the walls as they fled back from the bars, stumbling and toppling over each other in the darkness.

Benjamin heard muffled cries of pain rising from somewhere near his feet as children trampled each other in the panicking stampede. He opened his mouth to shout, but the earsplitting chaos stole his words. From the corner of his eye, he saw the veiled woman advancing. Lit by another violent torrent of lightning, she slid along the corridor toward them, gliding effortlessly and unnaturally, as if floating on air. In the brilliant flashes, Benjamin saw her drift past the neighboring cells, taking no notice of the children within, ignoring their screams. She moved with a relentless, singular sense of purpose, as if she were intent on one cell alone.

And then, all at once, Benjamin understood. It was a realization so dreadful every part of him went frigid: the orphans were in no danger at all. They had no loved ones to mourn their losses—no one to *punish*. The vengeful spirit of Rebecca Hale had no interest in them. She had come for one child and one child only.

The only child with a family.

"Duncan!" Benjamin's frantic cry burst forth from the pandemonium of screams. "Duncan, come to me! Come to my voice! *Do it! DO IT NOW!*"

A pair of small hands seized the old man's coat, but he couldn't tell if it was Duncan. In that instant, he caught the outline of the woman now standing outside his cell, looming in the darkness like a shadow upon a shadow. Benjamin felt himself withering under the malevolent hellfire of unseen eyes, glaring at him from behind her veil. When her black dress came apart, the old man's mind drained of its stability. He watched in horror as her figure disintegrated into bits, dissolving, turning to smoke, to mist, flowing through the bars, into the cell, slithering toward them.

Benjamin shrank back and clutched at the child clinging to his waist. His shameless screams were now a horrible counterpoint to the children's as he scrambled across the cell. Losing all sense of time and place, he fell back against the wall, collapsing among the children, melting into the huddled mass, screaming in the darkness and waiting for the inevitable.

Waiting to be engulfed by the mist.

Chapter 15

Magistrate Holm reined his horse to a halt on the edge of Salem Common and found the field empty. A swift spike of alarm shot through him as he dismounted and looked around. Captain Dennard was supposed to be here, coordinating and supervising the patrols of his militiamen.

Now, there was no one. The Common was a sprawling expanse of darkness, its silence broken only by the ferocity of the storm unfurling overhead.

A cold prickle stole up the back of Holm's neck. It was a sensation he knew well enough. He had experienced it at Bunker Hill when the tide of the battle had turned against him.

Something had gone wrong in his absence. Something terrible.

Holm withdrew his musket from the holster strapped to Eclipse's side and gave the exhausted horse a distracted pat on the neck. Her chestnut hide gleamed with sweat, the heat of it sending plumes of steam into the chilly night air. Holm had ridden the horse hard from the Northern Woods and made the journey a short one. But the ride felt like an eternity. It had been a very long time since he had known the bitter sting of failure. He had gone to find Sarah Bridges, intent on fulfilling his oath to defend his town and its people. Instead, he'd been sent fleeing by the unspeakable horrors that dwelt in her cursed woods.

Holm still couldn't believe what he had discovered in that dark and terrible place. It didn't seem possible; in one horrifying instant, all he held to be true was laid to ruin like cannon-fire decimating the front lines of his carefully arranged forces. He could still hear the echo of hellish voices. He felt the freezing grip of icy hands clawing at him.

Holm shifted his musket from one shoulder to another and shook his head to clear away the awful memories. His eyes swept across the grand homes surrounding the Common, now looming in absolute darkness.

The streets were silent and desolate, like yawning portals into windswept nothingness. Holm stood still for a moment, listening for the sound of boot-heels clicking off the cobblestones as the militiamen marched their routes through town. His ears strained to hear the call of the captains as they sounded their *all-clear!*

All he heard was the lonesome howl of the wind. What was happening in his town?

A violent peal of thunder erupted overhead. A rising sense of dread stole into Holm's gut as he made his way to the eastern edge of the Common. An enormous statue of Salem's founder, Roger Conant, stood perched atop a massive granite boulder. The scaffolding they had erected it with only a week ago still surrounded the monument. Flashes of lightning reflected in dull glints off the new and polished bronze. The wide brim of Conant's pilgrim's hat was pulled low over his eyes and his long cape billowed behind him, as if he was frozen in time while walking headlong into a harsh storm. The pointed collar of his heavy cloak was pulled high around his gaunt face, framing an angular jaw and a mouth that was pressed into a grim line. His left hand was hidden somewhere within the folds of his cloak; his right gripped a gnarled oak limb like a walking stick.

The idea for the statue had been among Holm's first initiatives when he was elected to public office. As a new, independent republic, it was time for America to pay tribute to its own pioneering forefathers. And Roger Conant was one of the few men that Holm truly admired. Conant had been a man of uncompromising principle, courageous enough to sacrifice everything—home, safety, companionship—for the sake of his beliefs. It was only right that they immortalize him in the center of the town he had raised from the rock and wilderness.

Over the past year, as Sarah Bridges' omens unfolded one-by-one and All Hallows' Eve drew nearer, the raising of the monument had become much more significant. Holm knew the importance of maintaining morale among a frightened populace, especially in times of uncertainty and unrest. He'd intended to give the people something spectacular, a distraction that would provide some comfort. The monument would stand as a reminder of the perseverance the town had been founded upon, of what they could accomplish when a group of courageous people held together against a common foe.

Now, with the memory of his narrow escape from the Northern Woods still lingering in his mind, Holm looked for reassurance in the monument's austerity. Instead, the statue only filled him with a staggering sense of inferiority. Holm gazed up at Conant's stern face and wondered what his own legacy would be. How would he be remembered? A coward who failed his people on the night when they needed him most?

The bold embodiment of Roger Conant's courage now reminded Holm of nothing but his own shame. He turned his back on the monument and clenched his jaw into a tight block. The swirling winds swept dead leaves across his boots. For an instant, the sensation of being completely alone left Holm hollow. It was as if he had been gone for years and returned to find Salem laid to ruin in his absence. For a military man accustomed to the constant company of friend or foe, this strange and uncomfortable sense of aloneness was unbearable.

With great effort, Holm struggled to find the confidence and determination that had kept him alive through so many battles. He's shed his own blood countless times throughout the war, and yet he had never relented. There had been retreats and disease and destruction and annihilation, but Holm had never once surrendered his hope for victory. Why should tonight be any different?

A comforting realization came to the magistrate: he was being tested, just like the great Roger Conant. What set a man apart was how he rose from the ashes of his own defeat. History would judge him by how he reacted at this very moment.

Holm took heart and forced himself to remember there was more than one way to win a war. It wasn't too late; he could still put an end to Sarah Bridges' evil. He had failed to find her home, but now, standing in the shadow of Salem's founder, Holm realized he didn't need to find the woman after all. A man needn't kill a general to defeat an army. Sarah Bridges may have had him at a disadvantage in the safety of her cursed woods, but the spirits she had conjured would soon come to him, to *his* town.

He would be waiting when they did.

Chapter 16

Alice stood at the ancient crossroads and gazed up at a massive crucifix looming over her in the darkness. Twenty yards ahead of her, the old Boston Road vanished into the darkness of the Northern Woods. To her left and right, the trampled remains of a long-forgotten Indian trail skirted the forest and extended into murky obscurity.

No one knew who had erected the giant cross where the paths intersected. The common belief was that it was planted there over a century ago in memory of a bloody massacre during the time of King Philip's War. A young minister had been traveling from Boston with his family when a Wampanoag Indian raid ambushed their carriage at the crossroads. The minister and his wife were slain and disemboweled on the spot, but their children had suffered a much worse fate. Both were made to eat morsels of their parents' entrails. The horrific incident was one reason the old road through the Northern Woods was abandoned and the newer one cut a few miles to the east, along the open and safer banks of the North River.

Alice didn't know how much time had passed since she had left the town streets behind her. The quaint cottages that clung to Salem's outskirts had given way to older and more rundown farmhouses. The open spaces between them had grown more expansive until there had remained nothing before Alice but wind and darkness and the hard ruts of the dusty road.

Out in the open fields, there was nothing to block the wind but the gnarled, claw-like trunks of the apple orchards. Alice had been lashed and rocked by the unimpeded gusts as she pulled the collar of Jonas's wool coat up around her chin and pushed into the teeth of the wind, lighting her way with the sailor's lantern.

Ahead—not too far away—she had made out the ragged tree line of the Northern Woods rising from the gloom. It stood silhouetted like a gaping fissure across the lightning-streaked sky.

Alice had clutched Samuel's journal tighter as she drew nearer, taking comfort in its weight. The leather felt smooth under her touch. For some strange reason; it made her feel as though her husband were there with her, holding her hand and accompanying her along this dark and frightening road.

Now, Alice held her lantern high and took a moment to study the enormous crucifix erected at the crossroads. There were slivers of white stuck in the cracks and recesses of the ancient wood. Someone had whitewashed it at some point, but the harsh New England elements had long since stripped the paint away. A closer look at the center of the cross revealed more faded paint stuck in an indistinct collection of gouges. Alice squinted in the dim light to make them out and thought they resembled engravings. Were they letters?

The yellow stalks of overgrown grass brushed against Alice's thighs as she waded closer, raising her lantern so that its light fell on the weather-beaten wood. Yes, they *were* letters. The shallow grooves were almost eroded smooth. Alice leaned forward and narrowed her eyes, straining to make out the crude carvings. There were numbers as well. A chapter and verse from the Bible:

Jeremiah 6:16

An unexpected spark of recognition struck Alice. Something about this reference to Scripture was stuck in her memory. She didn't know why it seemed so familiar, but it did. She had seen it before, recently. Then it came to her: Jeremiah 6:16 was a verse she had come across just a few hours ago… in Samuel's journal.

Alice backed away from the cross and knelt on the dirt at the center of the crossroads. She set the lantern on the ground next to the journal. Her eyes twitched from side to side as she skimmed through her husband's notes. She felt the briefest moment of doubt when she reached the end of the entries with no success. Had she seen the Bible reference somewhere else? No. It was here; she was sure of it. Resolute, she went back and started again, slower this time, scanning each page.

And then there it was, in Samuel's own writing, staring back at her: *Jeremiah 6:16— "Stand you in the crossroads and see and ask for the ancient paths; ask where the good way is and walk therein, and you will find rest for your souls. But you said 'We will not walk therein."*

Alice stared at the page. It couldn't be a coincidence; Samuel had *seen* this cross. There could be no other reason he had recorded this one specific scriptural verse. Samuel had been here! He had been here on his way to Gallows Hill, just as she had always suspected.

Alice stiffened.

There had been a sudden change in her surroundings. She was only now becoming aware of it, but something was different. It felt as if something had gone missing from the night air. She tilted her head, craning her neck to listen. It took her a second to realize what had changed, but when she did, an icy chill crawled up her spine.

The wind had stopped.

For one peculiar moment, Alice had the unpleasant impression of having been stricken deaf. It was as if a constant whispering in her ear had gone silent. She glanced around with a creeping sense of foreboding, taking in the empty expanse of the crossroads and the yawning blackness of the woods beyond.

Everything was absolutely still.

There were no creaking tree limbs. No rustling branches. No fluttering leaves. Nothing. The air had gone dead. Even the thunder fell away. The night had stopped breathing, leaving nothing but a lifeless and empty void.

Alice's pulse quickened as she waited and readied herself. Something was about to happen, she was certain of it. Something terrible lurked behind the eerie silence. The stillness of each passing minute hung like heavy stones on her nerves. Then—so slowly it was almost imperceptible—the air came alive again.

Only now, the night exhaled whispers instead of wind.

Alice rose to her feet, straining to make out the faint sounds drifting to her from every direction. At first they were soft, ethereal, fleeting—like raindrops landing with a *hiss* on a patch of scorched earth. Then the sounds grew and took shape, becoming more material. Alice could soon make out voices: dozens of men and women whispering in a language she didn't understand. Their strange words came to her as if snatched from the shadowy ether of another world.

Alice seized the lantern from the ground and held it up to illuminate the darkness. "Who is there?" she cried with an edge of panic. "Show yourself at once!"

The voices grew more substantial, more insistent, as if they were *willing* their way into existence.

All at once, Alice realized she *did* understand the language. What she had mistaken for a chant were fragmented syllables, repeated over and over with no discernible pattern like a mad incantation.

...uff... ring... fer... ing... er... suf...

The syllables came together, picking up speed, finding a common rhythm, pulling themselves into one single word.

...suff... er... ing... suffer.. ing...

Alice's heart went cold as it all came together.

...suffering... suffering... suffering...

The nightmarish chorus swelled, growing in numbers, dozens becoming hundreds, gaining strength with each recitation of that one terrible word.

...suffering... suffering... suffering...

It was deafening, swirling all around her.

Alice suddenly heard Samuel's voice in her mind. Even

above the chaotic din of the ghostly voices, she heard it as clearly as if he were standing next to her. He was saying something: a random anecdote she had overheard once without really listening. It was one of the silly superstitions he amused Abigail with before sending her off to bed. *If you stand at a crossroads on All Hallows' Eve and listen to the wind, you will hear what will befall you in the year to come.*

Alice's blood froze in her veins.

...SUFFERING... SUFFERING... SUFFERING...

Another sound arose from beneath the voices, one so high and keening its pitch existed only at the upper threshold of Alice's perception. The sound grew, took form, and she realized she was hearing screams—hundreds of them—merging into one perfect note of absolute agony.

Alice pressed her hands to her ears, desperate to mute the shrieking chaos that was every bit as ferocious as the wind had been. The voices were so intense, so overwhelming, she felt she would collapse under their weight at any moment. She had to escape.

She swung around and probed the woods for the animal trail that would deliver her from this pandemonium. In the feeble light of her lantern, her eyes fell on nothing but snarls of underbrush and trees. The dense woods seemed impregnable.

With the terrible screams piercing her brain like the razor-sharp point of an arrow, she finally found the trail. The narrow opening was but a slim and indistinct shadow among the trees. Alice snatched Samuel's journal from the dirt and broke toward the path, fleeing headlong into the black maw of the Northern Woods.

Chapter 17

Benjamin Emmons hadn't ridden a horse in ages. He couldn't recall how many years it had been; it could have been ten as easily as two. Every impact of his steed's furious gallop pounded at his old bones like the relentless blows of a blacksmith's hammer. As he charged across the narrow causeway connecting Winter Island to the mainland, Benjamin gripped the reins and grit his teeth against the bitter winds sweeping from the sea.

Ahead, the dark gloom of the forested mainland drew nearer. Jagged bolts of lightning blasted across the sky, battling for violent supremacy. Back beyond the wind-blown whitecaps churning across Cat Cove, the squat bulk of Fort Pickering loomed atop the hill. Its hulking silhouette was shrinking as Benjamin sped away.

Further in the distance, the lighthouse stood blazing in the night, engulfed in flames. Benjamin could smell the acrid stench of the smoke being carried inland by the howling winds as he reached the mainland and left the hellish scene behind.

The road to Salem from Winter Island was relatively smooth and well-travelled from years of military use. Even in the darkness, it was impossible to lose. The young quarter-horse Captain Dennard had given Benjamin seemed to know the way instinctively as she thundered onward. If the mare could maintain this pace, Benjamin guessed he could reach the outskirts of town within a few minutes. Another couple minutes of navigating Salem's winding lanes would see him at the Town Hall. There, with any luck, he would find Magistrate Holm.

With even more luck, the magistrate would have found Sarah Bridges.

The looming shapes of trees flew by on either side as Benjamin charged through the woods. He shifted his feet in the stirrups and forced himself to ignore the pain shooting through his aching joints. Instead, he bent his thoughts toward piecing together all that had happened since that terrible moment in the stockade.

He could remember the dreadful woman standing outside his cell, her face obscured by her awful mourning veil. There was no doubt it had been the spirit of Rebecca Hale, risen from Hell to seek her revenge. Even now, Benjamin could feel the scorching intensity of her baleful stare. He remembered screaming for Duncan as she came apart, dissolving into that terrible mist that slithered into the cell with a life of its own. There was darkness and confusion and trampling feet and tiny hands clutching at him and a vague sense that these were the last breaths he would ever take. There were screams and screams and screams…

And then there was nothing.

When Benjamin had awakened, Captain Dennard was standing over him. Duncan was gone.

What came next seemed to Benjamin like the fragmented memories of a fevered dream. He was still in his cell, surrounded by orphans crying and wailing in terrified fits of hysteria. As he told Dennard everything that had happened, he could hear his own voice crying and moaning. He had a vague recollection of the captain explaining he'd withdrawn his troops from town to fight the fire in the lighthouse once a patrol near the harbor had spied the blaze.

There was another memory—the only one that wasn't hazy —of Dennard describing what remained of the soldier they had found outside. *Shredded.* That's the word the captain had used. There were bits of flesh everywhere, scattered across a wide area as if the man had been torn apart by dozens of frenzied claws. They had found the head nearly thirty yards away. Half of the skull was gone. What was left was ripped and torn, the one remaining eye staring out from the gore with a look of infinite terror.

Benjamin had a dim recollection of being asked about Lieutenant Maddock—*Maddock, Maddock, Maddock…*

But Benjamin didn't know what to say.

Someone needed to apprise Magistrate Holm of their situation and Dennard needed every man at his disposal to help contain the damage to the lighthouse. Benjamin had a vague memory of being asked if he could ride, but all he could think of was the awful look on his daughter's face when she had lost her own child nine years ago.

Little Charlotte had been off on her own, exploring the woods as children often do, when she happened upon an abandoned well. It had been used to hide patriots during the war and was so artfully camouflaged it had resisted the detection of even the keenest redcoat. Six days had passed before a man from the search party spotted the little girl's body down in that dark hole.

Charlotte's death had nearly broken her mother's spirit. Consumed by grief, she'd begun wasting away, rarely leaving her bed and often refusing to eat. Only when she had become pregnant with Duncan some two years later did she regain her will to live.

What would Benjamin tell her now that Duncan was also gone? How could he put his daughter through that agony again?

It was these first stirrings of anguish that had brought Benjamin back to his senses. His daughter wouldn't be able to bear the death of another child. Her life would be lost if they didn't find Duncan. Losing her only remaining son would undo what remained of her already fragile health and finish her.

Benjamin wouldn't let it happen. He would find his grandson if it cost him his life.

The forest came to an abrupt end, and he now raced past the first of the board-and-batten cabins on the edge of town. Ahead, shrouded in darkness, the narrow lanes leading to the town-center lay empty and silent.

With great effort, Benjamin willed his thoughts away from the terrible events of the last few hours. *Had it really been just hours?* It all still seemed unreal, like a terrible dream. But the unbearable grief Benjamin carried with him on that ride back to Salem reminded him that every horrifying moment had been all-too real. He would have to keep his emotions under control if there was any hope for his grandson. Magistrate Holm would have questions and Benjamin would need his wits to answer them.

And if Sarah Bridges was with him, Benjamin would need his strength to kill her if she didn't tell him where his grandson was.

Chapter 18

Alice crashed across the threshold of the forest and found herself in absolute darkness. As she fled the hellish screams of the crossroads, she felt as if the night itself had swallowed her. The darkness was so thick—so unnatural—even the light of her lantern seemed fearful of straying too far from its flame. Its fragile radiance surrounded her with a trembling sphere beyond which nothing was visible. The world ceased to exist outside the shallow radius of the lantern's yellow glow.

The terrible shrieks receded into the distance as Alice tore through the underbrush. Eventually, her steps slowed and became more calculated. It was cold here among the dense trees, much colder than at the crossroads. The silvery steam of Alice's breath hung in the air. She shivered and pulled Jonas's coat tighter over her nightgown, clinging to Samuel's journal like a castaway hanging on driftwood. The narrow herd path led her ever deeper into the woods and she struggled to keep the faint line of trampled underbrush in her sights, trying not to think about the dangerous situation she was walking into.

If the trail escaped her, she would be lost and alone, with

no hope of finding her way out of the darkened forest.

A growing sense of unease gnawed at Alice's gut. The woods were devoid of life, as if nature itself had abandoned it and left it for dead. She softened her steps to quiet her footfalls, listening for frogs, bats, an owl—*anything*.

There was nothing but a dreadful silence.

The lantern trembled in Alice's hand as she picked her way ever deeper into the darkness. She was a tiny island of light drifting across a vast sea of eternal nothingness. Her shuddering breaths were too loud in her ears and she wished she could stifle them, fearing they would give her away—to *what*, she didn't know.

Utterly alone, Alice's fears fed on the silence. This was madness. What was she doing here, wading into this frightening wilderness? She had come this far on the slim assurances of a man she had just met, trusting that this murky trail would lead her to Sarah Bridges. What would she do if she found the witch? There was no longer any doubt in Alice's mind that a powerful evil had descended upon Salem. She had seen too much with her own eyes to deny it any longer. How could she stop it? If Sarah Bridges was strong enough to conjure such forces, what chance did Alice have against her? If she had any hope of rescuing Abigail, she would have to be ready to do anything—to *sacrifice* anything.

Suddenly, she froze. Was that a sound?

Alice scanned the yawning void beyond the lamplight and saw nothing but darkness. She tilted her head and raised an ear, listening. Seconds stretched into minutes as she stood in silence.

She heard it again.

Alice's breath died in her throat. The sound was distant and faint, but unmistakable.

A child was screaming in the black reaches of the forest.

"Abigail!" Alice's frantic cry rang across the darkness and echoed forever through the woods. She waited breathlessly for a response, but none came.

The child had fallen silent.

Alice surged forward, propelled by a renewed sense of urgency. She couldn't be certain—not with the way the child's scream had bounced from tree to tree—but she felt sure the cry had come from somewhere further ahead. The lantern swung crazily in her grip as she ran. The light flickered over dense tangles of shrubs and underbrush that ripped her nightgown and tore at her legs as she sped through. Alice didn't notice any of it. One solitary goal consumed her every thought: finding the child, finding her daughter.

Something snared Alice's foot without warning.

She stumbled and crashed to the ground. Her momentum sent her slewing across the forest floor, and her hands shot out to absorb the impact. She gasped as the sharp teeth of twigs, stones, and dirt bit into her palms. Stunned, she lay there for a moment, catching her breath and assessing her injuries. Her hands were bleeding and aching with a dull throb that felt like a burn. But nothing was broken. She flexed her foot and discovered she hadn't twisted her ankle. She still had the brass ring of the lantern's handle around her wrist, but she had lost her grip on Samuel's journal during her fall. Sprawled on the forest floor, she dragged herself to her hands and knees and glanced back to see what had tripped her.

There was nothing there but rotting leaves.

A sickening feeling took root in Alice's stomach as she staggered to her feet. She hadn't imagined it—*couldn't* have. Some *thing* had caught her ankle and sent her sprawling.

Alice had an instinctive urge to run. There was something evil about this place. She could feel it, sense it like an animal senses danger. She had to get further down the trail—and she had to do it *now*.

The lantern's light cut through the darkness as Alice searched for Samuel's journal. She felt more vulnerable with each passing second as she kicked at the underbrush, scattering the leaves and twigs.

At last, the leather surface caught a glint of light from beneath some cripple-brush just a few feet away. Alice's pulse raced as she went to retrieve it.

Something grabbed her ankle.

Alice gasped and looked down.

There was nothing there.

Alice's eyes went wide with fright as she tried frantically to kick her leg, but couldn't. An unseen hand held her in place

A child let loose a shrill laugh beyond the light of the lantern.

Alice flailed and jerked her foot, windmilling her arms to keep from toppling over. A blinding agony blossomed from her ankle as she fought to break loose from whatever invisible grip held her. Something was happening to her flesh, something unimaginably painful. Her skin was growing hot, blistering as if it were being seared by the white-hot tip of a firebrand.

Except this was the agony of ice—something invisible was

freezing her flesh to the bone.

A skeletal handprint materialized on the exposed white of Alice's ankle. She watched, too terrified to scream, as the imprint rose to the surface of her skin. The impression of finger-bones deepened to an ugly shade of blue, freezing and bruising her flesh under the crushing grip of the invisible hand. It twisted her leg out from under her and she tumbled forward, her ribs shuddering beneath her weight as she hit the ground hard. The lantern rolled from her hand and went out.

Alice had the horrible sensation of being stricken blind as the darkness swooped in to engulf her. She struggled against the hand clenched around her ankle and dragged herself to her knees. The lantern lay nearby. She crawled toward it and stretched for the ring. Her fingers brushed against the brass…

Another hand seized her wrist with crushing force.

The child's shrill laugh bounced out of the darkness once more. This time, others joined it. A bone-chilling chorus laughed at Alice's pain, taunting her like children in a schoolyard. *They're cold... So very cold... They want you... Need you... They want your flesh... They want your blood... Give it to them... Warm their graves...*

Alice's scream echoed in all directions as the invisible hands pulled at her, hauling her downward toward the earth.

Warm their graves… Warm their graves... Warm their graves...

The pungent smell of dirt and rot filled Alice's nose as her strength gave out and she collapsed to her stomach on the forest floor. She was screaming and sobbing at once now, unable to resist the hands dragging her down. She clenched her jaw, biting down hard against the pain of their freezing grip. A tooth cracked under the pressure.

The invisible hands continued their relentless downward pull, stretching her flat, crushing her chest into the soft carpet of leaves and earth. She opened her mouth to scream again, but the cry died on her lips when another hand seized her by the throat. Her eyes bulged in their sockets as she choked and gasped for air. Her chin was resting in the dirt now and she struggled as though she were trying to keep her head above water. Tears streamed down her cheeks in ruddy streaks as the nails of her free hand clawed and scrabbled at the forest floor.

The ghostly hands wouldn't yield. When they could pull no further, the ground beneath Alice softened strangely. To her absolute horror, her foot sank *into* the earth.

The unseen children still mocked her from the darkness, their sing-song taunts filling her ears like a nightmarish nursery rhyme.

Warm their graves… Warm their graves... Warm their graves...

In a moment of sickening clarity, Alice understood what was coming. She saw herself being dragged down, down, down—into the earth, beneath the surface, vanishing, rotting, becoming nothing. She had an image of Abigail alone and frightened, wondering where her mother was, wondering why her mother hadn't protected her, why she was left for dead. Alice saw all of this very clearly and spiraled into a chasm of despair. This was it, the end of everything. This is how she would die. Alone. In the darkness.

But then something else happened.

It began with a stirring deep within her, a sensation unlike any she had ever known. Alice's despair grew so great—so absolute—it became something else, something of immeasurable power: rage. Alice felt it rippling through her body, coursing in her blood like lightning through water. Her rage was a gift; a weapon unlike any other.

Alice summoned all the months of pain and sorrow and fed her anger, fueling it like a fire, giving it strength, giving it *life*. Everything—all the loss, all the frustration, all the heartache, all the hopelessness and despair and suffering—was channeled into an impossible force of will. Alice felt it blazing within her, boiling over, ready to be unleashed. She gave voice to her rage with a primal cry of might and fury.

"I will pass! Your guardians will not stop me, Sarah Bridges! *I will pass!*"

Driven by a strength she never thought she possessed, Alice pressed her hands into the dirt and pushed against it, tearing against the ghostly hands that threatened to drag her under. Inch by agonizing inch, she strained to raise herself up from the earth. She forced every muscle in her body to its limit and pushed past the point of endurance. Somehow, she knew this wasn't supposed to be possible; the grip of these terrible hands had never been broken.

And yet, it *was* happening. Alice was resisting, fighting back. She would not let herself be taken. The skeletal hands were losing their grip with every inch she gained. She knew they would relent; they *had* to relent.

With one final, supreme effort, Alice dragged herself to her feet and broke free of their icy clutches.

The laughing taunts of the children turned to shrieks of fury as she scrambled away, sucking in air, heedless of the discolored handprints she would bear like livid tattoos on her skin until the end of her days. Frantic, she dashed down the path, not looking back, leaving the wails of the children behind and forgetting all about Samuel's journal as she ran and ran and ran.

.

Chapter 19

Jonas Hobbes slumped against the doorjamb to his daughter's bedroom and stared at the empty tangle of blankets on the bed. The room before him was in shambles, the result of the grief-stricken fury he had flown into when he'd returned home to find Emily missing. Now he stood gazing blankly at the wreckage, cursing himself for his selfish stupidity. He had known the risk he was taking when he'd left Emily. Yet he'd left her anyway—left his little girl vulnerable and helpless while he went after a damned horse. A goddamned horse!

Now, his only child was gone.

Jonas closed his eyes and hung his head. He could hear Clara weeping somewhere downstairs. He knew he should go to her and try to comfort her. But he didn't have it in him. He didn't blame his sister for what had happened; Clara would have given her life to keep Emily safe. But how could he comfort her when he, himself, was so far beyond consolation?

Jonas hauled himself from the doorjamb and stepped into the room. He brushed aside the splintered remains of a shelf with the toe of his boot. Emily didn't have many toys. The few she had were now scattered to all corners of the room. Jonas stooped to pick up a ragged doll. It was the one he had brought back for Emily from the West Indies, one of her favorites. He gazed at it for a moment, not seeing the doll but remembering his daughter's delight when he had given it to her.

It wasn't particularly attractive to look at. The doll was crude, carved from some dark wood and clad only in bits of leather and twine. Most children would've thought it grotesque. But what had mattered most to Emily was that it had come from somewhere far, far away—somewhere like the magical lands she read about in the books Jonas sometimes brought her. Emily found the exotic doll enchanting and Jonas knew his daughter admired him for his travels. She never complained when he departed on another long voyage. Emily wanted nothing more than to go with him, following him everywhere, sailing with him to every point of the compass.

A bitter gall rose in Jonas's throat. He swallowed it and placed the doll on the dresser. He didn't know why he did it —his daughter was gone forever—but he just couldn't bear the idea of her favorite toy lying discarded among the wreckage.

Jonas picked his way through the mess of shattered furniture to sit on the edge of Emily's small bed. He remained there, staring at nothing, his tear-filled eyes seeing only a barren and meaningless future. Minutes passed before his gaze slid to the floor.

Half hidden amidst the remains of the shattered bedside

chair lay the slim book of fairy tales he had been reading to his daughter. Jonas leaned forward and plucked it from the debris. He flipped through the pages absently until came to where he had last left off. The realization that Emily would never know how this story ended crushed him.

Jonas's thoughts drifted to Alice, the woman so intent on journeying to Gallows Hill to confront Sarah Bridges for herself. What if she was right? What if Bridges *had* conjured the ghost of Rebecca Hale? An image flew into Jonas's mind. He envisioned Sarah Bridges roaming free and untouchable in her cursed woods while her wicked spirits rode the winds and did her evil bidding. He could still hear Alice's words echoing in his thoughts: *My life began with my daughter and it will end with her as well.* Didn't he feel the same about Emily? Wouldn't he do anything—risk anything—to get his daughter back?

Jonas imagined Alice traveling alone to that terrible place and was filled with a humbling shame. She had the courage to venture into the mouth of Hell to find her child. Yet here he was, wallowing in his own despair while his little girl was out there somewhere in the stormy darkness. If Emily was alive, she would be alone… and so terribly frightened.

Jonas couldn't live with the thought.

The book tumbled back to the floor as he rose to his feet, his jaw clenched in a grim scowl. Broken bits of wood crunched and split under his boots as he left the wrecked room behind and marched down the narrow hall to his own bedroom. There, he slid open the top drawer of his dresser and withdrew his flintlock pistol. It was a .69 caliber with a worn walnut stock, French barrel, and tarnished brass fittings.

Jonas filled his pockets with handfuls of lead balls, grabbed the powder kit, and headed for the stairs.

Clara was already on her feet and waiting for him when he reached the first-floor landing. Her face was dreadfully pale and her eyes were red and swollen from countless tears.

"Where are you going?" Her voice was hoarse and cracking.

Jonas didn't answer. Instead, he turned to the place where he hung his coat, only now remembering that he'd given it to Alice.

"Jonas, please! Tell me what you're doing!" When Clara spied the pistol in her brother's hand, she understood his intention clearly. "No! You can't go out there!"

"I must, Clara."

"What can you possibly do?"

"I am going to find Sarah Bridges."

"You can't! You will die, I'm sure of it!"

"I *will* go! And I will stop at nothing until the hateful woman returns my daughter to me."

Jonas turned, but Clara fell on his arm before he reached the door. "What will I do without you? You are all the family I have!"

Jonas's determination wavered when he saw the heart-wrenching anguish painted on his sister's face. But the crack in his resolve lasted only a moment.

"I'm sorry, Clara. But if I do not find Emily, then I am lost to you already."

He released himself from his sister's grip, turned his back on her, and stepped out into the raging night.

Chapter 20

Alice scrambled through the darkness, directionless, losing all sense of time and place. Minutes passed like hours until she saw dim flickers of light filtering through the shadowy forest ahead. They were faint, like the light that would sneak between her fingers if she covered her eyes with her hands. The flashes grew brighter as she plunged onward. Alice soon realized she was seeing the lightning piercing through the treetops again. There was a clearing ahead.

Alice sobbed with relief as she surged toward it, sprinting through the undergrowth until she burst into the small grove and skidded to an abrupt stop.

An enormous stallion rose like a monument atop the small rise of a hill.

The horse's hot breath streamed from its flaring nostrils in a billowing white cloud. Its smooth, ebony coat shined like satin and reflected the jagged bolts streaking across the open swath of sky.

Startled by the horse's unexpected presence, Alice let out a yelp and retreated to the edge the grove. She moved carefully to avoid spooking the massive stallion until she reached a safe distance, where she paused and eyed the animal. What was it doing out here? Was this the horse that Hobbes was after? It had to be. But what drew it to this place? Why would it have wandered so deep into these cursed woods? And why was it standing there as if waiting patiently for something to happen?

Just then, a bone-jarring *CRAAACK!* exploded overhead and Alice jumped. The thunder and lightning were detonating as one now, bathing the grove in a dazzling array of pink and purple and white. The air hummed and crackled with electricity as Alice returned her attention to the immense horse. She glimpsed a dark space gaping between the trees on the far side of the grove. It took her a moment to recognize it as the start of another path. Even obscured in shadows, it appeared much more distinct than the one she had followed into the woods. At the sight of it, Alice felt a spark of hope rekindling within her. Perhaps this was the trail that would lead her to Sarah Bridges. At the very least, it would give her a direction and save her from her aimless wandering through these terrible woods.

But the massive horse now stood in her way.

With a deep breath, Alice took her first cautious step around the stallion. She paused, testing its reaction, then started again. The beast could charge at any moment, but it remained still and calm, indifferent to her presence. She took another step, then another. Her eyes were on the horse as she angled around, watching for the slightest reaction and giving it a safe distance as she circled the grove toward the fresh path.

She took one step too many.

The stallion thrust its head out and looked directly at her.

Alice's heart lurched. She froze in her tracks. She saw the horse flatten its ears straight against its enormous head, pinning them back as far as they would go. Its tail stood rigid before it swished from side to side with agitation. The steam of its angry snorts filled the air. Alice could almost feel the ground quaking as the animal pounded its hoof as a warning. She felt an instinctive impulse to retreat, but the furious stomp of the stallion's powerful foreleg and the gnashing of its bared teeth kept her frozen in place. How long before the beast charged? Seconds? Maybe less?

She became aware of another sound.

Someone was approaching.

Alice heard the distinct tread of footsteps crunching across the forest floor somewhere deep down the path to her right. Caught between the path and the enormous horse, she felt a hot stab of panic. She was trapped. Any sudden movement could incite the nervous stallion to charge, but if she remained here, exposed, she would be discovered by whoever —or whatever—was approaching from the darkness. Even now, she could hear the footsteps growing louder, closer.

Time was running out. Whatever Alice decided, she had to do it now.

She darted for the cover of the nearest trees, praying she wouldn't hear the awful gallop of the horse's massive hooves thundering after her. To her relief, the stallion remained where it was. With only seconds to spare, Alice hid in the underbrush. She spun around in time to see a dark figure materialize from the murky gloom. It was cloaked in a filthy robe that was tattered and rotting. The robe's heavy hood was pulled low over its head, concealing its face in shadows.

Alice crouched unseen at the edge of the grove and held her breath. A second, smaller shape emerged from the darkness. Lit by a flash of lightning, it surprised Alice to see it was a small goat. Its short horns protruded at asymmetrical angles and its fur was brown all over except for a black stripe along its snout and two steaks of white that stretched from its muzzle to its strange eyes. The muted staccato of its plaintive bleating drifted across the clearing as it trailed behind the figure at the end of a long leather tether.

Alice's heart thumped as she squeezed the scar of her bottom lip between her teeth. Had the cloaked figure seen her? She had no way of knowing if she'd acted quickly enough to avoid detection. But if the figure *had* seen her, it was now choosing to ignore her. It circled around the stallion and came to a halt in front of it.

Alice's muscles tensed in anticipation of the beast's violent reaction to the blatant challenge. Amazingly, the horse had no reaction. Instead, it seemed overcome by a placid calm as it lowered its giant head and offered it to the figure. A hand slid from the folds of the figure's ragged cloak and laid itself on the stallion's black muzzle. The fingers were long and slender and white as bone.

Minutes passed as the figure stood with its hand on the motionless horse, as if holding the beast in thrall. Then the hand drew back. Alice watched as the spidery fingers traced invisible symbols in the air. There was something distinctly feminine about the gestures, an eerie, preternatural grace.

For the first time, Alice considered the possibility that a

woman was hidden beneath the cloak. The revelation filled her with a mixture of dread and relief.

Had she found Sarah Bridges?

The woman continued her eerie pantomime, swaying and moving rhythmically with the lithe grace of a dancer. A strange incantation murmured in a language Alice didn't recognize accented each of her fluid movements. Punctuated by the thundering chaos unfurling in the sky, the chant took on a melody that was beautiful and haunting and ominous all at once. As if sensing something awful was about to happen, the goat trembled at the woman's feet, growing more agitated with each repetition of the fearful incantation. It reared and bucked, its eyes rolling back to the whites with terror as it strained its neck against the frayed tether. The words of the woman's chant were barely audible over the pitiful cries of the animal's bleating.

Alice was careful not to make a sound as she inched forward in the bush to make out what was being said. There was a sudden flash of steel as the woman drew a long blade from the folds of her cloak. With the same eerie grace, the knife flew down in a long, swooping arc. The cruel blade glinted as it slashed the goat's throat from ear to ear.

Alice clamped her hands to her mouth to stifle her shock as a fount of crimson sprayed from the animal's severed artery. There was a gurgling sound, like liquid rushing through a perforated pipe. Then the air filled with an awful reek as the animal's bowels vacated themselves. The goat's hind legs pistoned spastically for a moment until there came a long, shuddering wheeze as its last breath escaped its cut windpipe.

Horrified, Alice looked on as the hooded woman lowered

the knife and rolled the dead animal onto its back. The woman gripped it by its forelegs and dragged the carcass around the grove, encircling the stallion and painting the ground with a trail of hot, steaming blood. When she came full-circle, the woman drew to a halt before the horse and sank to her knees among the dead leaves. The goat's legs twitched as the woman plunged two long, white fingers deep into the gaping gash in the animal's throat. The heat of the blood sent tendrils of steam into the chilly air as her slender fingers smeared a series of arcane symbols down each of the horse's front legs, ending with the hooves.

Alice's pulse thundered in her ears as the woman remained there for a moment, kneeling before the horse, head bowed as if in prayer.

And then the woman's hood turned toward her.

Even hidden in the darkness, Alice felt the heat of unseen eyes staring at her. There was no longer any doubt; the woman knew she was there.

She had *always* known.

A sickening dread struck Alice as the woman rose up to her full height. She panicked and shrank back through the underbrush as the figure advanced toward her, dragging the dead goat across the leaves with one slender hand and clutching the bloody blade with the other. The woman was taller than any woman Alice had ever known.

Alice collided with the thick trunk of a tree as she scrambled backward. She could only watch, paralyzed by terror, as the sinister figure drew ever closer like an unholy doom. Every impulse for self-preservation told her to run, to flee and never look back. She peeled away from the tree and spun around, on the verge of retreat…

Something stopped her. If she turned away now, she would lose Abigail forever. This was her only chance of finding the answers she sought.

Alice gathered all of her courage and turned. She stepped forward into the grove and stood her ground. "Sarah Bridges, I have come for my daughter." She hoped her voice sounded as bold as she meant it to.

The figure continued to advance, a menacing specter gliding across the shrinking distance between them.

Alice's courage faltered at the sight of the sharp blade gleaming red in the bursts of lightning. It was too awful; she had to look away. Her gaze fell to the ground without meaning to, unable to face the terrible darkness pooling within the advancing figure's hood. With her eyes lowered to the withered leaves, Alice waited, terrified yet refusing to yield her ground as the slow and steady footfalls drew ever closer, now only a few feet away.

A heavy boot strode into view…

Then another…

The figure drew to within striking distance…

It stopped.

Alice drew upon a determination she didn't know she had and willed herself to face the figure standing before her. She trembled as her gaze slid from the ground to the lifeless goat. Her eyes crawled up the woman's rotting cloak to the bloodstained blade. At last, she raised her head and stared at the hooded nightmare. Her heart pounded louder than the thunder above.

"I have come for my daughter," she whispered, her mouth

feeling parched. Then, calling upon her anger, her whisper became a shout. "*Where is my daughter?*"

A dreadful moment passed as the cloaked figure loomed over her in silence. Alice shivered as something cold and wet landed on her skin. The first raindrops were falling.

Alice lost all capacity for fear as she stood there, staring up at the terrible shape and not backing down. She had gone too far and seen too much. The nightmarish voices at the crossroads; her harrowing escape from the skeletal hands; this dreadful figure looming over her; losing Samuel; losing Abigail—all of it was too much to bear. She had already lost everything. What had she left to fear? If she died now, she would welcome death as a merciful deliverance from a lifetime of sorrow and despair. Only her grim determination to discover her daughter's fate kept her from sinking to her knees and offering her neck to the woman's blade.

The figure took a step toward her.

This was it; th*is was the end*. Alice squeezed her eyes shut and held her breath, expecting it to be the last she ever drew.

Another step…

Alice trembled as she waited for the inevitable. Would she hear the blade slicing through the air as it sped toward her throat? She heard the woman's cloak rustle and prayed the end would be quick and painless.

One last step…

And the figure brushed past her.

Alice's eyes snapped open. She bent doubled-over, hands on her knees, her chest heaving as she exhaled hard and swallowed deep gulps of air. She turned and saw the tall woman dragged the goat's limp body back down the path from which she had come. What remained of the animal's blood spilled across the leaves as it slid and bumped over the rocks and roots. Before long, the dark shape vanished into the gloom, leaving Alice alone with the stallion as the heavens opened and the rain came down upon her.

Chapter 21

Jonas was soaked to the bone by the time he reached the edge of town. The dusty path of the old Boston Road had disintegrated to muddy ruts in the downpour. The thin linen of the sailor's shirt clung to his brawny chest as he trudged through the storm on his way to the Northern Woods. His ponytail lay plastered to the back of his neck and fat drops of rain pelted the bare skin of his arms as he shivered with cold. It was all he could do to keep his powder kit dry in the pocket of his wool pants.

Jonas took no notice of it. His thoughts were in a dark place where he had Sarah Bridges at his mercy and all the time in the world to make her talk. He didn't need a lantern to show him the way. The dazzling bolts tearing loose from the heavens showed him all he needed of the road and the ramshackle farmhouses and the apple orchards beyond.

And then he saw something else.

A squat shape stood in the darkness on the side of the road.

Jonas shielded his eyes and squinted, trying to make it out through the driving rain. Was it merely a tree stump?

Then it moved.

Jonas's hand fell to his pistol as he slowed his pace and crept nearer. His muscles tensed and flooded with adrenaline. Nothing friendly would be out on this black night, not in this storm.

Each slow and cautious step brought Jonas closer to the shape. He kept his eyes on it, waiting for it to make a move as it stood there in the rain, waiting for him.

A violent flash of lightning fell upon the shape and Jonas's jaw dropped open.

A small girl stood tethered by the neck to a crooked fencepost.

The child couldn't have been older than seven or eight. Her hands were bound behind her back by a leather thong, and someone had gagged her with a dirty strip of burlap. She wore nothing but a simple cotton dress, and she shivered in the rain as she stared up at Jonas with a look of unspeakable terror.

Jonas rushed to her and dropped to his knees in the mud, pulling the gag from her mouth and releasing her hands. The tight leather binding left deep abrasions on the pale skin of her wrists. "What are you doing out here?" he demanded. "Who did this to you?"

The poor girl could say nothing through the merciless chattering of her teeth.

"Can you tell me where you live?" Jonas persisted.

The girl hesitated, as if unsure how to respond. Then she pointed at the rundown farmhouse looming behind her in the darkness.

"There?" Jonas asked, astonished. "You live *there*?"

The girl nodded.

"Come with me."

Jonas took her little hand and led her across the muddy footpath. They mounted the steps to the porch, where they found shelter from the downpour. Jonas pounded at the old wood of the front door. "You in there! Open this door at once!"

When no response came, Jonas stepped back and gave the door a vicious kick just below the handle. The wood shuddered and reverberated with the impact, but the door held. Jonas looked closer. The doorframe was old and brittle; it should have splintered and ripped free with the force of his blow. Someone had reinforced the door from the inside.

Jonas put it together in his mind: someone *was* inside. Barricaded. Hiding.

Jonas crouched before the girl and took her shivering shoulders into his muscular hands. "What is your name?"

The girl said nothing. Instead, she stared at him with round, fearful eyes. When she spoke, it was in a hoarse whisper that Jonas barely heard over the beating of the rain. "Nora."

"Nora, I know it's frightening out here, but I need you to wait here just a few moments longer. I want you to remain here by this door. I'll be right back for you. Do you understand?" Jonas waited for an answer but the girl only looked up at him and trembled. "Nora?"

Nora gave a slow nod.

Jonas rose to his feet and rounded the wraparound porch until he came to a large, dirty window. He did his best to wipe the grime away and peered inside. He saw nothing in the murky darkness. If anyone was in there, they were not to be seen. Jonas hesitated for just a moment before shielding his eyes and smashing the windowpane with his elbow. Clearing away the shards of broken glass, he peaked inside.

He saw the rifle pointed at him an instant before it was too late.

Jonas dropped to his knees just as the muzzle flash exploded from the barrel and sent a lead ball roaring past his ear. He was up again in an instant, vaulting through the empty window and lunging for the shadowy figure fumbling to reload the rifle in the darkness.

Jonas rammed his shoulder into the man's stomach and heard a wheezing grunt as the air burst from his opponent's lungs. Locked in a furious struggle, the two toppled backward, smashing through a flimsy table on their way to the floor. A thin hand clawing at Jonas's face. He batted it aside and shifted his weight just in time to block a bony knee that was driving up toward his crotch.

Something hard caught him in the jaw from the other direction. His mind exploded with a white flash as he reeled from the blow. His left hand found the fleshy stretch of a throat and clenched it. He balled his other hand into a tight fist and brought it down hard—again and again and again—each time hearing the satisfying *smack!* of his punches striking home and doing damage.

"Leave him alone!"

Jonas froze at the shrill cry. He turned, his fist still raised and quivering in the air.

Three boys stood in the doorway. Their shabby clothes were tattered and poorly patched. The tallest held a sputtering lantern, its glow casting a lambent light across what was supposed to be the parlor of the dilapidated house. He must have been about thirteen, if he was a teenager at all. The other two boys were smaller and younger. The trio gaped in shock at the scene before them.

"Pa!" The eldest boy's eyes narrowed. He saw the man Jonas held pinned to the floor by the throat and took an angry step forward.

With one quick motion, Jonas had his pistol in his hand and pointed at the boy. It wasn't loaded, but the mere sight of the firearm kept the child rooted to where he stood. Jonas looked down at the scrawny, barely conscious man beneath him. His broken nose was spewing blood, but in the yellow light of the boy's lantern, Jonas realized he knew the man. It was Fergus Hollins.

In that one terrible instant, Jonas understood. He looked back at the boys standing in the doorway. "That girl outside. Nora. She's your sister?"

The tall boy hesitated, then nodded. His eyes were round with fright as he stared down the barrel of Jonas's pistol.

"And this man, your father. He left her tied out there?"

Another slow nod of the boy's head. His trembling voice fell low with shame. "Pa said the witch would come for one of us. Better it should be her than one of us, he said."

An awful nausea swept through Jonas's gut. Fergus Hollins was a well-known drunk who often neglected his apple orchards in favor of the local tavern. The man had left his own daughter outside as a sacrifice to Rebecca Hale, hoping she would spare his sons. Hollins needed his boys to support the household while he drank his days away.

But his daughter was expendable.

Jonas felt a molten rush of fury as he gazed down at the man's pasty, grizzled face. Hollins was regaining consciousness and looking up at him through a smattering of blood. His thin jaw moved, as if he meant to say something, but Jonas snapped it shut with the barrel of his pistol.

"I've returned your daughter to you." The sailor hissed through clenched teeth. "You will do whatever it takes to keep her safe. You will give your own life if you have to." Jonas pushed the cold steel barrel further up underneath Hollins' chin. "If that girl isn't here when the sun rises, by God, I will return and thrash you within an inch of your life. And then I will drag that inch before Magistrate Holm himself!"

Jonas glared at the man to make sure he understood. Hollins' sons remained where they were, eyeing the sailor as he rose to his feet and crossed the room. He hauled aside the hutch they had used to barricade the front door and flung it open.

Nora stood looking up at him from the porch.

"Come inside," he said. "You'll be safe here now."

Chapter 22

Alice took shelter from the rain beneath the heavy boughs of an ancient spruce. Hidden from view, she kept her distance and watched as the cloaked woman dragged the dead goat up a few rickety steps to the dilapidated front porch of an ancient cabin that rose like a decaying sepulcher from the darkness.

Shrouded by a knot of twisted trees, the cabin's timber frame was green with moss and lichen and the walls seemed shaped from the forest itself, as if called together by some magic that was now losing its hold and crumbling. Streams of rain ran across the ruined shingles of a roof that sloped downward at warped angles and reached out over the sagging porch. A gnarled mass of ivy clung to the fieldstone chimney, coiling skyward and nearly obliterating the stones from sight. The orange glow flickering in two of the crooked windows burned in the night like the eyes of a pagan idol.

It was as if the cabin stood in the palm of a primordial hand that threatened to snap shut at any moment, dragging the whole thing back into the earth.

Alice spied the woman pausing on the porch to let the rain run off her cloak before she nudged the front door inward with the toe of a muddy boot. Firelight from within caught her shape and spilled a long shadow across the porch, bending at square angles down the steps as she stood silhouetted in the yellow glow.

For one fleeting instant, Alice thought she saw the hood tilt to one side. Her heart skipped a beat. Did the mysterious woman know I had followed her? Did she sense Alice watching from the shadows?

Alice held her breath as the woman remained motionless on the porch. She glided across the threshold without looking back, and the door swung shut.

Shivers wracked Alice's body as she waited to see if the woman would reemerge from within. The rain came down in torrents, even under the dense canopy. It plastered her hair across her cheeks and the soaked shreds of her nightgown clung to her legs. Her jaw was growing numb from the chattering of her teeth as she wrapped herself tighter in Jonas's wool coat, thankful for what little warmth it afforded.

Long minutes passed with no sign of the woman. Alice snuck from beneath the giant spruce and crept across the final fifty yards to the cabin. Explosions of lightning sent jagged patterns of shadows across the crooked roof. Alice kept to the cover of the trees and skirted around the porch, approaching it from the side. She was keen on avoiding the creaking steps that might give away her presence. She pushed through a snarl of underbrush to where the planks of the porch tilted toward the ground like a ship listing to one side. There, she mounted the decrepit platform and crouched beneath a boarded-up window.

The rain pattered relentlessly on the moss blanketing the decaying roof above Alice's head. Plump drops seeped through a crudely patched hole and fell with a splash on the nape of her neck. The damp stink of rotting wood filled her nose as she remained below the crisscrossing planks covering the window and listened for movement from within the cabin.

There was nothing.

Alice kept low as she slid toward the wavering square of firelight emanating from the next window. She did her best to tread lightly, wary of breaking through the sagging planks that flexed dangerously beneath her feet. Her heart beat furiously as she drew nearer to the window. Had her husband made it this far? Alice already knew Samuel had been at the crossroads. He might have found his way through the woods to this place. Was this cloaked woman somehow connected to the mysterious Giles Dicer, the man Samuel intended to visit on the day he had disappeared?

What if Samuel was being held captive inside?

Alice steeled her courage and rose tall. She had come here for a confrontation; now was the time to demand it.

She moved boldly across the porch and reached for the door. She barely hesitated before prodding it open. It swung inward with a tired and rusty groan.

A welcome wave of heat greeted Alice, as if the cabin itself was exhaling. Its warm breath was thick with fire smoke, candles, and exotic incense. Alice detected another smell as well, lingering somewhere beneath the first. This one was pungent and unpleasant: the cloying reek of mold, mildew, and rot.

Alice nudged the door open further and stepped across the threshold. A fire roared and crackled in an immense stone fireplace. The room was deceptively large, its limits hidden in the dancing shadows. Antique books and arcane objects cluttered the walls, strewn about the shelves with no apparent order. Glass jars of all shapes and sizes filled with ugly, opaque fluids stood in chaotic disarray. Crude dolls made of burlap, twine, seashells, and bone lay scattered among an assortment of dreadful animal skulls. The carcass of the goat was splayed on a large oaken table across the room near the fireplace. Books, skulls, and the molten stubs of candles littered the surrounding surface.

The cloaked woman stood at the table with her back to Alice.

"You interrupt my ceremony." The woman's whisper flowed from within the dark of her hood. Her voice was distinctly youthful, its timbre warm and husky and touched by an accent that Alice couldn't put a name to.

"A mother's love for her child moves me to no better end," Alice returned, keeping her tone low and even. "What have you done with my daughter?"

"The wolf, the rat, the cat, and the wild; I know of the shadows, but not of a child." The woman pulled back her tattered hood to reveal a darkly beautiful face. Her hair was long and thick and the color of a raven's wing, so black it almost consumed the light. She was tall and willowy, with a slender neck many would have considered elegant. She gazed at Alice with icy blue eyes that radiated intensity. But what struck Alice most was the woman's skin. Stretched tight across her slight and delicate features, it was as white as alabaster and so pale it seemed translucent. A threadlike constellation of veins was visible below the surface, like scratches of blue ink concealed beneath a pale sheet of vellum.

"Are you Sarah Bridges?" Alice asked. She made an effort to cover her surprise at the woman's youthful appearance. "Are you the one known to Salem as the witch of Gallows Hill?"

"I am that same Sarah Bridges, but I am no witch. I am an artisan." The woman's lips curled with the faintest trace of a disdainful sneer as she drew the long blade from the folds of her cloak. She turned her back on Alice and set to work at butchering the goat.

Alice couldn't conceal her revulsion as Sarah split the carcass from abdomen to throat and hauled handfuls of bloody viscera out onto the table. "And is this your art? Animal sacrifice? Black magic?"

Sarah cracked an amused smile. "Nay, my art be storytelling. I am a soothsayer—or *truth-sayer*—if by sooth we mean truth."

"Stories are seldom the basis for exile."

"Aye, but the *truth* may see you cast out." Sarah let out a bitter chuckle.

A hint of something unstable in the woman's voice led Alice to wonder if Sarah was losing her sanity from years of living in isolation amidst these dismal woods. It was a dismaying prospect. What could she hope to gain from a madwoman?

"The townsfolk scorn me, for I am their accuser," Sarah went on. She used the tip of her blade to separate one of the goat's femurs from its hipbone. Then she gripped the leg and tore it away from the joint with a loud *snap!* "Through my divination, all the secrets of Salem are known. Shall I tell you of Mary Barker's dalliances with George Colson? Of the babes Elizabeth Coombs has secretly buried? Of the milk Henry Sears steals every Sunday while the town is at prayers? Or what of Roger Willard's less-than-holy relations with his prize pig?"

With a sudden, vicious blow, Sarah brought the knife crashing down on the goat's neck, severing the vertebrae and sending its head spinning from its body. She ignored Alice's revulsion and flung what remained of the carcass into the fireplace. The flames leaped and blazed as they fed on the mangled mess of bone and flesh and sinew. Next came the limbs, the fire roaring to new heights with each dismembered piece it devoured. Alice fought back a wave of nausea and raised a hand to shield her nose from the stench of burning fur.

"We all have our scapegoats," Sarah continued, motioning to the fire. "I have mine; the townsfolk have theirs. It seems Salem has always had a problem with its judges."

"Is that why you conjured the spirit of Rebecca Hale?" Alice demanded. "To punish the town that judged you and cast you out?"

The impish smile vanished from Sarah's lips. Her blue eyes turned icy and her pale face grew dark and solemn. "The witch's spirit is conjured by no one, beholden to none. She rises unbidden from the realm of wrath and vengeance."

"I don't believe you," Alice said, losing her patience. "What have you done with my daughter? Tell me now!"

"What becomes of the children is no work of mine. If I

were the witch I am thought to be, would I not be offering your daughter to my bone-fire in the place of a goat? Would I have risked my own life to warn the hateful town of Salem of the coming of this terrible night? No. I have done all I can to save them from their fates. Now, they will reap what they have sown."

"You meant to warn them that night at the Harvest Moon Ball?" Alice asked warily.

"Aye. When my eyes stared in horror at what was to come."

"Why did you do it? Why return to Salem and put your life in peril to save the very citizens who banished you?"

"Because I scorn the hurt of any child." Sarah turned from the fire and leveled her cool eyes on Alice. "Mrs. Jacobs."

Alice felt physically struck as the echo of her name hung in the air. She stared at Sarah for a second, stunned, thinking she must have misunderstood. How could this woman know who she was? "Pardon… I… I have not given you my name."

"There was no need to." Sarah's blue eyes glittered.

"You were expecting me," said Alice. It was all becoming very clear to her now. Sarah had deliberately led her here, to this place.

"It was I who delivered you from the hands of those condemned to the earth," Sarah confessed.

Alice's thoughts strayed back to those awful moments in the woods when the ghostly hands had threatened to drag her under. She glanced at her wrists and the skeletal handprints emblazoned on her flesh. She could still feel the icy clutch of the hand wrapped around her neck and knew that she would bear the mark of its grip forever. "You released me? Why?"

"That you might find the truth you seek."

"The truth of what?"

"Rebecca Hale. Shall I show you her story?"

"Show me? How?"

Sarah motioned to the bones roasting in the fire. "Come. Look."

Alice hesitated before crossing the room to stand by Sarah's side at the fireplace. She waited while Sarah murmured words that sounded sibilant and enchanting, like a language without hard consonants. She followed Sarah's gaze into the fire and saw nothing but flames, embers, and ashes. But as Sarah's haunting chant rolled on, Alice soon discovered that she *did* see something.

Some kind of structure was taking shape within the fire. An image was drawing itself together before her eyes. The angles of the goat's bones became walls, and Alice soon had the impression that she was staring into a small room engulfed in flames. The image was mesmerizing, hypnotic. Alice was dimly aware of Sarah's voice somewhere beside her, her strange words rising and falling with an eerie cadence, lulling her into a trance.

As if pulled by an irresistible force, Alice had the strange sensation of being drawn *into* the blazing room. There was a moment of panic as the flames rushed toward her. She felt their heat, heard their crackling, was blinded by their brilliance. Then there was nothing but a serene calm as she left the cares of the present behind and stepped across the ages into the unalterable past.

Chapter 23

When Alice opened her eyes, she was kneeling in a filthy cell as narrow as an upright coffin. Her legs felt cramped and sore, but there was no room to stretch them. Somewhere beyond the heavy oaken door, the soft glow of a sputtering candle sent glimmers of yellow light flickering through iron bars set into the wood.

A spasm of panic and claustrophobia gripped Alice as she tried to make sense of what had happened. Where was she? What had Sarah Bridges done to her?

Alice looked down and discovered she was wearing the tattered remains of an old-fashioned dress. It was black and severe, with straight sleeves and a bodice laced from her navel to her neck. She ran her hands across the soiled linen and somehow she knew it was the dress Rebecca Hale had worn on the day she was arrested.

Scratches raked across the stone walls above Alice's head. She traced her fingertips across them and had the uncanny impression that she *was* Rebecca.

Like a bubble rising to the surface of a black lake, a dim

realization came to her: she wasn't merely being shown Rebecca's story; in this strange reality Sarah had conjured, Alice had somehow *become* Rebecca. It was Alice's hands that had flailed at the stone walls. It was *her* nails that had torn loose against the hard stone.

Alice trembled with fright and struggled to stand. There was no bed or chair in the tiny chamber. Lying across the floor was impossible. Kneeling on the cold stone had been Rebecca's only respite from endless hours standing upright.

Alice's muscles ached as she rose to the level of the bars of her cell door and peered into the gloom. A dingy corridor stretched away in either direction. The flickering flame of a tallow candle set on a ledge sent a line of oily smoke into the darkness that shrouded the heavy ceiling beams of Salem's witch dungeon. The weak candlelight gave off no warmth and no consolation. Cold and dampness filled the air. Water ran down the stone walls in thin but constant trickles, leaving behind sticky streams of orange mildew. The foul scent of burning tallow was coupled with the stench of unwashed bodies and human filth. Moans and whispers haunted the dim corridor.

Through the bars, Alice watched in horror as a rat materialized from the shadows and scurried down the corridor. Others quickly followed, filthy creatures with loathsome eyes and diseased flesh who were drawn from the nearby harbor by the enticing scent of the dead and dying. Alice heard their chatter in the hushed quiet of the jail as they scuttled by her door and disappeared into a neighboring cell.

"Ann Foster is dead!" A tormented voice wailed. "Please! She is being devoured! Somebody please have mercy on her!

Please! Oh God, please deliver me!"

Other inmates joined the screaming as the rats glutted themselves on the remains of Alice's neighbor. But such cries were common in the witch jail.

The candle's flame guttered and went out with a sudden hiss.

Plunged into darkness, a rising tide of panic swelled from deep within Alice as she cowered, blinded and trapped in her narrow confines. The icy walls felt like they were collapsing inward. Her arms flew out to keep them at bay. Her foot kicked against something round and metallic. There was a splash, and the awful reek of excrement and urine flooded the darkness. A rush of nausea rolled from Alice's gut and scorched the back of her throat. She whimpered when the distant clink of iron keys rattled from somewhere far beyond her door.

The hysterical wailing of the other inmates came to an instant halt.

Alice's heartbeat reverberated like cannon-fire in the silence. Two men spoke at the end of the corridor. Alice cocked her head to listen, but their words came to her as if she were underwater. They were too far away to understand. There was the scrape of a heavy door being swung open, then a dull *thud*. A sallow light spilled through the corridor.

Alice's breath halted.

Heavy footfalls approached.

Each step resonated down the narrow passage and echoed toward her. Alice recognized the menacing stomp of the jailor, and she realized she now possessed Rebecca's memories as if they were her own. She had somehow grown accustomed to the sound of the jailor as he came and went, escorting prisoners to their trials. She could even remember him taking the time to stop and whisper cruel taunts through Rebecca's door—through *her* door.

But now it was the sound of two men walking with an unmistakable sense of purpose.

Alice's pulse quickened, the accelerating rhythm of her heart hammering against her ribcage as if it were pounding to be released from her chest. The thin slivers of light flickering into her cell grew brighter as the booming footsteps drew nearer. Then the glow vanished. The footsteps halted outside her door and an enormous silhouette stood in the way.

Alice went rigid and cowered in the darkness. She smelled the stale odor of a man's breath wafting through the bars and realized that it was familiar, as if she had smelled it a hundred times before. There was the shuffle of fabric and a sharp *clang* as a key rammed into the iron lock.

Alice recoiled from the door and pressed her back to the damp stone wall as the hard gaze of Edgar Fisk, Salem's jailor, appeared between the bars. She shrieked as he flung the door open and seized a fistful of her hair. He yanked her from the cell with a vicious snarl and hurled her into the corridor. Alice rebounded off the wall with a sickening *thud* and collapsed to the floor at Fisk's feet. Her world went blank. No sight, no sound—just a searing white pain.

More of Rebecca's memories thrust their way into Alice's mind, like the surreal twists of a dream spiraling into a nightmare.

Months after Rebecca's arrest, Alice stood with her at the meetinghouse where Rebecca was being examined by Judge

Hathorne. Rebecca had once been pretty, but her teeth had long since turned a sickly shade of yellow. Grime smeared her pale skin, obscuring the spattering of freckles that marked her face and arms. She had thick red hair that was now a tangled mess of impossible knots. Her mouth was a dry crack stretched between two sunken cheeks. Her dull green eyes stared from the depths of hollow sockets like tarnished emeralds tossed in a well. The limp remains of her simple black dress hung from her emaciated frame, the delicate linen now little more than soiled rags.

Alice watched in horror as Salem's afflicted girls fell to their knees, screaming and writhing in agony each time Rebecca denied the judge's accusations of witchcraft. Ann Putnam twisted her limbs into impossible angles and wailed that Rebecca's spirit was tearing her apart. Mercy Lewis pointed at Rebecca and cried that she could see Satan at her ear, whispering curses from his black book.

Alice watched in disbelief as people leaped to the aid of the shrieking girls, soothing them, comforting them, embracing them. For the first time, she understood the awful power Salem's afflicted girls wielded. As they screamed and writhed on the old wood of the meetinghouse floor, she understood that Rebecca's innocence was worthless. What could the woman have said to defend herself against such a wicked performance? What hope did she have when even the sanest among them believed the testimonies of these teenage fiends?

The nightmare twisted again. Alice saw Rebecca being flung into her squalid cell and chained to the wall in irons. At dawn one dismal morning, they snatched her and led down the foul corridor. In a small stone chamber, they stripped her naked and made her stand on a rickety chair to be searched for witchmarks. Exposed and ashamed, trembled in the cold as the rough hands of Edgar Fisk probed every inch of her naked flesh. A greasy leer slid across his face as he paid particular attention to her most delicate areas.

Unable to stand the sheer humiliation of the man's hands slithering across her skin, Rebecca's mind had fled. The damp walls dissolved around her and she was no longer a captive in the witch dungeon. She was in the vast meadow she had played in as a girl. Honey-yellow sunshine poured across rolling acres of tall prairie grass that brushed across her thighs. The aroma of milkweed filled the air, syrupy and spicy and dripping with memories of her youth. Lush fields of violets and prairie asters spread before her, a riot of blues and whites. The soft and vivid spires of lupines swayed in the breeze, cascading down a gentle hillside before giving way to the tall thickets of silky pussy-willows and tiger lilies stretching along the banks of a cool brook. A flight of swallows soared and swirled above her. Rebecca closed her eyes and sank to her knees, glorying in their music.

Countless days sped by. With every new degradation, Rebecca's mind fled to the comfort of the meadow. She felt as if she were watching herself from a distance, as if it was all happening to someone else, someone she didn't know, someone she didn't care to know. In the silence of her cell, Rebecca often wondered what had become of her children. She demanded they not be brought to visit her. No matter the heartache it brought her, she refused to risk their safety by seeing them. The power of Salem's afflicted girls was now fearfully absolute—and children were not beyond the aim of their accusations.

Summer came and went by the time Rebecca was hauled before Judge Hathorne again. Her eyes were vacant, overcome by that now familiar sense of detachment, as they led her accusers into the meetinghouse. They fell into hysterics at the sight of her. Rebecca's spirit was biting them, choking them, burning them, drowning them…

All at once, Rebecca's memories vanished. Alice's mind reeled as her senses flickered back to life one by one. Her sight was dim and unfocused. Sounds came as if from a great distance as the world spun around her. She struggled onto her back and saw Fisk looming over her in the dingy corridor. A hulking mass of brute force, he was a pitiless blacksmith who blamed Salem's witches for his wife's death. He had been the first to volunteer to keep them behind bars—and to serve as a hangman if needed.

Sheriff Corwin stood behind the jailor. Alice didn't know how she recognized him, but somehow she did. It was as if his image lurked somewhere deep in the corners of her own memory. He was round and middle-aged, with a pockmarked face notable only for its unpleasantness. He wore a dusty overcoat and a wide-brimmed hat. Both were new and expensive, paid for with the money he made seizing and selling the possessions of accused witches like Rebecca Hale.

Corwin looked down at Alice as she lay slumped on the floor. He raised a hand to his face to shield his blunt nose from her appalling stench.

"Apologies for the smell, Sheriff," Fisk mumbled as he lumbered out of Corwin's way. "The witch has yet to pay for the price of her chains, let alone the upkeep of her cell."

Corwin nodded once and pressed his thin lips into a frown. "Let us put this matter to rest."

Alice screamed and shrank away as the jailor's massive hands shot toward her. She fought against them as best she could, gritting her teeth as the rough leather of his gloves closed on her wrists and bit into her dirty skin. Fisk grunted as he fixed her in a pair of rusty iron shackles. Alice gasped as the cold metal scraped and dug into her pale flesh.

Fisk spat on the stone floor and let her squirm, savoring the moment before seizing her by the hair and dragging her along the dingy corridor. A searing agony bloomed from Alice's scalp and raced down her spine. She caught passing glimpses of miserable eyes staring at her from behind the bars of the neighboring cells as she struggled against the jailor.

Corwin trailed behind as Fisk hauled Alice up a creaking wooden staircase. Her legs bounced painfully from step to step with a series of dull *thumps* until they emerged from the dank pit of the dungeon and crossed the floorboards of a small room. The furnishings were plain and spartan: a desk, a couple of chairs, nothing more. The walls were bare except for a small rack of iron keys.

Light from an overcast sky seared her eyes. Alice squinted against it, feeling like she hadn't seen daylight in months. It was a dreary morning and the damp chill sank into her exposed skin. She shivered as Fisk dragged her toward a makeshift cage sitting in the back of a wooden cart. Hitched to the wagon was a scrawny mare as gray and battered as the cart itself. No one would waste a good horse on such grim work.

Fisk gripped Alice by her arm with one powerful hand and

swung the cage door open with the other. She felt Corwin's eyes on her as the jailor heaved her off her feet and tossed her into the cage. She rolled to her knees and flung herself back toward the door, but Fisk slammed it in her face and snapped the lock shut with an ugly sneer.

Corwin took his seat on the wagon bench and snapped the pitiful horse into motion with a sharp flick of the reins. Fisk walked alongside the rickety cart as it lurched, groaned, and rumbled through the rutted mud.

A gloomy morning mist had settled on the deserted streets of Salem Village. The smell of chimney smoke filled the chilly air. Inside her cage—Rebecca's cage—Alice shivered in the cold as the cart trundled past a row of small, square cottages. She could make out the shadowy silhouettes of Salem's villagers through the leaded panes of the unlit windows. She felt their eyes on her as the grim procession rumbled by, and she sensed their relief when the cart that bore her disappeared into the gloom at the edge of town.

Engulfed by the thick, white mist, Alice strained to see as Corwin steered the cart across a narrow bridge spanning a shallow brook. The constant rush of the North River in the murky distance accompanied them. Alice gripped the bars of the cage to keep from sliding backward as the cart lumbered up the steep incline of a hill until it creaked to an abrupt stop.

The fog was incredibly thick here. The vague shapes of the forest loomed like hulking shadows. The air was silent. Nothing moved.

Fisk stood next to the wagon with his arms folded across the bulk of his gut. His menacing eyes fixed on Alice while he waited for Corwin to dismount.

Through the gloom, Alice saw the road ahead was too steep and rocky for the rickety wagon to navigate. She strained to see what lay beyond.

An immense oak tree stood at the top of the rocky hill.

A noose hung from one of its enormous limbs.

Alice shrieked and threw herself against the door of the cage when she saw the rope dangling in the mist. The bars shuddered but held under the impact. She reared and hurled herself again, this time nearly overturning the cart.

"Restrain the witch!" Corwin lunged as the wagon rocked to one side.

Fisk hurried to the door and fumbled with the keys. He snapped the lock open and made a grab for Alice, but she caught his arm and sank her teeth deep into his flesh. She felt his skin split and tasted the coppery blood rushing warm and thick into her mouth. She spat it out and seized her opportunity as the big man howled with pain. Bolting from the cage, she broke into a desperate run into the mist.

"After her!" Corwin joined Fisk, and they charged off in pursuit.

Alice fled from the road and crashed through the woods, dashing through the dense fog. Cruel tree limbs ripped at her exposed skin and sharp rocks tore into her bare feet as she raced through the underbrush. A gnarled root snared her ankle and gave it a nasty twist, sending a bolt of pain up her leg as she tripped and pitched to the forest floor. Sprawled in the sodden blanket of leaves, Alice heard the heavy footfalls of the men chasing her, moving fast. Their shouts echoed off the trees and came from all around her. She sprang to her feet and ran on, too terrified to feel the stabbing jolts darting from her swelling ankle, until the trees came to an end and she burst into a small hollow.

The lifeless bodies of seven little children hung from the trees.

Alice's face contorted with anguish. Her legs went soft, and she crumpled to her knees among the dirt and leaves. She heard a voice shrieking hysterically and realized it was her own. She closed her eyes, willing the awful sight to go away.

But when she opened them again, she was still in the hollow. She reached her shackled arms toward the lifeless corpses of the children hanging from the trees.

One of them looked like Abigail.

The little girl's lifeless face was ashen and limp. Her cloudy, empty eyes were fixed in a horrible stare, the whites streaked red with the threadlike lines of burst blood vessels. Her head sagged at a hideous angle, no longer supported by her broken neck.

Alice crawled through the dirt toward her and screamed and screamed and screamed.

Chapter 24

A dizzying rush of sound and light broke the spell. Alice hurled forward across a century to her own time. She fought off a nauseating sense of vertigo as she staggered and caught herself on the heavy table in Sarah Bridges' cabin. There was nothing to be seen but bones and flames in the roaring fire. The images of the past had dissolved and vanished.

"What happened next?" Alice demanded, spinning to Sarah. "Please, I must know! Show me!"

"I cannot," Sarah replied. "I have shown you all I can. The windows into the past are shifting and fleeting. To conjure the correct moment is to capture lightning in a bottle. Were I to try again, I could show you the instant of your own birth, or the crucifixion of Christ, or the creation of the stars, or any number of random moments in time."

Alice fell silent, her thoughts revisiting all that she had witnessed in her visions of the past. "Hale's children weren't spared, were they?" she said in a voice that was low and hollow. "They were hanged in secret. Is that why she has returned? To claim our children as her own?"

Sarah said nothing for a moment. Her face remained dark and grave as she nodded grimly. "The people of Salem branded her a witch and so a witch she became. For most, All Hallows' Eve marks the end of the harvest. The season of sun passes to the season of darkness as the fertile fields are left to decay. But tonight, there is one who harvests in the town of Salem, one who reaps the freshest crop… the souls of the young."

"Can her ghost be stopped?" Alice asked.

Sarah lowered her eyes to stare into the blazing fire. "Not by the hand of man. But her spirit lurks among us on this night only. At dawn, she is bound to return to the black abyss whence she came."

"And my daughter will vanish with her," whispered Alice.

Sarah kept her eyes fixed on the flames and said nothing.

"Is Abigail still alive?" Alice asked. "Can I yet be save her?"

"I am merely a voice for the voiceless, Mrs. Jacobs. I know nothing of your daughter." Sarah turned from the fireplace, her tone growing low and somber. "But at your bidding, I may conjure one who may."

"Yet you would deny you are a witch?"

"Simple divination, nothing more."

"Was it by this same divination that you foresaw the coming of the omens?"

Sarah gave a nod. "All Hallows' Eve is a night of tremendous power. Tonight, we stand at the boundary of many worlds: day and night, sun and winter, living and dead. On this night, the spirits will tell the fortune of any with an ear to listen." She paused and raised her cool eyes to look deep into Alice's. "Shall I ask them of your daughter?"

Alice hesitated, unconsciously squeezing the scar of her lip between her teeth. Her thoughts escaped her and her gaze fell to the floor. What was she thinking? Why was she even considering this possibility? Conjuring? Divination? Just this morning, she was certain that such things were ridiculous. But now that comfortable certainty was gone, snatched away with her daughter. In its place stood a terrible need for answers by any means necessary. Alice felt the boundaries of her rational mind straining to their limits. This all seemed unreal, impossible. How could this woman foretell the future?

"Mrs. Jacobs?"

The husky purr of Sarah's voice brought Alice back to the moment. She lifted her eyes to meet those of the tall woman standing next to her. With a slight tilt of her head, Alice nodded. "Yes. Please, if you can… tell me what has become of Abigail."

Sarah's teeth gleamed in the firelight as she smiled and whirled around, plunging her bare hands into the fireplace. Alice gasped and lunged for her, then stopped. Rooted in place, she watched in disbelief as the flames leaped and danced around the woman's pale flesh, but left it unscathed.

Sarah collected the charred skeleton of the goat and spread the bones across the heavy table. She studied them for a moment. Her eyes narrowed as they passed from one bone to the next. Each seemed to speak to her, revealing something only she could read. Minutes passed before Sarah used her finger to draw a sequence of arcane shapes in the congealing blood smeared across the table's surface. The crude diagram looked to Alice like the outline of some gruesome map.

Sarah moved on. She jabbed her slender hand into the

hollow of an overturned deer skull, withdrew a handful of acorns, and scattered them across the blackened bones. Her eyes shone with intensity as she studied the bones and acorns, seeing the details of each all at once, a unified whole instead of a scattered collection of individual pieces. She kept her gaze fixed on the grisly heap as she murmured strange words to herself.

This time, Alice recognized the language. It was similar to the one Sarah had used to conjure her images of the past. Only now, the woman was speaking the words in reverse, opening a window not back through time, but *forward* into the future.

The eerie inflection of Sarah's voice was mesmerizing. Alice soon had the impression of time slowing down. It was an awful feeling, as if she were being drawn into a space where all human sensations ceased to exist. Suspended in a void where nothing was born and nothing died, she stared into the awful face of eternity. She felt the thumping of her own heart slowing, the empty spaces between the beats stretching longer and longer as time continued to falter.

The intervals extended until the rhythm of Alice's heartbeat was no longer discernible. each *thump* followed another at an agonizing crawl. All sound drained from the room. The spidery words issuing from Sarah's mouth, the crackle of the fire, the pounding of the rain on the roof, the crashing thunder—all of it receded into the shadows where they waited for the woman to complete her divination.

Suddenly, Sarah's head snapped up. Her blue eyes flew wide open as if she had gazed into the fires of Hell and saw the devil himself glaring back up at her.

"What do they say?" Alice asked, alarmed by the fright painted on the woman's pale face. "What do the spirits tell you of my child? Please, tell me what prophecy you have seen!"

"The legacy of the witch did not die at the end of a rope." Sarah's whisper barely crossed her lips. All at once, she burst into a flurry of movement. She swept the charred bones into her arms and brushed past Alice as she hurried across the room.

"Wait!" Alice whirled as the woman's tall form disappeared through the front door. "Please!"

Alice left the warmth of the cabin behind and strode across the porch. She halted beneath the shelter of the dripping roof.

Sarah knelt in the downpour at the foot of the crooked steps, digging in the mud with her bare hands.

"Can the artisan no longer bear her own masterpiece?" Alice shouted to be heard over the driving rain and thunder.

"On the contrary, I trust no other protection!" Sarah tossed the bones into the muddy hole. "I have opened a breach in the Veil, a window to the world of the spirit and the damned. But as with all windows, one can be seen as well as see."

"And so you bury bones at your doorstep for protection?"

"Aye, and for the same purpose, I must send you away." Sarah pushed the drenched clumps of soil back over the bones. "You have seen the harvester with your own eyes, Mrs. Jacobs. Your soul has been marked for it. Even now, your presence here could lead the witch's spirit to my very door!"

Sarah's eyes met Alice's as she rose from the mud to her full height. She mounted the sagging stairs and extended a hand streaked with blood, dirt, and broken fingernails. Something cold and metallic slid into Alice's palm.

"Press this talisman to your flesh as you travel the woods," Sarah said. "It will guard you from those condemned to the earth."

"Mrs. Bridges, please…" Alice's voice trembled. "I don't understand. What have the spirits told you? What has become of my daughter?"

"Justice Hathorne traded hate for seven, yet one remains beyond the shadows of heaven."

That was all. Without another word, Sarah spun around and dashed into the cabin. The door slammed shut behind her.

"No! Please! I beg you!" Alice threw herself at the heavy wood, pounding at it with her fists and pleading for answers. The door wouldn't yield.

It was no use. Sarah would say no more.

Alice turned away and opened her hand. A small charm sat in her palm. Forged of iron, it was bent in the shape of an ancient rune. Alice recognized it from Samuel's journal. That book was gone now, lost, like her husband himself. What did the rune signify? And what had Sarah meant with her final, enigmatic words? *Justice Hathorne traded hate for seven, yet one remains beyond the shadows of heaven.* Were they just the ramblings of a madwoman? Sarah's riddles had done nothing to help and Alice was still no closer to finding Abigail.

Alice struggled to keep from succumbing to her despair as she left the cabin behind and ventured down the rain-beaten path. Her encounter with Sarah Bridges had yielded as many questions as answers, leaving her certain of just one thing: she couldn't stop the coming of the dawn. It was inevitable, and her time was running out.

Chapter 25

Jonas Hobbes stood at the crossroads and prepared to meet his fate. The town of Salem stood in the distance behind him. That was all it was to him now—merely a town. Home was no longer back there; Salem held nothing for him anymore. His life had been taken from him and its merciful end now lay in the cursed woods ahead.

Jonas's eyes never left the forest as he drew his powder kit from his pocket and loaded his pistol.

The torrential rain had ended somewhere between Jonas's encounter with Fergus Hollins and his arrival at the threshold of the Northern Woods. He now shivered in the calm breeze the storm had left in its wake. He did his best to keep his hands from shaking as he poured the gunpowder down the pistol's muzzle and tamped it with the ramrod. Next came the lead ball, followed by a small amount of powder to prime the flashpan. His movements were calm and automatic, perfected through practice and repetition.

Jonas cocked the hammer and aimed the pistol, closing his eye to look down the barrel. Satisfied that it was true, he lowered the weapon and took a last glance at the massive crucifix looming over him at the crossroads. He was glad to make his peace with God one last time; he was embarking on a journey from which he would not return.

With his hand wrapped around the pistol grip, he searched the murky tree-line until he found the faint impression of the animal trail he hoped would lead him to Sarah Bridges and his daughter—to redemption or death. His throat felt dry as he swallowed. He kept his eyes on the path and started toward it when a sudden sound held him in place.

Something was coming towards him.

Jonas froze and listened. The sound grew louder. Closer. An animal? It had to be a big one. A frightened deer? Whatever it was, it was moving quickly, crashing through the underbrush on its way toward the crossroads. Jonas recalled the reports of wolves prowling the outskirts of town, the ones that had attacked Timothy Ruggles' sheep. Ruggles' farm was out by the western cornfields, but the pack could easily have moved north.

Jonas's finger flew to his pistol's trigger. The cold brass pressed against his skin as he braced himself and held his breath. He peered into the darkness, hoping he'd been able to keep his powder dry enough to fire. He knew acutely that his flintlock was dreadfully inaccurate at a range of over fifteen feet.

The thing in the woods was coming at him fast. It would be on top of him by the time he got a decent shot off. He would only have one chance to bring it down, whatever it was.

The sound drew nearer, closing the distance to where he

stood…

Twenty yards…

Ten yards…

Jonas aimed the pistol and readied to fire.

Five yards…

Two…

Jonas's finger squeezed the trigger. The hammer clicked loudly against the flashpan.

Nothing happened. The powder was too wet.

A shape exploded from the gloom, crashing through the forest.

Jonas backpedaled and raised an arm to defend himself before the figure revealed itself. His breath caught in his throat.

It was Alice Jacobs.

Frantic and out of breath, she caught herself against the giant cross and thrust what looked like an iron charm back toward the forest.

"Come no further!" she cried to the unseen horrors chasing her from the woods. "In the name of God, come no further!" The sound of her voice echoed through the night. Her chest heaved as she stared into the gloom. Her eyes were wild and terrified, as if expecting something to lunge at her from the forest at any second.

Alice remained oblivious to Jonas's presence as she sank to her knees in exhaustion. Not wanting to alarm her any further, he lowered his pistol to his side and remained where he stood, trying not to think about how close he had come to shooting her.

Alice looked like she'd been dragged through Hell itself.

Wet strands of hair hung before her eyes and clung to her flushed face in tousled streaks. She still wore the dark woolen coat he had given her, its collar pulled up high around her neck, but the tattered skirt of her nightgown was soaked and filthy. Bloody cuts and a crisscrossing array of scratches covered her bare legs. The steam of her heavy panting hung in the cold air as she struggled to catch her breath and calm her racing heart.

When Alice realized she wasn't alone, she whirled and screamed, brandishing the talisman and recoiling before she could catch herself.

"Shhh… easy, easy…" Jonas raised his hands and used the soothing voice he usually reserved for his daughter when she had bad dreams. "It's alright. It's only me, Jonas Hobbes…"

Through her panic, Alice recognized the rugged face of the sailor standing over her. "Oh, Mr. Hobbes…" she gasped with relief. Her blue eyes glistened with tears.

"Mrs. Jacobs, what has happened to you? Are you hurt?"

"No, I… I'm all right." She took a deep, calming breath to compose herself. There was something hollow and flat about Jonas's voice. He was uncharacteristically stoic, and although he was attempting to attend to her, his eyes strayed to the darkness of the woods. "Mr. Hobbes, why are you—"

"Mrs. Jacobs, under the circumstances, I would not consider it too forward if you would call me Jonas."

"Very well. Mr—I mean… *Jonas*…" Alice fumbled with the unaccustomed familiarity. "Why have you come here?"

Jonas's face darkened into a hard line. "Someone has taken Emily."

"Your daughter," Alice said.

He nodded. "I returned from our encounter in the street to find her bed empty. I do not intend for it to remain that way." With his jaw set, he took a step past Alice toward the woods, pistol in hand.

"Where are you going?" she asked.

"To hunt the witch. To bring our children home."

"I have just come from Sarah Bridges," Alice said, leaping to her feet and catching his arm.

Jonas paused in his tracks but kept his back to her. "Impossible. No one has ever crossed the threshold of these woods. I fully expect to die trying. Some of Salem's bravest fathers have—"

"Then perhaps what was called for was a courageous *mother*," Alice interrupted. "I *have* been to the home of Sarah Bridges. I have no reason to lie. Our daughters are not with her. She is harmless."

"You have been deceived," Jonas said. "The devil is a liar, as are his servants." He released his arm from her grip and started again for the trail.

"Continue down that path and you will die. Of that, you can be certain. I have seen its horrors with my own eyes." Alice shrugged the heavy coat from her shoulders and raised her chin high into the air, exposing the ghastly handprint emblazoned across her milk-white throat. "Look! Look at what they've done to me!

Jonas's eyes went wide at the sight. "My God!"

"'Tis the hand of those condemned to the earth," Alice explained, "the mark of those hanged for witchcraft and left to rot in these woods. Sarah Bridges is the one who saved me from their clutches. I would have perished in that terrible place without her intervention." Alice slipped the coat back over her shoulders and pulled the collar up to hide her throat again. "I still intend to find my child, Mr. Hobbes. If your daughter is with her, she'll be looking for her father when this is over."

Jonas hesitated. A look of suspicion crept into his eyes when they fell upon the iron charm dangling from Alice's hand. "What is that?"

"A gift from Sarah Bridges." Alice showed him the talisman. She had clutched it so tightly in her flight through the woods that its edges had dug into her flesh.

Jonas gave it a disapproving shake of his head. "What else did she leave you with?"

"The truth about Rebecca Hale."

"Who?"

"A woman tried and hanged during the witch trials, along with her seven children."

Jonas shook his head. "She lies. Nothing of the sort ever happened, even at the height of the witch madness."

"I can assure you it is true, as appalling as it may seem. Hale's vengeful spirit has now returned to Salem to claim the souls of the young and avenge the deaths of her own children. We have only until dawn to find our daughters."

"What will happen then?"

"Her ghost will return to Hell, and I fear we will never see our children again."

Jonas was dimly aware of the chilly breeze passing across his wet skin. Tiny goosebumps had risen to the surface, but he couldn't tell whether it was from the cold or Alice's tale. "Did you learn anything else? Is there no way to stop Hale's spirit?"

Alice shrugged and shook her head, recalling Sarah's cryptic words. "She said Justice Hathorne traded hate for seven, yet one remains beyond the shadows of heaven."

"Hate for seven?" Jonas shook his head. "Useless riddles. Begging your pardon, but I'm naught but a simple sailor, not a poet."

Alice heaved a heavy sigh and hung her head. She repeated Sarah's words as she hunched in the tall grass. *Justice Hathorne traded hate for seven, yet one remains beyond the shadows of heaven... Hate for seven... Hate for seven... Justice Hathorne...*

Alice let her thoughts travel back to the visions Sarah had shown her, those terrible moments when she had relived Rebecca's memories of her jail cell. She remembered hearing Rebecca's thoughts, experiencing Rebecca's horror when the woman recognized that no amount of innocence would prevent Hathorne from seeing her hanged. That was the key, wasn't it? There had been some kind of revelation there, something so dreadful it drove Rebecca to make her pact with the devil. Alice couldn't see what it was. The insight was too obscure, too buried in Rebecca's unraveling mind. There had to be something to it, some kind of clue. But what was it?

Alice leaned back and felt the solid wood of the cross press into her shoulders. Time was running out. The passing of every second felt like precious blood dripping from a fatal wound.

Sitting there in the grass, Alice felt so very, very tired. She noticed for the first time that her feet were torn and bleeding from her frantic race through the woods. Her wool slippers were now little more than useless shreds. She let her eyes slide closed, feeling the sweet oblivion of her exhaustion creeping closer. How much longer could she go on like this? How much more could she endure?

Then it came to her. It happened all at once; a sudden clarity of thought that banished her despair and propelled her to her feet.

"What is it?" Jonas asked, reading the abrupt urgency written on Alice's face.

"Where does the town keep its records?"

"Its records?"

"Yes! Its official papers! Births, deaths, marriages. There must be records of them somewhere. Quickly! Tell me where they are kept!"

A look of confusion gathered on Jonas's face. "Anything since the war is kept at the Town Hall."

"What about before the war? From the time of the witch trials?"

Jonas thought about it for a second. "'Tis hard to say. For the most part, we've tried to forget the memory of those dark days. I suppose they could be in the keeping of Benjamin Emmons as part of his collection."

Alice swung around and started toward town.

"What do you propose we do?" Jonas called after her as he jogged to catch up.

"We must go to the museum."

Chapter 26

The waters of Salem Harbor were black and calm as Jonas and Alice hustled along the desolate expanse of Derby Street. The storm had left behind stray flickers of lightning and the occasional stubborn growl of thunder. Salty brine hung thick in the night air and the shadowy shapes of the deserted wharves rose like phantoms from the water. There were many empty berths where the fleet had been. A gentle rattle and clattering of bones lapping against the hollow hulls of the few ships that remained at anchor.

"Where have all the ships gone?" Alice asked.

"Out to sea." Jonas jerked a thumb at the grand homes that stood clustered in darkness along Derby Street. "Salem's ship-owners were more than willing to profit from frightened families who would pay a price to have their children spend the night aboard a ship, far from town."

"Far from the curse," Alice mused.

Jonas nodded and glanced at Alice from the corner of his eye. She hurried along the uneven cobblestones with feet that were now practically bare. She was limping slightly. He had offered her his boots, but she insisted they were far too big and would only slow her down. Instead, she simply did her best to ignore the pain. There wasn't any time to waste. Midnight had come and gone and dawn was creeping ever closer.

On the long walk from the crossroads, Alice had recounted what had happened in the Northern Woods. She told Jonas of her harrowing escape from the spirits in the forest; of finding his stallion in the grove and the terrible visions of the past that Sarah Bridges had shown her. And she had told him of the sudden horror in Sarah's eyes when looked into the future saw what it held.

Now, with Jonas in the lead, they turned left and crossed the rickety wooden gate of the East India Museum. Alice followed him up the creaking steps to the museum's heavy doors, where he gripped the tarnished handle and gave it a tug. The door flinched but wouldn't open.

"Locked," Jonas said. "I suppose it would be useless to knock." He stepped back to study the solid wooden frame, gauging if he had enough force to break in.

"We must get in there," Alice insisted. She gazed at the small panes of stained glass set into the old wood of the door. "I must see those records."

"What exactly do you hope to find?"

"The names of Rebecca Hale's children… *all* of them."

Jonas's eyes narrowed. "I don't take your meaning."

"Sarah Bridges spoke with a strange accent, one that was sometimes difficult to grasp. As I think about it now, 'tis possible that I misunderstood her. She didn't say *hate* for seven, she said *eight* for seven. Justice Hathorne traded *eight*

197

for seven, yet one remains beyond the shadow of heaven. Those were Sarah's actual words."

"I'm afraid it's still no clearer to me."

"The town believed Rebecca had seven children. But what if there was an *eighth* child?"

Jonas frowned, unconvinced. "How could she have kept her pregnancy a secret? The townsfolk would have known such a thing."

"Yes, but what if they *chose* to forget? You said it yourself. Salem has tried to erase all memories of those dark times. What if it were true? What if there *was* an eighth child?"

"The witch's legacy did not die at the end of a rope…" Sarah's cryptic words came together for Jonas.

"Precisely," said Alice. "Rebecca Hale's legacy wasn't her pact with the devil, but her eighth child, the one who was spared."

"But how does this help us stop her?"

"What if her spirit isn't collecting children to punish the town of Salem, but to find her last living descendant?"

Jonas gazed at her as the implications of what she was saying hit home. "Are you suggesting we attempt to trade this person to her ghost for our children?"

Alice said nothing. Her silence told him all he needed to know.

"Then I suppose we should find this person before she does," he said. He drew his pistol from his waistband, gripped it by its barrel, and turned to the door, ready to shatter the delicate window with the butt of the gun's solid walnut stock.

Alice laid a hand on his shoulder and stayed his arm. "Wait."

"What is it?"

"Listen."

The gentle knell of ship bells rose from the silence.

Jonas looked across the street to the harbor. He saw the dim outline of flags fluttering from the masts. They had been hanging limp in the stillness just a few moments ago. A stiff wind was picking up without warning, as if the night was stirring and coming alive.

"Ready yourself," Alice said as a nervous shiver ran across her skin.

"For what?"

"Anything."

Jonas's hand went to his powder kit.

While he primed the pistol, Alice narrowed her eyes and peered around at the deserted streets. A growing sense of dread threaded its way up her spine. Something was about to happen, something awful. She could feel it in the air.

A powerful gust swept a tornado of wet leaves across the museum's muddy footpath. To the west, Alice heard the low rumble of distant thunder as the storm pushed further inland.

Then she saw it.

"Look! There!" Alice pointed to where the street disappeared into murky darkness. A strange fog was taking shape in the shadows. Thick and white, it materialized from the gloom and spilled into the lane, rolling across the ground like a wave breaking across a rocky beach. Imbued with a life of its own, the spectral mist slithered across the cobblestones toward them.

"My God…" Alice watched, petrified, as the ghostly mass slid ever nearer. It churned and swirled with supernatural life as it closed the distance between them, swelling and engulfing everything around it in its thick, white depths. The cobblestones, the harbor, the ships, the houses—everything was obscured and obliterated from sight.

All at once, shrill and ghastly voices rose like a hellish chorus from within the mist's swirling reaches.

Too terrified to move, Alice stared in horror as the shadowy forms of young boys and girls rose and receded within the fog's churning mass. Writhing and twisting as a horde, the shapes drew themselves together, merging; the mist going from white to black as it coalesced into the single figure of a woman shrouded in a black veil.

Alice screamed as Rebecca Hale's ghostly shape floated toward the gate.

"Stand aside!" Jonas leveled his pistol on the woman's heart and squeezed the trigger. With an earsplitting blast, the lead ball roared from the barrel in an explosion of fire and smoke.

The ghost vanished, splitting apart and dissolving instantly back into a mass of roiling white mist.

Jonas could only gape as the mist gathered and writhed over the cobblestones just beyond the museum's rickety fence. It spilled through the gate and across the footpath.

"The door!"

Alice's frantic cry brought Jonas back to himself. He spun around and shielded his eyes in the crook of his elbow as he drew his arm back, pistol in hand. With one powerful blow, the stained glass shattered into thousands of gleaming pieces.

"Jonas!"

He glanced over his shoulder and saw the mist swarming its way up the museum steps. It was just yards away now.

"Stay behind me!" Alice shrank back and pinned Jonas between herself and the door as the mist surged across the porch toward them. She thrust her arm out with a terrified gasp, brandishing Sarah's iron talisman in a desperate attempt to ward off the surging mist.

Ghastly voices filled the night, shrieking with rage as the spirits slid to an abrupt halt inches from her feet. Alice's heart beat madly in her chest as she stood her ground. The shifting mass of vapor swirled at her toes like an enraged animal, but it stayed where it was, held back by the talisman's power. Alice kept her eyes on the mist, the iron charm trembling in her outstretched grasp as she whispered over her shoulder.

"The lock…"

Jonas stretched his arm through the hole in the window, reached down, and released the bolt. A jagged shard of broken glass pierced his skin as he removed his hand from the opening. He winced and drew his arm back, grimacing as a crimson slash of blood fell across the wooden planks of the porch.

At the sight of the sailor's blood, the blanket of white churning at their feet coiled about itself like a hungry serpent ready to strike. Alice gasped and thrust the talisman toward it, repelling it. The roiling mass seethed with staggering fury.

"Get inside," Alice whispered. She kept the mist at arm's length while Jonas cracked the door open and slipped into the museum. Then she backed through the narrow opening and inched her way into the darkness after him.

Chapter 27

Jonas slammed the door shut and bolted it while Alice rushed to hang the talisman from the handle. She prayed it would be enough to keep the fog from breaching the threshold. She remembered the way the mist streamed like smoke from beneath her own bedroom door at the inn. If the talisman didn't work now, they'd be trapped.

Through the jagged hole of the broken window, Alice saw the swirling mass rearing up with unrestrained fury. Her heart nearly stopped as it surged toward the door, battering it with impossible force. The heavy wood shuddered, but the bolt held. *BAM! BAM! BAM!* The mist hammered at the door again and again and again.

An enraged roar erupted from outside. Alice's hands flew to her ears to shield them from the furious shrieks. As she trembled in the darkness, she made out the faint outline of the talisman glowing with an effervescent light. As quickly as it appeared, the mist dissipated into the night air. It was gone without a trace within seconds.

For long minutes, Alice could only stand there, shaken to

the core. Only when she was sure the terrible fog had truly vanished did she allow herself to collapse into a small leather chair. Moments passed in silence as she fought to calm her racing heart.

Jonas still stood by the door, examining his wounded hand. A stream of blood seeped from a ragged cut slashed across the fleshy web where his index finger met his thumb.

"Are you badly hurt?" Alice asked.

"No worse than you are," Jonas replied with a nod at her torn and bloody feet. He pressed his wound against his shirt to stanch the bleeding and started toward the rear of the room.

"Where are you going?" Alice asked, rising from her chair.

"To find some light and something to dress our wounds."

Alice watched his shape disappear into the gloom at the far end of the hall where Benjamin Emmons kept his small study. Her eyes had adjusted to the darkness and she could now distinguish the rectangular forms of the museum's display cases. The ancient building creaked and groaned all around her. To her right stood the supposed man-eating clam that had so captivated Abigail.

Alice swallowed the lump gathering in her throat and pushed the memory from her thoughts. It wasn't too late to find her daughter. Not yet.

Alice turned her back on the glass dome and went after Jonas. Dozens of dead, glassy eyes stared at her as she marched across the hall, passing rows and rows of darkened cabinets. When she reached the far wall, she paused before the stacks of shelves where Benjamin housed his collection on the infamous witch trials. Alice didn't know where to begin.

Her hopes crashed to the floor; it would take all night to examine them all. They didn't have much time.

Alice squinted and did her best to make out the titles embossed on the ancient leather spines. She could see next to nothing in the gloom. The futility of the situation wore on her until a yellow light fell across the aisle.

Jonas was approaching from Benjamin's study with a small storm lantern in his bandaged hand. In the other, he carried a pair of worn leather slippers and some strips of cloth torn from a plush chair cushion.

"It seems Old Man Emmons likes to make himself comfortable while he naps," he said, offering Alice the slippers and the cloth strips. "Here, wrap your feet with these."

Alice shook her head and went back to searching the book titles. "We haven't the time. We must find the town records."

"I assure you I can read, Mrs. Jacobs. And finding the records will be useless if you can no longer walk."

Alice gazed at him for a moment. His face looked drawn and tired, and she thought he had aged years since she had first encountered the brash and easygoing sailor back at the Ingersoll Inn. She wondered how she must look to him: scratched and dirty and wrapped in nothing more than a tattered nightgown and his soaking wool coat. Any further objections fell from her lips and she reached for the bandages.

While Jonas took up the search of the books, Alice sank to the wooden floor and tended her wounds. Minutes later, with her feet bound and clad in Benjamin's leather slippers, she joined him in the hunt. Her eyes scanned title after title. There were countless histories and manuscript accounts of the witch trials, but nothing resembling what they were looking for, nothing related to the town's births and deaths.

Alice began to doubt herself. Maybe the records no longer existed? Maybe they had never existed at all?

Time was running out—and so were the shelves of books —when Alice realized her mistake. "They're not here," she said, standing back from the stacks. "This can't be all there is. There must be more, somewhere else."

"How can you be so sure?" Jonas asked.

"The documents we're looking for contain secrets the town has tried to conceal for a hundred years. Benjamin Emmons wouldn't keep them here with his public collection. He would hide them somewhere else, somewhere safe and secret."

Alice's thoughts went to the tidy bookcase the old man kept behind his desk, the one from which he had drawn Samuel's journal. Could the old town records be among those volumes? No, that would be too obvious. But maybe that was the point: to hide them in plain sight where no one would think to look for them.

"The storm cellar," Jonas said.

"What?"

"This building has stood perched on the shoulder of the North Atlantic for decades. It would have a storm cellar, somewhere to hunker down when a hurricane or a big Nor'easter blows in. All of these old buildings have them. The patriots hid powder kegs in them during the revolution."

Alice's eyes gleamed with sudden hope. "Yes! That could be it! Quickly, how do we find the way in?"

Jonas drew a blank as he tried to recall everything he knew about this building; how and when it was built and by whom.

He knew they had repurposed it several times over the decades, but the details were vague in his mind. The storm cellar would have been part of the initial construction, built into the stone foundation itself. They would likely find the entrance in the oldest part of the building, an area unlike the rest, some place leftover from its early days. It would be somewhere near where they now stood, in the museum's rear. A moment passed Jonas thought it over. He remembered a peculiar sound he had heard in Benjamin's study, the hollow groan of a floorboard as he strode across the rug to fetch the storm lantern from the old man's desk.

"I know where it is." Jonas spun on his heels and marched away, with Alice trailing close behind.

When they entered the study, Jonas crossed the room and set the lantern on the desk. Alice glanced at the clock. It was now just past one in the morning. There were only five hours until sunrise.

Jonas grunted as he hauled aside the heavy wingback Alice had sat in earlier in the afternoon. Stretched across the floor beneath it was an intricate Oriental rug, no doubt another of Benjamin's exotic treasures gleaned from his voyages abroad.

"Stand away," Jonas said. He gripped one of the rug's tasseled ends while Alice stepped back against the wall. With another grunt and an eruption of dust, he flipped the rug over, exposing what lay beneath.

There was a trapdoor in the center of the floor.

Alice rushed forward, her spirits leaping as Jonas threw open the door and was met with a cool draught of rotten air. She retrieved the lantern from the desk and played its light into the space, revealing a wooden staircase descending into a chasm of darkness.

Alice gasped and nearly staggered at the sight of the ancient steps.

Even in the dim light, Jonas saw her face had drained of all its color. "Mrs. Jacobs, what is it? What's wrong?"

"I know this place." Alice's voice had become a choked whisper.

"What? How?"

"I've seen this place before, in the visions shown to me by Sarah Bridges."

"What is it?"

"The witch dungeon."

Jonas understood in an instant. Salem had been founded on the shores of the sea. The town's earliest buildings were erected as close to the water as possible. Many were torn down to make way for the new. Benjamin Emmons' museum of natural curiosities now stood on the foundation of the old Salem jail.

Alice stared down through the hole into the yawning darkness. She couldn't go on. Her thoughts flooded with unwanted images from the past. She remembered cruel Edgar Fisk dragging her up from the pit and back into the light, her body thudding painfully from step to step…

"Mrs. Jacobs…" Jonas was speaking, looking at her. "Shall I go alone?"

Alice blinked and shook her head to release her mind from the awful memory of her vision. "No. I will follow."

With a deep, trembling breath, she fell in behind Jonas and descended the creaking steps into the darkness.

Alice didn't need the light of his lantern to illuminate what lay below. She knew exactly what was down there.

They reached the landing and stood at the head of a long, narrow corridor. Alice recognized it instantly. The air was fetid and saturated with the reek of mold and rot. Thin streams of water dripped in streaks down the stone walls, leaving behind orange rivulets of limescale that glistened in the pallid light. A gossamer network of spiderwebs dripped from the ancient oak beams over their heads.

Alice's skin crawled. She felt like she could still smell the fear and misery in the air. She tried not to think about the suffering she had experienced here in her vision. It was almost too much to bear to be back in this horrible place. Standing there, her thoughts consumed with memories that weren't her own, she knew exactly where they would find the documents they were after.

"Down the corridor," she murmured. "Near the end."

"Are you sure?" Jonas asked.

Alice gave a grim nod and said nothing.

Jonas held the lantern high to fend off the oppressive gloom and led the way past the long row of abandoned jail cells. The heavy wooden doors had been removed decades ago, salvaged for other buildings around town. Now the cells stood like gaping alcoves, packed with an assortment of strange curiosities that had never made it into the museum's vast collection upstairs.

When they could go no further, Jonas halted and shone his light into a tiny cell no larger than a coffin. Alice knew it well. For a moment, she couldn't look at it. Her mind quaked at the very thought. It was too terrible, too *real*. With tremendous determination, she willed herself to look up and face it, expecting to see the disheveled wreck of Rebecca Hale cowering in the darkness.

Instead, the narrow chamber was crammed with rows of ancient ledgers arranged on makeshift shelves.

"This is it," Alice whispered, stepping into the light to examine the faded titles inscribed on the cracked leather spines. "The town records. We've found them."

She ran her finger across the rows, scattering dust as she scanned the years, searching for one in particular. The ledgers got thinner the further back in time she went. She hesitated, her hand hanging in the air, before withdrawing two slim volumes from the rest. Both were stamped with the same faded title: *The Sixth Volume of Record of Salem Village: 1691-1693.*

"Here." Alice passed one book to Jonas. "Search this one."

"What am I looking for?"

"Any reference to Rebecca Hale."

Jonas turned from the cell and placed his lantern on a narrow ledge—the same ledge on which Edgar Fisk had laid a tallow candle every night. The pages of the ancient ledger were covered with long lists of dates and names scrawled in the thin, flowing script of some long-forgotten clerk. Births, deaths, marriages, baptisms—every man, woman, and child who inhabited Salem a century ago were accounted for here. The ancient parchment rustled and cracked beneath Jonas's calloused fingers as he searched the entries, looking for Rebecca Hale and coming up empty.

At his side, Alice's eyes gleamed in the pale light as she scanned the pages of the other volume. Minutes passed as she flipped through page after page after page, finding nothing and growing more anxious by the second. There had to be *some* record of Rebecca Hale. What had the townspeople done with them? With every passing page, Alice found it more difficult to deny the lingering suspicion that any reference to the woman's children had been destroyed long ago.

Then—quite suddenly—Alice went rigid. She stared at an open page; her face was a perfect mask of shock. "God no…"

"What is it?" Jonas asked, struck by the intensity of her gaze.

Alice said nothing. Her eyes studied the page, re-reading it, making sure she hadn't made a mistake, committing the contents to memory. She cast the book aside with a sudden flurry and spun back to the tiny cell.

Jonas watched as she pulled volume after volume from the shelves, cracking them open, sliding her finger down the pages, letting the books fall to her feet when she didn't find what she was looking for. He was about to ask what she was after when she froze. Something in the middle of the page arrested her attention.

"Mrs. Jacobs, what have you found?"

Alice held a hand in the air to silence him and the sailor fell quiet to let her concentrate. Her fingers trembled as she turned from one page to the next. Her eyes twitched as she scanned the words, absorbing them, making connections. She looked up from the page in horror, overcome by a sudden, sickening realization. "Oh, Lord…"

In that instant, she understood everything.

Alice turned to Jonas, her eyes gleaming. "We must go to the Burying Point!"

"What?" he exclaimed, glaring at her incredulously.

Alice slammed the book shut and brushed past him, reaching for the lantern. "There is no time to explain! We must go! *Now!*"

Chapter 28

The gate of the wrought-iron fence screeched on rusty hinges as Jonas swung it open and crossed the threshold of the graveyard. Alice followed, holding the storm lantern high. Tucked in her other arm was the volume of records she had taken from the witch dungeon.

A fine mist hung in the night air, diffusing the lantern's yellow glow and bathing the tombstones in a ghostly light. The bare branches of the cemetery trees creaked and rattled in the breeze, warning the intruders to turn around.

Jonas shuddered as they moved deeper into the gloom and threaded around the graves. It felt lonely here, like a place forsaken of warmth and soul. All around him were the darkened husks of the jack-o'-lanterns the children had left as offerings. Dozens of ghastly faces grinned and scowled at him from atop every tombstone. Overhead, the faint glow of moonlight struggled to break through the remnants of the retreating storm clouds.

"I don't like this," he whispered. "We've been running from the dead all night. Now we've delivered ourselves to their door."

"We'll be leaving soon enough," Alice promised. She had been quiet since leaving the museum. Jonas could tell that whatever she had discovered in those ledgers had disturbed her much more than she was letting on.

"Let's just hurry and get this business over with," he muttered. He eyed the mist, expecting it to come alive at any second. "Which one is it?"

Alice paused and squinted into the gloom, straining to see through the veil of mist. "It would be one of the larger ones. There…" She pointed to a hulking shape barely visible on the far side of the cemetery. "I believe it could be that one."

"It *could* be? You don't even know what you're looking for, do you?"

"A mausoleum."

"Which one?"

"I'll know it when I see it, and I will explain soon enough. For now, you must trust me."

Jonas shaking his head in resignation and led the way across the cemetery.

The mausoleum loomed in the darkness on the shoulder of a small hill. It stood shrouded within a knot of elms. A mantle of fallen leaves spilled from the steep pitch of its roof, tumbling down the slopes on either side and wreathing the limestone walls in a blanket of yellows and oranges and reds. Alice held the lantern higher to illuminate the details of the decaying stonework as she mounted the uneven slabs to the mausoleum's mouth. A pair of Doric columns rose on either side of an ornate iron gate. Eroded and green with lichen, they supported an impressive arch stretching over the recessed entrance.

Alice saw the name chiseled into the crumbling stone overhead and felt the air stolen from her lungs.

DICER

The name stared at her in large gothic letters.

"Is this what we've come here for?" asked Jonas, following her gaze up to the arch.

Alice nodded. "Giles Dicer."

It was a name that had haunted her ever since she had seen it in her husband's journal. Now she knew what it meant. "We must go inside."

Jonas swiveled around and glared at her with undisguised disbelief.

He didn't need to say anything. Alice knew he had reached the limits of his faith in her. She could see it in his eyes. "Jonas, I believe my husband may have visited this place on the day he disappeared. And thanks to what I've discovered in the town records, I'm beginning to understand why. The key to finding our daughters may very well rest inside this tomb. But in order to be certain, I must see what lies beyond that gate."

Jonas remained motionless. Every instinct told him this was madness. They should turn away and leave this place immediately. But then he remembered that moment at the crossroads only hours ago. He had been so eager to sacrifice his life in the Northern Woods in search of his daughter. What was he clinging to now? Emily was still gone, and he still had nothing to lose.

Jonas exhaled and reached for one of the gate's iron bars. The pitted surface dug into the palm of his bandaged hand as he gave it a firm tug. The ancient gate swung open with a rusty groan. Alice stepped to Jonas's side and played the lantern's light into the breach. The short radius of its glow failed to illuminate anything beyond a few feet. Stealing a glance at Jonas for reassurance, she hesitated for only a moment before stepping inside.

There was a brief chattering of vermin as a dozen creatures fled the light, scurrying for the cover of hidden cracks and crevasses and leaving nothing behind but an eerie silence. Alice wrinkled her nose as she crept further into the vault. The air was thick with the dank stench of mildew and rat droppings. Once her eyes adjusted to the dimness, she took in her surroundings.

A pair of stone caskets stood at the center of the chamber. Their heavy lids were covered with a layer of dust that had taken decades to accumulate. The walls on either side were bare except for two narrow windows, each protected by intricate ironwork. Cobwebs hung from every crevice. The flagstone floor was buried beneath a thick coating of dust that lay undisturbed except for the tiny tracks of the scurrying rats.

Alice felt a crushing disappointment as her eyes moved around the vault. No one had been here in years. If Samuel had intended to come here, he'd never made it. Not for the first time, Alice wondered if she would ever know the truth of what happened to him on that fateful day. She raised the lantern and crossed the chamber to the first of the caskets. The stone was cold against her fingertips as she brushed the dust from its smooth surface. There was an inscription chiseled into the solid granite.

"This is it," she said. "Giles Dicer."

"And his wife, Mary Winthrop Dicer." Jonas stood by the second casket, gazing at Alice impatiently. "Mrs. Jacobs, I trust there is some purpose to this."

"I assure you there is," Alice replied. She laid the lantern and the volume of records on the stone lid of Giles Dicer's casket and cleared away more dust to expose the rest of the engraving: *1691-1775*. She studied the years a moment longer before gripping the edges of the heavy lid with both hands. "Will you help me?"

"I'll do no such thing! Disturbing the dead! And on *this* of all nights! The ghost of Rebecca Hale is not the only one who has freed tonight. On All Hallows' Eve, *all* manner of spirits are free to roam the earth."

"Jonas, if I am correct, there is no one in this casket to disturb."

The sailor flinched ever so slightly and Alice could tell she had piqued his curiosity. But he still refused to move.

Alice ignored his disapproving glare and positioned her hands on one side of the lid. She pushed with all her strength. The heavy stone groaned as it yielded a grudging inch, but nothing more. Out of breath, she relented and looked once again to Jonas, her eyes pleading for help.

A moment passed in silence before he gave in, shaking his head and muttering to himself. He pressed his hands to the lid and lent his strength to Alice's. There was another dull, hollow groan followed by the sound of stone grinding against stone as the massive lid inched aside. Soon, a narrow opening appeared. Alice rushed to peer into the void.

The casket was empty.

Alice's hand went to her mouth as she backed away. "Dear God… It can't be possible. It can't—"

"Mrs. Jacobs!" Jonas's eyes flew wide.

A tall shape stood in the open door behind her.

Alice whirled and screamed, recoiling as the figure stepped from the shadows and into the chamber.

It was Benjamin Emmons.

The old man's wrinkled eyes flew wide at the sight of the open casket. "What in the name of—"

"Mr. Emmons, what are you doing here?" Jonas demanded. He stepped forward while Alice slid aside to conceal the volume of records behind her back.

"I've a mind to ask you the same," Benjamin replied, studying them both.

"Emily has been taken," said Jonas.

"Abigail is missing too," Alice added.

Benjamin removed his hat and hung his gray head. "I am sorry for your losses. Now I may add your sorrow to my own." He paused and swallowed bitterly. "The witch has claimed Duncan as well."

Benjamin's voice was low and sullen as he recounted the terrible events that had led him to this moment. After failing to find Magistrate Holm at the Town Hall, the old man had tracked him down at Salem Common. There, he had learned of Holm's doomed attempt to apprehend Sarah Bridges.

"He remains at the Common, waiting for the witch's spirits to come to him," Benjamin explained. "Holm had the air of a man possessed, and I got the sense he will stop at nothing to see Sarah Bridges defeated." He clenched his bony hand into a bitter fist. "I only wish to God I could get my hands on the hateful woman myself."

Alice didn't bother telling the old man about her own encounter with Sarah. It was too long a story, and they had too little time.

"Since leaving Holm, I've been riding the streets aimlessly," Benjamin went on. "I was trying to find the words to tell my daughter that I've lost her only remaining son. Then I saw your light from the street."

"Perhaps all is not lost," Alice said. "Mr. Emmons… who was Giles Dicer?"

"Dicer?" The old man's tired eyes clouded with confusion behind his spectacles. "What has he to do with anything?"

"Please, Mr. Emmons. If my suspicions are correct, this man may be our only hope of seeing our loved ones again. What can you tell us about him?"

Benjamin frowned and went quiet as he gathered his thoughts, trying to recollect the details of what he knew. "Dicer was a man of independent wealth who came to Salem in his thirties. I seem to recall he was an acquaintance of my father's. Dicer's goal was to become a sea captain in the East India trade. He prospered, too… until crewmen refused to sail with him."

"The Jonah ship," Jonas murmured. "I believe I've heard of this man. His story is the stuff of tall tales among the seamen on the docks, isn't it? Dicer's crews would return to shore with terrible accounts of what transpired aboard his ship. They called it a *Jonah* ship—doomed by God—and every man who sailed it vowed to never set foot on its decks again."

Benjamin nodded. "Dicer himself claimed to be the son of a notorious murderer and that the spirits of his father's victims haunted him—his mother among them. When the eldest of Dicer's children one day went missing, the poor man saw it as evidence of a terrible curse brought upon his family by his murderous father. In his panic, he sent his only surviving son to live with a family in Boston. The lad was merely a newborn. Soon after, Dicer's heartbroken wife drowned herself in a small lake near their home."

Benjamin motioned to the massive block of the second casket. "Dicer again blamed the spirits for her death. The loss of his entire family was too great for him. With his sanity unraveling, he withdrew from society and spent the rest of his days living as a recluse until his death."

Alice bit her lip and chose her next question carefully. "What of Dicer's claim that his father murdered his mother?"

Benjamin shrugged. "Little is known about his life before he came to Salem."

"Mr. Emmons. I think you know more about this man's family than you realize."

"How so?"

"Dicer's murderous father was Judge Hathorne… and his mother was Rebecca Hale."

"What?" Benjamin gaped at her in disbelief. "How can you possibly—"

"Shhh! Listen…" Jonas broke in.

Benjamin's protests hung on his lips as the sailor raised a hand for silence.

Voices were drifting from out in the cemetery.

"Douse the light!" Jonas hissed.

Alice reacted quickly, blowing out the lantern and plunging them all into darkness.

Jonas crept to one of the narrow windows and peered through the intricate ironwork.

The silhouettes of two men crept their way among the tombstones in the misty gloom of the graveyard. Jonas strained to get a better look.

Each man was carrying a shovel. Their progress was slow and halting as they examined each grave, as if looking for one in particular.

There was a quiet shuffle to Jonas's left. Alice and Benjamin moved to the other window.

"Fools…" the old man muttered and shook his head.

At the sight of the men outside, Alice quickly withdrew from sight. "Grave robbers?"

"Worse," Benjamin replied. "Body snatchers."

"Aye. They'll have come for Silas Painter," Jonas added.

"I'm sorry, I don't understand," Alice confessed.

"Modern medicine has its price," Benjamin whispered. "Unfortunately, the supply of specimens for the school of anatomy at Harvard has yet to meet the demand. They lay poor Silas to rest only yesterday; he should fetch a fair price."

Alice's mouth fell open. "Are you to tell me that those men intend to unearth the unfortunate man's corpse and sell it for a fee to be dissected?"

"Lower your voice," Jonas warned. "Any man bold enough to dig up the remains of a dead man would gladly forgo the effort in exchange for the corpses of three people much more recently deceased. Their clients pay more for freshness and they do not ask questions."

With a sudden, terrified gasp, Benjamin spun away from the window.

Even in the darkness, Alice could see he trembled. "Mr. Emmons, what is it? What did you see?"

The old man was too paralyzed with fear to speak.

Jonas returned to the window and peered outside.

And that's when he saw it too.

"The dead, Mrs. Jacobs," he said. "Silas Painter has returned to defend his earthly remains… and he's brought some new acquaintances."

Chapter 29

Davey Liddle plunged his shovel deep into the loose dirt of
the fresh grave. He stomped his boot on the head of the blade
to drive it even deeper before hauling it free and flinging
another load of wet earth onto a mound that was growing
taller by the minute. Davey had never dug up a body before.
What would six feet of dirt look like? He drove his shovel
back into the soft earth and struck a rock with a jarring *clang!*
that echoed forever through the silence.

"Keep it quiet!" Davey's big brother, Jack, hissed from
across the grave. "You'll bring the whole town down on us!"

"Sorry," Davey mumbled, lowering his head like a dog who
was just kicked. How he could have predicted that he'd hit a
rock, and could he avoid it in the future? Davey's hands still
rang from the impact and his palms were already blistered,
but he knew better than to complain. Davey's big brother
couldn't stand complaints. Jack Liddle was someone who *got
things done*, not someone who complained. *Complainin's as
useless as prayin', and prayin's the same as beggin'.* That's what
Jack always said. And it was more than just words; Davey's

brother lived by his motto too.

It was Jack who had met with the university man from Boston. It was Jack who planned this job once he'd heard that Old Man Painter had died. And it was Jack who was kind enough to bring his little brother along to share in the profit. All Davey had to do was keep his mouth shut and dig. It didn't matter that his pile of dirt was twice the size of Jack's or that his brother was spending more time watching him than digging. This was Jack's idea, and as long as Davey did what he was told, he would be entitled to a whole two percent of whatever they got for the old man's corpse. Davey was never very good at mathematics, but two percent seemed like an awful lot for a couple hours of digging.

"How much did ya say we'd fetch for 'im?" Davey asked.

"We'll fetch naught but the gallows if we're discovered," Jack snapped. "Now keep quiet and keep diggin'."

Davey did as he was told and put his back into it. It wasn't easy work, but life had never been easy for the Liddle brothers. Now, digging up the muddy grave, it seemed to Davey like their luck was changing. He admired the way his big brother had put this plan together.

Ever since he could remember, Jack had always been the one with the brains. With the whole town too scared to even look out their windows, they had the entire cemetery all to themselves. There had been a few ugly moments around sundown when Jack saw the militiamen patrolling the streets. He'd been some kind of furious then—the kind of furious that Davey tried to stay away from. But then the soldiers just went away. *All part of the plan*, Jack had said with that grin that showed off his cracked tooth. And it really was a brilliant plan. Davey often thought his brother could have been a military man—one of those generals who came up with the strategies to win wars—if only he'd been given a chance.

The muddy hole was getting deeper and Davey guessed it wouldn't be long now. Just a few more feet to go.

"You'll have to get down in it," Jack said.

Davey obeyed, keeping quiet as he slid down into the pit.

The moon broke through the clouds. Round and full, its pale light filtered through the veil of mist and spilled across the crooked tombstones.

Davey glanced around at the gloomy cemetery. He could see how the townspeople could get so spooked. It certainly was creepy out here. Jack said they were all stupid; there was no such thing as ghosts, and if the townspeople were dumb enough to fear some old wives' tale, then they deserved what they got. Still, there was something unnerving about the moan of the breeze through the trees, the creaking of their bare limbs, their murky shapes looming in the mist. Davey shuddered and picked up the pace. It might be a brilliant plan, but he'd be glad when this job was over.

Despite the chilly air, Davey was soon coated in sweat from all the exertion. He took a second to wipe his brow with his threadbare sleeve.

And that's when he stopped digging for good.

"Damn it, Davey!" Jack sighed. "This bloke's not going to dig 'imself up, no matter what anyone in this town thinks. Now get to work!"

But Davey's eyes were fixed on a spot over Jack's shoulder.

Something was stirring in the darkness.

"Davey!" Jack whispered.

"Jack… what is *that*?" Davey pointed into the gloom. Jack turned.

The fine mist hanging in the air seemed to gather itself. The brothers watched, spellbound, as it grew denser, coming together into a thick, white mass. Davey had seen nothing like it. It was as if the mist was alive and moving with a will of its own. He knew it was impossible, and he told himself as much as he clambered up from the ditch. But, possible or not, the mist continued to take shape until it blanketed the ground in a churning layer of white.

It surged forward without warning.

Jack whirled around. "Get outta here, Davey!" He hit a note of panic that Davey had never heard from his brother before. "Get the hell outta here while ya can!"

It was too late.

The mist moved too quickly as it spilled around the tombstones and closed the distance to the brothers.

For one fleeting moment, Davey saw Jack shrouded in the murky whiteness. In that instant, he saw his brother's face split in two. Something warm and sticky sprayed onto him and everything went red.

Davey tasted his brother's coppery blood on his lips and he blinked dumbly, like a man who had just had water thrown in his face. The shovel fell from Davey's hands and then Jack's mutilated face was gone, engulfed in white. For one last and terrible moment, all Davey Liddle could hear was his big brother shrieking in the roiling depths of the mist.

An instant later, it was upon him too.

Chapter 30

The brothers' screams reverberated off the thick walls of the mausoleum. Jonas spun from the window, unable to endure the sight any longer. Benjamin huddled in the dust next to him, his lips mouthing the words of a desperate prayer while Alice shut her eyes and slid to the stone floor, pressing her hands to her ears to deafen herself against the terrible wails.

Alice clutched her iron talisman in her trembling grip as the shrieks of the dying men built toward a sickening crescendo. Its cold edges dug into her flesh. She thought she would go mad if the wailing didn't stop, and she bit her tongue to keep her own screams from escaping. She felt Benjamin reach for her hand and take it into his own in the darkness.

The cries ended suddenly. Silence filled the vault. Along with it came a stillness as awful as the men's terrible screams. The trio remained huddled in the darkness, trembling with shock.

Jonas was the first to rise. "Stay where you are." He snuck to the window and raised his eyes to peer outside.

There was nothing there.

The mist had dissipated into the night. Nothing remained of the two body snatchers.

Jonas looked deeper and spied dark stains splashed across the tombstones. They gleamed wet and red in the moonlight. With a shuddering breath, he sank back to the floor, saying nothing; the sight was too terrible to describe. A sideways glance told him that Alice was shaken, but he didn't have the words to comfort her. Her breathing came in shallow fits as she strove to regain composure. The collar of her coat had fallen away, revealing the ghastly print of the skeletal hand tattooed across her throat.

Benjamin saw it and gasped. "Mrs. Jacobs! What has happened to you?"

"We haven't the time for explanations," Alice replied. She pulled her collar back up around her neck, dragged herself to her feet, and released her white-knuckle grip on the talisman. She flexed her fingers and laid it on the stone lid of the casket to retrieve the volume of records with both hands.

Benjamin scrambled to his feet at the sight of the book, his eyes flying wide. "Where did you find that?"

"Where we found this isn't important, Mr. Emmons," Alice replied. "What matters right now is what this ledger reveals… the truth about Giles Dicer."

"Mrs. Jacobs, I don't know how you might possibly believe —"

"The physician of Salem declared Rebecca Hale's husband, Philip Hale, impotent in 1679. We have it right here in the records." Alice flipped through the ledger to the page and spun it around for Benjamin to see. "Rebecca used it as a justification for the petition of divorce she filed with the Court of Assistants the following year. And yet, she gave birth to the first of her children just a few months later."

"How can that be?" Jonas asked.

"Perhaps the rumors of her prostitution bore some truth," said Alice. "Whatever the case, over the years, Rebecca gave birth to *eight* children, not seven. Her youngest was born in the fall of 1691, but the baby is recorded here as having died in his crib." Alice turned the pages and pointed to a spot on the old parchment. "Just a few short months later, Rebecca Hale was accused of witchcraft and hanged along with the rest of her children."

"That's not correct," Benjamin protested. "Rebecca's children were saved. They fled to the safety of Maine."

"No, Mr. Emmons. That is only the comforting story the townspeople *chose* to believe once they were left with the terrible guilt of what they had done. The truth is—because no one could identify who their father was—Rebecca's children were hanged on suspicions of being the devil's progeny. But one man knew the truth. Judge Hathorne was determined to see Rebecca hang, regardless of her innocence."

Benjamin's eyes grew wide and round as it all came together. "You believe Hathorne condemned the woman to death to conceal his affair with the tavern prostitute?"

"Yes. But Rebecca's eighth child—Hathorne's child—was spared."

"*Justice Hathorne traded eight for seven…*" Jonas recalled the words of Sarah Bridges.

Alice gave a grim nod. "Hathorne felt no remorse in condemning the offspring of other men, but he couldn't hang his own son. Rebecca's eighth child never died in his crib. Hathorne claimed the baby and spent the remainder of his life living as the judge's illegitimate son... Giles Dicer."

Benjamin shook his head. "Hathorne had a wife and children of his own. He couldn't have brought another child into his home unnoticed."

"Perhaps Hathorne didn't raise the boy under his own roof. Perhaps he simply spared the child from the fate to which he was about to condemn the baby's siblings."

Jonas nodded. "Hathorne could have given the boy to an orphanage, a relative, anybody."

"Precisely," Alice said. "But somehow Dicer learned the truth, that Hathorne traded the life of Rebecca's eighth child for those of the other seven."

A silence fell as the weight of Alice's words hung in the air.

"This is impossible." Benjamin shook his head. "There is hardly enough evidence here to support such a theory."

"Mr. Emmons, why were these records hidden in the museum's storm cellar?" Jonas asked.

The old man's face tightened. "My father served as town clerk for many years. Before his death, he entrusted the records to my care. At the outbreak of the war with Britain, I hid them to preserve our history in the event the redcoats captured the town. But I swear to you, I never knew what terrible secrets lay within those pages."

Alice could see by the look in the old man's eyes he was telling the truth. But that wasn't what she cared about right now. Something Benjamin had said stuck with her, like the image of a puzzle being revealed.

"Your father was the town clerk?" she asked.

Benjamin nodded.

"And you say he was a friend of Giles Dicer?"

Another nod. The last piece of the puzzle fell into place.

"Then your father must be the man who forged Dicer's death certificate," Alice said.

Benjamin lowered his head and said nothing.

"'Tis true, isn't it? Dicer enlisted the help of his friend—your father—to help him disappear, to fool the world into thinking he was dead. He even had this mausoleum built to keep up the pretense. But it didn't work, did it? Giles Dicer still lives, haunted by his family legacy."

"It doesn't matter!" Benjamin raised his head and Alice could see his eyes were red and glistening with tears. "Despite the lies my father put his name to, Dicer would have died of old age years ago. Were he to be still alive, this would mark his one hundredth year!"

"No, Mr. Emmons. Somehow, Giles Dicer is still among us, somewhere in Salem. *He* is the one who conjured the spirit of his mother, Rebecca Hale, and bid her to claim our children. He intends to avenge himself for the deaths of siblings and break the curse that has haunted him for a century." Alice paused for a breath. "Mr. Emmons, you must tell us where we can find him."

Benjamin stared at her. "Mrs. Jacobs, did you not just witness the fates of those two wretched men out there? How can you think of going off into the night in search of a man who has surely passed from this earth? No, Jonas and I will accompany you back to the inn. God willing, in the morning you might yet return to some sort of life in Boston."

"Mr. Emmons," Alice's voice was soft as snow. "My

husband has been missing for three months. Samuel loved me and not a day passes that I don't hope and pray for his return. But in my heart, I have known that he is gone forever. My daughter is all I have left of him. I confess I am afraid. I have seen things this night that have split my very soul with fear. But I have no choice. Without my daughter, I have no life to return to."

Benjamin's hard gaze melted when he saw the tears rising in her eyes. He thought of his own daughter and how she had deteriorated after losing her first child. How could he condemn Alice to the same fate? What if he could save her from it? What if her plan worked? If there was even the slightest chance of rescuing his own grandson, didn't he have to take it no matter the risk?

"Dicer was last known to inhabit an old farmhouse," he said. "It still stands out past the western cornfields."

"Thank you!" Alice threw her arms around him before she could stop herself.

Benjamin turned to Jonas. "Take my horse. 'Tis tethered just beyond the cemetery gates. But I pray God will send you more speed than the beast herself can yield."

Jonas nodded and rose, as did Alice. "Where are you going?" he asked.

"I'm coming with you."

"No. I'll go alone. Benjamin will see you back to the inn."

"Mr. Hobbes, when my daughter is found, I intend to be there to comfort her," Alice said.

Jonas could tell by the firm set of her jaw that there would be no talking her out of this. "Can you ride?"

Alice bit the scar on her lip and nodded.

"I'll be riding fast," he said. "Be sure to hold on." With a grim nod to Benjamin, Jonas headed out the door.

On her way after him, Alice paused and gave the old man a warm smile. "Thank you, Benjamin. You've given us a reason to hope."

Benjamin nodded, his eyes twinkling as Alice turned and followed Jonas into the night.

Chapter 31

In a decaying farmhouse on the edge of a lonesome cornfield, the old man gripped an axe and waited in the darkness. He remained still, his shallow breaths rattling in his bony chest as he listened to the night. The wind howled through the house's crooked shutters. There was a haunting cry from a distant owl. The old man tightened his grip on the axe, knowing the eerie silence would soon be broken. His long and unnatural life would end with it.

Giles Dicer had realized long ago he wasn't meant to die like a normal man. He had tried to end his own life so many times that he'd lost count. But the spirits of his dead brothers and sisters wouldn't let it happen. Eventually, the old man understood that they would *never* let him die, not until they were finished with him, until his dead mother had paid her debt to Hell and he had done his part to see his siblings avenged.

Not until tonight.

"You'll come now, won't you, devils?" he muttered to the air. The hard lines of his grizzled face tightened as he strained his ears, listening even closer for any sound at all. All he heard was the shrill whine of the wind. "Yes. You'll come now…"

The last time anyone ventured this far into the western cornfields was years ago. Everyone knew the old Dicer house was haunted. Giles lived alone, unnoticed and unbothered, dead to the world as far as the town was concerned. For decades, he did all he could to break the curse his father, the hanging judge, had brought upon him.

Three months ago, there was a knock at his door and everything changed.

When the man from the city had come knocking on that fateful day, Giles did everything the spirits demanded, awful things for which he would never forgive himself. Now, the old man's time had come. By now, the Jacobs woman would be on her way to him, to this place… to *them*. Giles hated himself for his hand in what they would do to her.

With the axe raised and ready, he crept through the darkness to a dirty window. The old farmhouse still shook with the rumbling thunder of the passing rainstorm. Giles peered through a space between the sagging shutters and saw the pale radiance of lightning falling upon acres of cornfield that had been neglected for decades. The corn grew wildly now. The tufted tops of the stalks swayed and rustled in the steady breeze, undulating and rippling like the surface of the ocean.

Giles strained eyes that were dull and yellow with age. He made out the shadowy outline of the woods that bordered his land. A veiled hint of moonlight twinkled on the stream that ran along the edge of his pasture. Somewhere in the gloom upstream was the lake where his children used to swim—the lake his wife had drowned herself in when her two sons were taken from her.

The old man backed away from the window and moved across the room to a lamp on the mantel of the unlit fireplace. He had long ago lost the strength to haul firewood into the house. The dingy lamp was now the best he could do.

Giles rested his axe against the stone hearth. His wrinkled hands shook as he removed the soot-stained chimney and struck a spark with the flint. A soft yellow flame rose from the wick as he replaced the lamp's glass chimney, took the axe back in his hands, and surveyed the wreckage of the surrounding room. He had been wielding the axe blindly in the darkness for hours now, smashing everything in sight as he swung at devils he saw lurking in every shadow. The parlor lay in ruins around him, strewn with the shattered remains of a lifetime of accumulated possessions.

Giles had no memory of where many of them had come from. Too many years had passed, and he had long since stopped caring. The splintered fragments of a chestnut hutch lay heaped in a corner, the fine porcelain plates now smashed into thousands of tiny pieces that lay scattered around the room. With a grunt, the old man stooped for a smashed portrait vignette. The faded image of a young woman stared back at him. For the life of him, Giles couldn't remember who she was.

Just then, the flame of the oil lamp flickered and died.

Giles froze and stared into the darkness where the lamp was. He knew full well what it meant. It was the reason he'd lit the flame in the first place: to reveal when the spirits were near.

They were here. Coming for him.

BAM! BAM! BAM!

A flurry of tiny feet pounded across the floorboards upstairs.

Frozen in the darkness, Giles could hear the sounds of children running and laughing on the second floor. "Devils! Come out!" he cried.

The footsteps died, leaving only the wind and the distant cry of the owl. The old man's breath came short and shallow as he spun in slow circles, searching the murky shadows.

BAM! BAM! BAM!

Tiny feet reverberated off the rickety planks of the porch outside.

Giles whirled. "Leave me be, devils! I've done you no harm! I've done all you asked! Haunt me no more!"

The house erupted with nightmarish laughter.

Seized by terror, Giles let loose a hoarse scream and brought the rusty axe slicing through the darkness, aiming for apparitions he saw coming at him from all directions. The old man was no longer afraid of dying. But he was terrified of the suffering they would force him to endure before the spirits finally ended his life. He swung the axe, intent on delaying that terrible fate for as long as possible. His wild blows smashed through the decaying furniture as peals of hellish lightning illuminated the room.

As quickly as it began, the piercing laughter came to a stop.

Giles shook all over and his chest heaved as he looked about in the darkness. "Devils, please take me quick. I did not ask to be spared your fates. It was my father's doing. Why do you visit *his* sins upon me?"

BAM! BAM! BAM!

More children running on the second floor.

Giles's heart thundered in his ears as he crept through the darkness to the staircase. "Is it not enough that you have taken my wife? My children?" The axe handle shook in his bony hands as he went up the creaking stairs. His tread was slow and wary as he reached the second-floor landing. The hallway stretched before him in silent darkness.

An involuntary shiver wracked Giles as he gazed into the gloom. It was cold up here, unnaturally cold. The old man gripped the axe even tighter as he took his first tentative steps into the blackness. Holding his breath, he approached the first bedroom to his right, inched his head into the doorframe, and peered inside.

There was nothing there but smashed furniture.

With a deep, shuddering exhale, Giles gathered his courage before moving further down the hallway. The next bedroom revealed the same darkness and ruin. Giles's blood turned to ice in his veins as he backed away from the threshold.

A faint light was flickering in the bedroom at the end of the hall.

It wasn't there a moment ago.

Giles's ancient heart pounded with furious intensity as he stood rooted in place, paralyzed with fright. He knew with every part of his being that he should turn and flee; that he should run from this house and all the unholy terrors it held. But he couldn't bring himself to move. He felt the weariness of his many years hanging on his soul as he stood gazing at the dim light flickering like a beacon in the darkness. He'd been running from his fate for a century. Now he would run no more.

Giles raised the axe and went to the bedroom. His slow steps along the floorboards creaked in the silence as he approached the open door.

His mouth fell open at what lay within.

A tall figure sat in a rocking-chair at the very center of the room. A long sheet of burlap completely concealed it as it waited for him. Motionless. Breathless.

The window across the room was open to the howling wind. The tattered curtains billowed inward toward Giles. A lit jack-o'-lantern sat on the windowsill. Its dreadful face grinned wickedly at him as it cast an eerie orange light across the room.

Giles's eyes narrowed, his old spine hardening with resolve. "For a century, I have endured your torment," he whispered to the motionless figure before him. "You have taken my wife, my children, my name, my sanity… I will suffer it no more." He took a step, gripping the axe. "Tonight, I wake from this nightmare."

Another step forward…

The old man paused within an arm's reach of the motionless shape.

Another step…

He reached for the burlap with a trembling hand.

Closer…

Closer…

Inches away…

The burlap sheet slipped off.

Giles's axe fell from his hands and clattered to the floor. His eyes went to an impossible size, and he shrank away as the ghost of Rebecca Hale rose from the chair. Too terrified to even scream, he felt the hatred in his mother's baleful stare searing him through the shroud of her mourning veil.

Giles lost all awareness of control and free will as he scrambled from the room. He ricocheted from wall to wall as he dashed down the hallway to the stairs. A chorus of hellish laughter burst forth behind him. The mocking voices chased him from the house as he charged through the ruined parlor to the front door and out across the porch into the night.

He raced across the wet grass of the pasture before plunging headlong into the thick murk of the cornfield. His rusty heart hammered dangerously in his chest, and he waited for when it would finally burst. He almost welcomed the bliss it would bring, the long-awaited release from the awful fate that haunted him at every step of his life.

Erratic bursts of purple lightning raked the sky as Giles fled through the tall cornstalks. An enormous scarecrow sprang up from the darkness. It was tattered and rotting from years of decay.

Giles shrieked and changed direction, crashing through the cornrows, fleeing further and further into the shadowy maze. At last, he could go no further. Overcome with exhaustion, he staggered to a halt, gasping for air and struggling to ease the burning agony in his chest.

The night remained deathly still. Giles shivered and waited among the cornstalks, listening for the sounds of his unearthly pursuers.

None came.

Minutes went by—two, three, five, ten. From somewhere nearby, the cry of the owl pierced the air once more.

All at once, the mist thickened around him.

The hairs rose on Giles's neck as the voices of children crowded around him with their whispers. The old man froze, chilled by a sensation that gripped his very soul. There was a presence behind him. He turned—very slowly.

A small girl in a white nightgown gazed up at him. Her eyes were the blue of a winter sky, and Giles thought they were strangely like his own.

"No! No!" Giles recoiled in horror. "Get away, devil! Away!" He turned to flee, only to find the same little girl standing there behind him. "*NO!*"

The girl's angelic face twisted into that of a hideous corpse.

Skin rotted…

Flesh fell away…

Eyes went white and rolled back…

Giles shrieked, his voice shrill and keening as the hideous creature lunged for his neck. The last thing he heard at the end of his long, tortured life was the mocking laughter of his dead siblings rising from the cornrows.

Chapter 32

Alice clung to Jonas with her arms wrapped around his waist as they raced along the darkened country roads. The young quarter-horse Benjamin Emmons had lent them was lean and powerful and bred for running. The spotted mare charged through the night at breakneck speed, her hooves thundering through the mud and kicking up a long trail of leaves that swirled and scattered in her wake.

Jonas stood in the stirrups, gripping the reins in one hand and holding the storm lantern high in the other. Alice sat in the saddle behind him, deafened by the rush of the wind in her ears. It brought tears to her eyes, and she wiped them away with the back of her hand, careful not to lose her grip on the sailor.

Soon, the bright sphere of the moon broke through the dissipating clouds and spilled its cold radiance over the cornfields. The looming silhouettes of grinning scarecrows flew by.

Alice peered over Jonas's shoulder and made out the hulking shape of a covered bridge spanning a stream ahead.

The rushing water glistened and twinkled in the moonlight. Beyond the bridge was something else, something much larger and darker.

"There!" Alice pointed to where the shape of the farmhouse rose from the fields.

Jonas saw it too. He switched the lantern from one hand to the other and he leaned forward in the stirrups to dig his heels into the horse's sides. Now at full stride, the mare sped down the muddy track toward the bridge. With every second, Jonas could discern more of its rotting planks revealed in the moonlight. The rickety shingles of its mossy roof were barely visible through a green canopy of vines.

A sinking feeling took shape in Jonas's gut as they hurtled toward it at full speed. The decrepit wreck of a bridge would never support their weight. He had an image of them smashing through the planks, pitching through space and crashing to the rocks below. His hand tightened on the reins, but it was too late to stop. Darkness filled the gaping mouth of the bridge as they sped headlong toward it.

Jonas grit his teeth.

Just a few more yards…

A few more feet…

Without warning, the horse skidded to a careening halt.

Seized by a sudden panic, the mare neighed and squealed with unrestrained terror as she reared on her hind legs, inches from the bridge's wooden deck. It threw Jonas crashing backward into Alice and sent her flying from the saddle. She hit the ground with a heavy *thud* that took her breath away. By sheer instinct, she rolled to her right in time to avoid the horse's hooves as they came smashing back down to earth.

Alice scrambled to safety and spun around to see the mare rear up again. Her breath caught in her throat as the horse reeled dangerously close to the steep precipice that tumbled down to the rocky stream-bed below.

Jonas hung from the mare's neck, the lantern swinging crazily from his arm as he hauled on the reins with all his might. Incredibly, he managed to bring the terror-stricken animal back under his control. Alice found she could breathe again as he guided the horse back from the brink.

Jonas leapt from the saddle and rushed to her. "Are you injured?" He pressed his fingers to her forehead and came away with a trace of blood.

"No… Just… Just shaken,." Alice ignored the cut above her eye and returned her attention to the distraught horse.

The mare's eyes were wide and round, the whites clearly visible. She whined fearfully as she gazed at the bridge, ears pressed flat back, tail twitching. Alice felt faint tremors through the ground as the animal pawed at the dirt with her front hoof, insisting that they turn away and run.

"I've seen nothing like that," said Alice.

But Jonas had. It had been just hours ago when his own stallion had broken loose from his stable. This horse wasn't just spooked; it was terrified. Jonas turned and raised the lantern to illuminate the shadowy span of the bridge. What could have sent the animal into such a terror-stricken panic?

Alice hung back while Jonas crept forward, his keen eyes scanning the darkness swimming within the bridge's hollow passage. He paused at the threshold for a moment before taking a tentative step onto the sagging deck to test the strength of the planks. The rotten wood creaked and groaned under his weight as he moved ahead to look deeper in the gloom.

Nothing.

Jonas listened as he waited for his eyes to adjust. There was only the rush of the stream and the whine of the wind whistling through the cracks in the timber. His gaze fell on the farmhouse looming in the moonlight on the far side of the stream. They had little choice. Riding the horse across the ruined span of the bridge would be too risky.

"We'll walk," he said. He handed the lantern to Alice and gave the horse's reins a gentle tug. The terrified mare thrashed her head and refused to advance.

"Wait. Look…" Alice whispered.

Jonas followed her gaze past the lantern's radius of light into the darkness of the bridge passage. He narrowed his eyes and glimpsed it too.

Something was lurking in the shadows.

"What is it?" Alice whispered.

Jonas silenced her with his hand. The sudden look on his face was chilling.

A rumbling growl answered Alice's question. She gasped with fright as a dark shape prowled from the shadows and drew into the light.

Glaring at them from the threshold was an enormous wolf.

Alice's blood stopped running at the sight of it. The predator's lips were curled back, its fangs bared.

Jonas's hand went for his pistol but it was already too late; there was no time to load it. The wolf lowered its massive head and stalked toward them with a deep-throated snarl. Its eyes burned with murderous intent.

"Jonas!" Alice cried.

In a flash, the sailor was dragging her back toward the horse. "Get behind the—"

Something huge and snarling sprang at them from the darkness of the cornfield.

The second wolf caught Jonas and toppled him onto the muddy road. The lantern fell from Alice's hand as she shrieked and jumped back. It shattered on the ground, its fuel igniting into a wall of flame.

Jonas rolled backward and used the momentum of his fall to flip the wolf off of him. He sprang to his feet and whirled to face his attacker. The immense beast glared at him from across the slash of burning lantern oil. Its fur bristled and saliva dripped from fangs as sharp as a steel trap.

Jonas faced it squarely, guarding Alice with his body and keeping the fire between them and the growling predator as it tried to circle around. Its yellow eyes blazed with hunger as it stole forward, but the heat of the flames held it back. With a furious snarl, the wolf retreated and circled around again, stalking them, waiting for them to make a mistake.

Jonas was aware of the squeals and grunts of the horse as she fought off the first wolf. The mare couldn't get away with the wolf ready to pounce on her the moment she turned her back. But Alice might have a chance at escaping if the horse could somehow separate herself for just a moment.

"Alice, take the horse!" Jonas shouted.

"Jonas, I…" Alice's thoughts froze with panic.

A blood-curdling howl unfurled in the distance. The rest of the wolf pack was drawing near.

"We haven't much time!" Jonas cried. "Take the horse! I'll

draw them away!"

"No! I can't! I…"

The wall of flame separating them from the snarling wolf was shrinking and growing dimmer as the lantern oil burned itself out. Across the fiery divide, the beast lowered itself into a crouch, muscles contracting, ready to pounce. Only seconds remained before it was on them, maybe less.

"Alice, go now!" Jonas shouted. "Find our children! Please!"

Then it happened.

The wolf launched through the fire, its snapping jaws aimed at Jonas's throat. He spun to the side and Alice jolted into action.

She whirled away just as the first wolf scrambled to take down the horse from the rear. The terrified mare spun and caught her attacker with one powerful kick of her hind leg. The wolf hit the ground with a yelp and rolled a few times before coming to rest about ten yards away. Stunned, it tried to stand, but staggered and slumped in the mud instead.

This was it. If Alice had any chance, she had to act now.

She rushed forward and hurled herself at the saddle, but the horse was too terrified to recognize her. It reeled and kicked, seeing only another shape charging at her from the darkness.

Alice dodged and fell to the side as the wind of a massive hoof blew past her cheek. She sprang to her feet and lunged for the saddle again, catching it with her hand. Her palm was slippery as she reached for the pommel and hauled herself up, swinging her leg over in time to avoid the snapping jaws of the wolf.

The beast leapt at her again with a vicious snarl, its fangs narrowly missing her exposed leg. The frightened mare reared back once more, oblivious to her rider as Alice stood high in the stirrups. With tremendous force, the horse's powerful hooves came down hard on the wolf's spine, shattering it. There was a sharp *crack!* followed by a raspy, sputtering hiss as the air left the predator's ruptured lungs and it went perfectly still.

Alice spun in the saddle in time to see the remaining wolf sink its jaws into Jonas's forearm. Even across the distance, she could hear the awful *snap!* of his bone fracturing. She screamed as the sailor somehow shook himself loose and hurled the animal to the side. Blood poured from the wound as he whirled on Alice.

"*GO!*" he cried.

Alice dug her heels into the mare's sides and it bolted for the rickety bridge, driven by sheer terror. Strained past their limits by the weight of the charging horse, two of the rotted deck beams split apart and plummeted into the stream below. Without their support, the wall to Alice's right buckled under the weight of the roof. The framework slumped lower and lower as she raced past. There were a series of sharp *cracks!* as the overhead trusses splintered and burst with the strain. The entire structure was coming down around her.

Alice clung to the horse as it sped for safety. She was thirty yards away when a huge portion of the roof caved in behind her. The heavy timber smashed into the deck, and the entire bridge began collapsing into the stream. There was a deafening crashing of wood and Alice felt the mare jolted as the deck lurched to one side. The ancient planks rumbled and quaked beneath her and she held her breath, certain they would never make it, waiting for the deck to fall away beneath her…

Then they were across.

A geyser of water sprayed into the air as the rest of the bridge crashed into the stream. Seconds later, Alice was leaving the wreckage behind and speeding off into the night.

Left alone with the remaining wolf, Jonas let his good hand drop to the pistol tucked in his waistband. He cradled his wounded forearm against his body as he and the snarling animal circled each other.

Without warning, the wolf sprang at him. In a flash, Jonas brought the heavy butt of the pistol grip down on the beast's skull and sent it sprawling into the sputtering flames. The stench of burnt fur filled the air as the animal yelped and scrambled from the fire.

The enraged wolf spun around and sprang at him again, throwing the sailor to the ground. Sprawled on his back, Jonas's hand shot up in time to catch the beast by its scruffy throat. Pain shot up his fractured forearm as he squeezed and pushed, keeping the wolf's snapping jaws inches away from his neck. Strands of warm slobber fell to his face from the yellow fangs. The heat of the animal's fetid breath was stifling as it snarled and snapped at him until the cracked bone in his forearm broke. Jonas barely had time to register the pain before the wolf sank its fangs into his hand and tore away two of his fingers.

The pain was blinding. Jonas clenched his teeth against it while his free hand clawed in the dirt and closed on a shard of the broken lantern. With a grunt, he swung it with all his might and drove it deep into the wolf's eye. The animal shrieked in agony and bowled to the side, shaking its head in a vain effort to dislodge the jagged piece of glass stuck in its eye socket.

Jonas rolled to his feet and glanced at the empty gulf where the bridge had been. The shattered wreckage lay in the stream-bed below like a ruined dam. Following Alice was no longer an option. From the corner of his eye, he caught the wolf rocking its head. It wouldn't be long before it dislodged the glass shard. Jonas had to get out of there—*now*.

Alice was on her own.

Jonas looked into the distance, across the moonlit pasture to the farmhouse. "God be with you, Alice Jacobs," he murmured. He was losing blood rapidly as he fled down the dark road toward town, leaving the injured wolf howling in the night.

Chapter 33

Magistrate Holm studied the faces of the soldiers gathered around the fire. Twelve young men—thirteen, if he counted Captain Dennard. Would it be enough? Thinking back to those terrible moments in the Northern Woods—the ghastly voices, the skeletal hands clutching at him—he wasn't so sure.

Thirteen men. It was an unlucky number.

In the hours since Holm had arrived to find Salem Common deserted, Dennard had returned with a quarter of the fort's garrison. The others were behind to help the orphans and sift through the rubble of the lighthouse. The rains from the fearsome thunderstorm had helped extinguish the fire, but not before it had reduced the tower to little more than charred ruins. It would probably take months to restore the beacon, perhaps even years.

And it was all because of Sarah Bridges.

Some time after midnight, the first of Salem's grief-stricken fathers had arrived on the Common to join them. The trembling young man had emerged from the shadows, his face streaked with tears. He spoke of a dark woman who had taken his son, a woman made of smoke and mist. Holm felt a chill deep in his bones as he listened to the man's awful tale. Other fathers soon trickled in, drawn to the Common by the light of the fire Dennard's soldiers had raised. All had lost sons or daughters to the witch.

Most of these men stood by Holm now. Their faces were long and drawn as they gazed at him in the firelight. Captain Dennard was saying something, and the sound of his raised voice brought the magistrate back to the moment.

"We must strike *tonight*, while there is still time," Dennard said, clenching his skinny fist for emphasis. "Every moment the witch of Gallows Hill eludes us is another moment this town lives in terror. We must not tolerate it. We must end it *now*."

A murmur of agreement passed through the men. Holm had to say something, to *do* something. His plan had failed. He had thought he could defeat the witch and her spirits once they left the shelter of their cursed woods and came to *him*. He was wrong.

Sarah Bridges' spirits had already come and gone with the storm, leaving nothing but misery and sorrow behind. Holm now had to show leadership. But how? How could he tell these men that he'd seen the witch's evil with his own eyes and been sent running for his life? Worse yet, what if he told them and they didn't believe him? Any man who ventured into those terrible woods would surely meet his end. Holm couldn't let that happen; he had to convince them. As much as he hated her, he had to keep them from going after Sarah Bridges.

"I say we wait until first light," he said. "Sunrise is only hours away. Under the cover of darkness, the witch has us at a disadvantage. Otherwise, I would not have failed to apprehend her." He omitted *why* he had failed.

"If we wait until sunrise, these men may never see their children again," Dennard argued, waving a hand at the grieving fathers gathered around the fire.

"Captain Dennard, just this afternoon you suggested that I not go to the Northern Woods after dark for fear of what I might encounter there," Holm countered. "Why the sudden change of heart?"

"That was before I returned to my fort to find it breached and three of my men ripped to shreds."

Ah, there it is, Holm mused. Dennard was allowing his emotions to guide his actions. By all accounts, he was a good soldier who had the right heart. But what Dennard had in spirit, he lacked in vision. It was the reason the man had never risen higher than his present rank of captain. Now, his desire for vengeance was clouding his judgment. Such rash decisions could spell disaster for them all.

"The woman cannot elude all of us," Dennard persisted. "If we simply—"

But the men were no longer listening. Instead, their attention turned to a spot across the moonlit Common. Beyond the orange glow of the firelight, the mist hanging on the ground was drawing itself together.

"What in God's name...?" Dennard whispered, mesmerized by the sight. It was happening quickly, the mist gathering itself, growing denser, glowing with an ethereal radiance as it reflected the moonlight.

Then it rushed forward.

The men fell back, stumbling over each other, trying to get away. Holm heard frantic shouts and cries as he pushed through the throng and raised his musket. He had been waiting for the moment he could put an end to this once and for all. He squeezed the trigger, and the musket roared with a fiery blast.

The ball passed through the swirling white depths like a stone hurled into the wind.

For one frozen instant, Holm felt like he was back in the Northern Woods, paralyzed by terror, unable to think, turn, flee. His thoughts failed him as he watched the mist surging toward him, covering the distance.

Yards, feet, inches…

Holm readied himself for death.

All at once, the mist evaporated. There was an earsplitting shriek of unfathomable rage, and then it was gone, vanishing into the night like wisps of smoke.

A long moment passed as silence descended on the Common.

"What was *that*?" Dennard spoke at last. Even in the warm glow of the firelight, his face had gone terribly pale.

"The dead," Holm answered. "Sent by Sarah Bridges to seek our destruction." His cold eyes lingered on the empty air where the mist had been. Something about this wasn't right. Why had the spirits turned away? Why had they let him live?

An uncomfortable hush fell before Holm spoke again. "That settles it. I'll not risk the lives of these men fighting an enemy that is already dead. We'll wait until dawn, and *then* we'll go for Sarah Bridges."

"By dawn, it will be too late." A brittle voice spoke from

the darkness behind them.

Holm whirled, his pistol already in his hand as Benjamin Emmons stepped into the firelight. The magistrate exhaled and relaxed his trigger finger at the sight of him.

"You are wise to fear Sarah Bridges," Benjamin said. "I believe she does seek our destruction. But by sunrise, it will be too late to stop her."

Something cold in the old man's eyes set Holm's teeth on edge.

"But I have found something that may help us right now," Benjamin confided.

Chapter 34

Alice tugged on the reins and brought the mare to a cautious trot. The muddy road from the bridge followed the stream as it snaked around the pasture to where the farmhouse stood in silent darkness. The steady *clop* of the horse's hooves carried maddeningly through the night air, announcing Alice's arrival with perfect clarity to anyone—or any *thing*—who was listening.

The infuriated howls of a wounded wolf echoed in the distance. Alice thought of Jonas. What had become of him? Would she see the sailor again when this nightmare was over?

The remains of a dilapidated fence came into view as Alice rounded a curve. She reined the horse to a halt where the road turned into a narrow lane running up the final fifty yards of pasture to the house. She dismounted, led the mare to a crooked fence post, and lashed the reins to it. With a soothing rub of the horse's neck, she turned and surveyed the gloomy scene.

The old farmhouse rose from the cornfields and loomed like a giant tombstone in the moonlight. It was a square, two-story Colonial with a gabled roof that was stripped of its shingles in at least a dozen places. The outline of a stone chimney stood silhouetted like a finger-bone against the moon. A single, darkened window gaped at her from the shelter of a small gable perched on the second floor. Two more dingy windows were set into the faded clapboard exterior of the ground floor, one on each side of the weather-beaten door.

Above the slumping front porch, the pitched slope of an overhanging roof stood supported by four spindle columns that looked ready to split at any moment. The hulking wreck of a barn with a caved-in roof stood behind the house. To the left, an immense oak rose high into the air, its skeletal branches twisting toward the house like an outstretched claw. Its bare limbs knocked against each other in the steady breeze with an eerie creak and clatter.

Alice steeled her resolve and left the horse behind as she crept up the lane to the porch. There, a chilling discovery gave her pause. Three dead bats hung suspended from a beam over the front door. Their sharp talons were stiff with rigor and clamped to the wood as if they had died instantly and frozen in place. Alice peered up at them, her misgivings swelling into an icy tingle of fear.

None of this felt right. The house was too calm. Too quiet.

Alice wanted nothing more than to turn and leave it all behind. Something awful waited for her inside this house. But Samuel had come here, to this place. Her husband was here the day he vanished. It wasn't Giles Dicer's tomb he had been investigating; he had been after Dicer *himself*. That's why Alice had found Dicer's mausoleum undisturbed.

Somehow, Samuel had discovered the man still lived, a direct descendant of the woman whose spirit had snatched Abigail from her bed. The disappearances of Alice's husband and her daughter were linked. She was sure of it. Everything she had learned in her search for Abigail had led her *here*, to this derelict farmhouse, to the very place where Samuel had vanished.

The ancient home of Giles Dicer stood at the center of both mysteries.

It was time to step inside.

Alice turned the doorknob with a trembling hand, pulled the door, and peeked within. As her eyes adjusted to the darkness, she made out the bulky shapes of smashed furniture strewn about the parlor. As if a ferocious battle had been waged in the room, there was nothing but ruin everywhere she looked. Alice hovered at the door, listening, waiting for the creak of a floorboard, the soft tread of a footfall, any telltale sign that someone was home. None came. The house was silent except for the constant howl of the wind through the eaves.

"Giles Dicer!" Alice's shout echoed forever throughout the empty rooms until the silence eventually swallowed it. The floorboards creaked with unnerving volume as she crossed the threshold and stepped inside. She picked her way through the darkness to the center of the wreckage, her eyes sweeping around the crumbling room. Broken pieces of furniture lay scattered everywhere. She bent to pick a shattered rosewood table-clock from the debris. The brass hands were bent and useless, but when she held it to her ear, she could still hear the mechanism ticking within. A tremor of dread passed through her. What in God's name had happened here?

"Giles Dicer! I have come to claim my child!" Alice shouted again, letting the ruined clock fall back to the floor with a clatter. As if in response, the old house creaked and groaned as the wind mounted outside. The shrill cry of a nearby owl shattered the eerie calm. Something was happening; the night was coming alive.

Alice felt the abrupt shift in the air and readied herself.

Just then, a stray blast of lightning lit the room.

Alice gasped and raised a hand to her mouth.

The words to a lullaby covered the dusky walls, scrawled in streaks of blood. *Hush-a-bye baby, on the tree top. When the wind blows, the cradle will rock. When the bough breaks, the cradle will fall. And down will fall baby, cradle and all.*

The lightning subsided and Alice was left trembling in the darkness again. It took all of her courage, all of her will and resolve, to keep from running from this hellish place.

BAM! BAM! BAM!

A child ran across the floor upstairs.

"Abigail!" Alice spun and darted for the staircase, bounding up the creaking steps to the second floor. The hallway yawned in the darkness before her. "Abigail, where are you? Mother is here! I've come for you!"

A sudden shiver stole up Alice's spine. It was cold up here, incredibly cold. She could see her own breath as she squinted into the gloom. She remembered those moments in the Northern Woods when she had felt a similar cold—the frigid chill of the grave that followed the dead wherever they went.

Alice wrapped herself tighter in Jonas's wool coat as she crept into the darkness and approached the nearest bedroom.

Nothing remained within but smashed furniture. Another peal of lightning erupted outside the window. Alice jumped. Lit by the brilliant flare, she found the same awful lullaby scribbled across the walls. She retreated into the hallway, where she froze in place.

A faint light danced through an open door at the end of the hall.

Alice stared at it, her breath trapped in her chest. She wasn't alone; somebody *was* home. It took all of her courage to cross the creaking floorboards and peek inside the bedroom.

A tall figure was waiting for her. It sat at the center of the room, hidden beneath a long sheet of burlap.

Alice's blood ran slow and cold like drops from an icicle. "Giles Dicer," she said. "I have come for my daughter. You'll offer the lives of no more innocents to save your own."

Nothing happened. The figure remained motionless, silent.

Alice's heart battered her ribs as she stepped into the room, moving cautiously, keeping her eyes on the sinister shape. She took another step, expecting the figure to lunge for her at any second.

Another step…

Alice reached for the burlap sheet.

Closer…

Closer…

Inches away…

The burlap slipped away from a scarecrow propped in a rickety rocking chair.

Alice drew a deep breath and let it out with an unsteady shudder. She let the burlap drop to the floor, the beating of her heart ebbing as she looked around. A grinning jack-o'-lantern perched on the windowsill sent shadows dancing through the room. Illuminated in the dim light were the lines of dozens of lullabies scrawled in blood across the walls.

Alice was about to exit the room when a horrific sound stopped her cold.

Out in the night, her horse was shrieking in agony. The animal's pitiful wails went on and on until the shrieks came to an awful, abrupt halt.

Silence descended once more.

A child laughed somewhere downstairs.

"Abigail!" Alice dashed from the room and raced for the stairs. Another blast of lightning brought her to a skidding halt. She looked up and screamed with sudden horror.

Giles Dicer's corpse swung at the end of a noose strung from the rafters high above the staircase. Explosions of lightning illuminated his lifeless body as it spun in slow, steady arcs. The remains of the old man's face were now a hideous mess. His wrinkled flesh was scratched and torn to unrecognizable pieces. The gray mass of his tongue protruded over a ragged jaw that dangled limp and useless from his mangled skull.

Alice's screams came fast and loud as she scrambled from the house and sprinted across the porch, desperate to leave the horrible sight behind.

The end of the narrow lane was even worse.

The mutilated remains of her horse lay splattered across the pasture. A grisly swath of blood and flesh and viscera soaked the ground in all directions, as if a thousand vicious claws had torn apart the mare. Only a thick portion of the animal's brown neck remained hanging from the fence post, the tawny hide still lashed to the sagging stake by the leather reins.

Sickened beyond all restraint, Alice stumbled and collapsed to her knees, retching violently into the tall grass at the water's edge. She shrieked as hopeless tears came and fell in a warm rush down her cheeks. The tomb, the farmhouse, Giles Dicer—her entire search had yielded nothing but horror. Dawn was a mere few hours away now, and she had nowhere left to turn. Everything was lost—daughter, husband, hope— everything. Alice's wail echoed among the trees of the distant woods, mocking her anguish.

Another sound made its way to her ear.

Alice stiffened and strained to listen, certain she had been mistaken, that she'd imagined it in her grief. But no. It was faint but there, drifting through the silence from somewhere in the fog upstream.

A woman was singing a lilting lullaby.

Goosebumps rose on the surface of Alice's skin. The woman's voice was haunting in its fragility and called to her like a Siren's song.

Alice wiped a hand across her cheeks, dragged herself to her feet, and crept to the stream's rocky shore. She lingered for a moment on the edge of the rush of cold water, listening to the ghostly melody before pursuing it deep into the murky fog.

Chapter 35

Alice kept the rushing stream to her right as she followed its meandering course through the fog. The haunting tones of the woman's lullaby still called to her from somewhere ahead. It drew Alice to it like a child under a spell as she ventured ever deeper into the gloom. The shredded hem of her nightgown dragged and pulled against the wet underbrush, but she paid it no attention.

Minutes went by until Alice found herself at the spot where the rushing stream drained from the deeper water of a murky lake. The fog was even thicker here. It glowed a ghostly white in the moonlight, clinging to the water's surface and obscuring the boundaries of the lake. The air was flush and pregnant with moisture.

Mist lighted on Alice's skin with a cold, wet tingle as she remained among the cattails and reeds at the water's edge and surveyed her surroundings with a wary eye. Nothing moved, but the delicate melody of the woman's song still floated in the air. It was louder and clearer now, coming to Alice from somewhere in the shadowy reaches of the mist-shrouded lake.

There was another sound too, a faint but familiar creaking that Alice couldn't identify. About twenty yards to her left, the decaying span of a dock extended across the still waters of the lake. A dense tangle of bulrushes rose on either side of it, drooping and languid in the cold night air.

Alice pushed through the reeds along the shoreline to the dock and mounted the sodden timber planks. They were gray and green with age, groaning under her leather slippers as she stole across to the end of the small wharf. There, she discovered the source of the strange creaking: a line of rope stretched out into the fog. Tied to one of the dock's crooked pilings and pulled taut by something hidden deep in the gloom, it creaked eerily with the tension as it hovered inches above the water's surface.

The woman's song came from somewhere at the other end of the line.

Alice stood perched at the brink of the dock, her eyes following the rope to where it vanished into the mist. She squinted and strained to make out whatever was floating out in its depths, but it was useless. The fog was too thick, too impenetrable.

With her pulse beating a slow and steady tattoo in her ears, Alice lowered herself to a crouch. Her hand trembled as she stretched her arm out over the dark water, reaching for the rope. Her fingers grazed the rough cord and she faltered. Did she really want to know what was tied to the other end? Overcome by a sudden apprehension, she let go of the rope and retreated toward the shore. But the chilling beauty of the woman's song held her from retreating any further. She needed to know where the voice came from.

Alice crouched and reached for the rope once more. A cold gush of water squeezed into her palm as she gripped the line and pulled. The tension on the rope released and the sound of the woman's singing grew louder. Alice hauled on the rope again, reeling in the slack so that it coiled in a soggy pile next to her on the dock. With each steady pull, the haunting notes of the woman's melody swelled in volume as it drew closer.

The tune changed. The eerie lullaby became shrill and piercing, like the wail of a banshee.

Alice's heart leaped into her throat, but she couldn't stop now. She had to see the woman. Small ripples emerged from the mist. They spread across the water in miniature waves, pushed toward the shore by whatever Alice was drawing in. A cluster of water lilies bobbed and dipped as the awful wail of the woman's song continued to swell, becoming unbearable. Alice cringed as she pulled at the rope, hand over hand, eyes straining for whatever was approaching.

The singing stopped.

Alice's eyes widened. The rope fell from her hands.

A small rowboat slid from the gloom of the fog.

Alice stared at it, confused and relieved at the same time. She took up the rope again, her breath quivering as she reeled the decrepit boat until it struck against the dock with a hollow *thunk*. The gentle sound of the ripples lapping at the shore carried through the stillness.

Still crouching at the edge of the dock, Alice studied the empty vessel. It was small, perhaps twelve feet long. The paint of the whitewashed hull had long since peeled away and the exposed wood was now green with rot. The iron oarlocks were pitted and caked with rust. Only one oar remained. It lay in the hull's bottom, gray and weathered and half-submerged in a puddle of dirty water.

Alice sighed and turned around.

Behind her stood Rebecca Hale.

Alice screamed and backpedaled as the ghostly woman floated across the dock toward her. Panicking, her foot slipped off the edge of the wooden planks. As she fought for balance, Alice caught the vivid green of the woman's eyes glaring at her from behind her black veil. Then she pitched from the dock and plunged into the cold, dark water.

Alice sank like a stone into the black depths of the lake. The frigid water stole the air from her lungs and arrested her breath. She struggled against the weight of her clothes, thrashing about to stop her descent. Pale moonlight shimmered over her head. Below her, there was nothing but murky darkness. Freeing herself from the heavy wool coat that dragged her ever downward like an anchor, Alice cast it off and swam toward the surface. The twinkling gleam of the moonlight grew steadily brighter as she rose toward it.

Something grabbed her ankle.

Alice's eyes shot downward and saw the pallid form of a woman's hand clutching at her from the darkness below. A spectral face materialized from the depths, young and pretty, with eyes like sapphires. The woman's long yellow hair billowed around her in the swirling water as she dragged Alice down. Alice's eyes grew wide with terror as the flesh of the woman's hand clamped around her ankle began to decay. The livid discoloration spread up the woman's arm to consume her pretty face. Skin rotted and eyes disappeared. The woman's mouth stretched impossibly wide in an awful, silent scream.

Alice fought madly against the corpse's iron grip, kicking at it in a desperate struggle to regain the surface. But the hand still clung to her, dragging her further downward into the darkness. Alice's lungs burned in her chest, screaming for air, ready to burst. Her mouth opened involuntarily and flooded with cold water. Darkness crept into the corners of her eyes as a shadowy nothingness closed in on her. She clung to consciousness as she stretched her hand up over her head, reaching for the moonlight in one last vain attempt to escape.

A warm hand plunged through the surface and grabbed her wrist.

Alice was suddenly hauled up from the water. Pulled in two directions, she had the brief impression that she would be torn in two until the hideous monstrosity below released its grip. With a furious shriek that resounded through the deep water, the undead woman sank away and vanished into the darkness as Alice was hoisted up onto the dock. She choked and sputtered, gasping to fill her lungs.

"Get away!" Alice was out of her mind with fright, kicking and flailing against the firm hands that held her. "Get away! Don't touch me! Get away!"

The hands pinned her to the wooden plank.

"Alice, stop it!" A man's voice was trying to soothe her. "It's alright, Alice! Please calm down!"

The familiar voice cut through her terror and Alice realized she recognized it, that she had heard it countless times. She opened her eyes to look up at her savior.

Her husband looked down at her with tender eyes.

Overwhelmed, Alice fainted and collapsed into Samuel's

arms.

Chapter 36

Adrift in a dream-like unconsciousness, Alice saw Samuel sitting at the shabby writing desk he kept in the modest bedroom of their Boston cottage. She remembered him as he was: handsome and lean with dark, curly hair and eyes as warm as cinnamon.

Samuel never could keep the desk tidy and it was now cluttered with stacks of manuscripts, letters, official records, and, of course, his precious journals. An oil lamp poked from among the clutter and Samuel was bent toward it, hunched over a large volume.

Alice remembered entering and pausing at the door without her husband noticing. She wore her flannel nightgown, and she had pinned her hair for the night. Samuel continued to read, oblivious to her presence as she crept closer on her tiptoes. She threw her arms around him and he jumped with fright at the unexpected jolt.

"I think you've read enough ghost stories for one night, Samuel Jacobs." Alice laughed. She removed his wire spectacles and tossed them onto a pile of letters on the desk.

Samuel smiled and pulled her into his lap. Still giggling, she kissed him before glancing down at the open book in his hands. "Is this one of your frightening stories?"

"Terrifying."

"Tell me more."

"'Tis about a man and a woman in love."

"And no doubt some terrible doom awaits them?"

Samuel closed the book and gazed up at Alice, admiring her exquisite eyes. "Most terrible. The man grows so enamored of his wife's beauty that he can think of nothing but her."

"How is that so bad?"

"The two are forced to live forever on the meager salary of an academic."

"But they are together forever in love?"

"Yes. Forever."

"Then it is not so terrible after all." Alice leaned in to kiss him again.

Samuel pulled her close and tightened his arms around her before carrying her to the bed.

The memories drifted like leaves caught in the wind.

Alice saw a modest coach waiting in the street in front of their home on North Square. She stood on the steps, holding Abigail's hand while Samuel helped the coachman load his worn baggage into the carriage.

With the last valise stowed away, her husband turned to her. "'Tis not too late. I don't have to go."

"Yes, you do," Alice replied. "This is your passion, Samuel. You must pursue it."

Samuel returned her smile and kissed her before crouching

and folding Abigail into a tender hug. "You be a good girl for your mother, Abigail."

"Who will read me my bedtime stories?" Abigail groused, her voice falling low and quiet. "How do I know you'll return?"

Samuel looked deep into his daughter's eyes and saw them glossy with tears. "Because of the riddle."

"What riddle?"

"There was once a man who had been away from his family for a very long time. Every day he was gone, he missed them dearly, until the time came when he was to return to them." Samuel took Abigail's tiny hand into his own. "Excited to see his family, the man leapt onto an enormous black horse and rode quickly for his home. He carried no lantern, and he carried no candle. The moon did not shine its light. But when he arrived, he could see his daughter's beautiful face waiting for him in the street. Tell me, Abigail... how was he able to do that?"

Abigail's adorable face crinkled in thought. "I don't know, Father. How was he able to see his daughter?"

Samuel winked, his eyes twinkling. "I will tell you when I return." He left a gentle kiss on Abigail's forehead and turned back to Alice. "I love you."

"And I love you."

Samuel smiled again as he broke away and took his place in the carriage.

Once again, Alice's memories washed over her in a flood. She tumbled with them, carried along through time until she found herself seated in the worn wingback of her humble parlor. Pale light streamed through the windows. Samuel's journals lay scattered on the surrounding floor. She hadn't slept for days and she looked tired.

There was a knock at the front door and Alice leapt to her feet. She hurried across the room and flung the door open for a gray-faced man in an austere uniform.

"Constable Dimsdale." Alice ushered the man back into the parlor. "Have you any news? I have been reading Samuel's journals but I've not—"

"I regret to say that I have learned nothing new, Mrs. Jacobs," Dimsdale replied, taking his hat into his hands. "Nor can I reasonably expect to discover anything."

"What of the historian with whom he was lodging?" Alice asked, gaping at the constable in disbelief. "Surely he must know something more?"

"I have spoken with Mr. Emmons myself, along with anyone else in Salem who may have come in contact with your husband. None have been able to assist us."

"Constable, a man does not simply disappear from the face of the earth," Alice insisted as she sank back into her chair. "There must be a clue to what happened."

The constable's thick fingers plucked at the brim of his hat. "Mrs. Jacobs, in cases such as this, there comes a time when the likelihood of a resolution can no longer be a reasonable consideration. Two months have passed since you first reported your husband's disappearance. We have exhausted our resources. I am sorry, but I am afraid we must now expect the worst."

"But Samuel wouldn't have…" Alice had gone pale. She swayed in her chair, her eyes fluttering. The room was suddenly too hot. Her breath escaped her.

"Mrs. Jacobs, I am truly sorry. Are… are you alright?"

Constable Dimsdale lunged for her as she slumped forward in a faint and plunged into darkness.

Chapter 37

Samuel's gentle voice drifted through the wandering vastness of Alice's unconscious mind, calling her back to herself.

Alice… Wake up, Alice…

For a fleeting moment, Alice had the strange sensation that she was rushing upward from somewhere deep and shadowy, hurtling through space toward a brighter point until her eyes fluttered open. Still dazed, she glanced around.

She was lying on her back on the old wooden dock. Mere minutes had passed since Samuel had hauled her from the water and she still lay cradled in her husband's arms. The night was still and calm.

"Samuel… How…" Alice's thoughts raced as she gazed in wonder at his face. Was it real? Was he truly there with her? Holding her?

"Shhh… You're freezing." Samuel rose to a crouch beside her and rubbed her arms to warm them. "Let's get you back to the house. I'll explain everything."

"No! We mustn't!" Alice's eyes flared with sudden fright and she clutched at him, pulling him back down to her.

"Samuel, the house is a nightmare! 'Tis dreadful! That man... Giles Dicer..." She trailed off, unable to continue as a bitter lump rose like bile into her throat. "Samuel... Abigail has been taken."

The stricken look that came over her husband's face was too much for Alice to bear. "I'm so sorry, Samuel! I had no choice! I didn't know! When you disappeared I... I..."

"It's alright, Alice. It's not your fault..." Samuel's voice was tender as he smoothed her wet hair and brushed away her tears. But lingering behind his reassuring words lay an unspoken sense of heart-rendering grief.

"Why didn't you come home?" Alice asked. "All this time? Why...?"

Samuel's eyes welled with anguish. "I tried, Alice. God help me, I tried with every shred of strength in my being. But he wouldn't let me."

"*Who* wouldn't let you?"

"He waited all this time for me to return," Samuel went on, not hearing her. His voice had grown distant, his thoughts lost somewhere else. "He waited all these years for me to unearth the truth about my father. Once he had me, he wouldn't let me go."

"Your father? Samuel, I don't understand. What do you mean by your father?"

"That man in the farmhouse..." Samuel's face went dark.

And then Alice understood.

"The only surviving son..." she whispered, recalling what she knew of Giles Dicer's family history. She looked at her husband's face, as if she were seeing it clearly for the first time. "It was you, wasn't it? *You* were the child sent to Boston to escape the curse. Your father was Giles Dicer."

Samuel nodded and looked into the fog. "My father was the eighth child of Rebecca Hale, the boy whose life they spared."

Alice's eyes went to the lake. "And that woman in the water…"

"My mother, Mary Winthrop Dicer. I was a baby when they sent me to live with the Jacobs family of Boston. My mother was driven mad with grief…" He followed Alice's gaze into the dark water. "My father's fate would not prove to be as merciful. For one hundred years, he suffered the wrath of his dead siblings. They returned every All Hallows' Eve, tormenting him, waiting with undying patience for the day his son would return—waiting to claim their terrible vengeance."

In that instant, Alice realized her greatest mistake. The words of Sarah Bridges echoed in her mind. *She is conjured by no one, beholden to none.* "Your father didn't summon the spirits."

Samuel shook his head. "Summoned? No. They commanded *him*."

"Samuel, your father is dead. I saw him back in the farmhouse."

Samuel gave a grim nod. "I know. But his death isn't enough, Alice. They won't stop, not as long as the blood of Judge Hathorne flows through living veins. Once I discovered the truth of my ancestry, I did everything I could to hide it."

Alice remembered the missing page in his journal, the one that was removed with such careful precision. "Your journal. You're the one who removed the one and only reference to

Giles Dicer."

Samuel nodded. "I swear to you I tried everything to keep you safe, to keep you from following me here."

"But why?"

Samuel didn't seem to hear her. His voice trembled now. "It was already too late. Once my father had me, he held me captive." He paused and looked at her. "They made him use me as bait, Alice."

"Bait?" Alice blinked in confusion.

"Don't you see? They used my disappearance to lure you here."

"Me?" None of this made sense. It was all coming at her too fast. "For what purpose?"

"To bring them the last of the Hathornes."

"What? Who—?" Suddenly, the full impact of his words struck Alice like a blow. "Abigail!"

Samuel closed his eyes and lowered his head. "Our daughter is the last of Rebecca Hale's bloodline, a direct descendant of the witch and the judge who hanged her. Rebecca's spirit will stop at nothing to claim our child as her own. At dawn Rebecca will return to Hell… and she will take Abigail with her."

"No! Samuel, we must find her! We…" Alice's mind reeled as another thought stole upon her. I must tell you something. Abigail isn't the only one. I—" Her eyes widened with sudden terror. "Samuel, behind you!"

A thick mist was coalescing among the reeds and cattails where the dock met the shoreline.

Samuel didn't look back or turn. Instead, he kept his eyes on Alice. "Get in the boat. They cannot cross water. They're bound to the earth, bound to their graves. We must get in the boat."

"No, we can stop them…" Alice fumbled for her talisman, but realized she had forgotten it in her rush to leave the mausoleum. It was still resting on the stone lid of Giles Dicer's empty tomb.

"Alice! Come now!" Samuel hauled her to her feet and hustled her to the edge of the dock. Behind them, the spectral mist glided forward, writhing and coiling with supernatural life as it slid across the ground.

Samuel supported Alice by the arm as she stepped into the old rowboat. It rocked unsteadily in the water while she gained her balance and sat on the rickety seat, waiting for Samuel to untie the rope that fastened the boat to the dock.

Instead of getting in after her, he pushed the boat away.

Alice stared at him in shock. "Samuel!"

Samuel remained at the edge of the dock and kept his eyes on her as the boat drifted away. "They've come for me, Alice."

"Samuel, please!" Alice scrambled from the flimsy bench. "Why are you doing this? Come with me! Leave this place!"

"I cannot," he said, shaking his head. "I can *never* leave. They've waited for me all these years… and now they've come for me. They will drive you mad, Alice, as they did my mother. As long as I live…" Samuel's voice trailed away and he clenched his fists. "It must end tonight. I must make the sacrifice."

"No! Samuel! Don't leave me!"

The writhing mist slithered forward and surged across the dock toward him. A hellish chorus of ghastly voices erupted from within its reaches.

"Find Abigail, Alice!" Samuel shouted. "Take her away from here! It may not be too late! Tell her… tell her the man could see his daughter because it was a bright and sunny day."

"No!" Alice screamed as the mist overtook her husband. "Samuel!"

Engulfed in the swirling depths, Samuel's screams burst forth and shattered the night air.

Alice wailed miserably and pressed her eyes shut. She sank into the hull of the boat and curled into a ball, clutching herself and sobbing while her husband's agonized shrieks echoed across the water and resounded throughout the surrounding forest. For long, awful minutes, she could do nothing but moan, willing herself to die, to somehow escape the horrific cries.

Then it was over.

The echoes of Samuel's voice sailed across the water until they were gone and there was nothing but Alice's moans and the surrounding silence. She had no memory of the time she stayed curled in the boat's bottom, trembling and sobbing. Minutes passed like hours until she opened her eyes and raised her head.

The mist was there, waiting for her.

It coiled around itself like a predator stalking prey and lashed out toward her, only to dissipate into the night air the instant it left the shore and crossed the water.

Still choking on her tears, Alice reached for the splintered oar and slid it into the water, guiding the decrepit rowboat away from the shore and floating deeper into the thick depths of the fog.

Chapter 38

Jonas would die if he didn't stop the bleeding. The trail of blood he was leaving behind would soon bring the rest of the wolf pack right to him. He would have to think of something fast if he had any chance of making it back to town alive.

After fleeing the wolf at the bridge, he had paused long enough to strip the cord waistband from his pants and tie it around his left wrist in a crude tourniquet. It wasn't easy. With only one good hand to work with, he had to use his teeth. The knot wasn't tight enough to stem the flow of blood to his amputated fingers, but it had at least bought him some time.

That time was now running out.

Jonas hurried down the darkened country road and ran his good hand over his body, searching for something, anything, that would help stop the bleeding. If only he had some way of cauterizing the wounds. He'd seen the procedure once or twice when accidents happened at sea and an unfortunate crewman was at risk of infection. But he needed fire, and all he had was his pistol and his powder kit.

His pistol…

Jonas froze in his tracks. Yes, it could work.

He stole an uneasy glance over his shoulder. He hadn't heard the howls of the wolves in some time, but they were out there, prowling the darkness and drawing closer. From the timbre of their calls, he'd been able to detect at least two of them on his trail. But wolves were notoriously good at hiding their numbers. He prayed he would have enough time to get this over with as his good hand went to his pocket for the powder kit.

Jonas raised the leather pouch to his mouth, bit off the stopper, and held the sack between his teeth as he sank down to sit in the middle of the road. Next, he reached for the pistol and kept it squeezed between his knees, positioning it so that the barrel faced the sky. Then he carefully retrieved the pouch from his mouth, poured a small charge of powder into the muzzle, and tamped it down with the pistol's ramrod. Returning the pouch to his mouth, he took the pistol in his good hand, cocked the hammer, and tilted his head to pour a pinch of powder on the flashpan.

When the pistol was loaded and ready to fire, Jonas hesitated until a chilling howl from somewhere nearby gave him a start. The wolves were much closer than he had expected. His time was running short.

He had to do it now.

Jonas aimed the pistol into the darkness and grit his teeth. This was going to hurt like hell.

With a squeeze of the trigger, the pistol erupted in an explosion of flame and smoke. At the same instant, Jonas pressed the bloody stump of his missing ring finger to the super-heated iron of the muzzle.

The pain was incapacitating. The smell of his own searing flesh rose to Jonas's nostrils, and he struggled to fight off a rush of nausea. Only seconds passed, but they seemed like hours before the gun-barrel cooled. At last, he withdrew his hand and examined the wound in the moonlight. The flesh was scorched and damaged forever, but it had worked. The gaping hole where his missing finger had been was seared shut.

Jonas reloaded the gun with a shuddering breath. Now that he knew what was coming, his second finger would be even worse. With the pistol loaded, he paused, dreading what would come next and gathering his courage. Then he fired.

This time, he didn't bother trying to stifle his scream. The earsplitting roar of the blast echoed through the night. If the wolves weren't immediately drawn to it, his cry wouldn't make any difference. He opened his mouth and let the agony out as the red-hot iron seared his flesh.

Jonas gasped for air and forced himself to steel his nerves. The wolves could descend on him at any moment, but he had to risk reloading the pistol one more time. This time, he fumbled in his pocket for a lead ball, dropped it down the barrel, and tamped it down into the powder. When the wolves did catch up to him, he would at least have one shot ready to fire.

And if there *were* only two of the beasts, he'd be damn sure only one remained to tear him to pieces.

Chapter 39

Alice's boat drifted listlessly through the gloom. The night was perfectly still. There was nothing but murky fog in all directions. The gentle lapping of the water at the boat's decaying hull provided the only sound.

Alice had spent countless minutes wasting her energy rowing until she realized it was useless. The gentle current had carried her downstream into what had grown into a wide river. Adrift in the endless fog, she could see nothing of the shore. Finally, she had given up trying.

She now lay motionless on the bottom of the boat, clinging to the oar, heedless of the cold puddle that sloshed around her. With her head propped on the gunwale, she remained content to float with the current. She trembled with cold and shock as she gazed across the dark water with a dull, unseeing stare until something roused her from her daze. Her eyes fluttered to life, and she raised her head to get a better look.

On the horizon, perhaps a hundred yards away, she made out the dark outline of trees along the shoreline. The fog was dissipating.

Alice gripped the oar with her shaking hands, slipped it into the water, and paddled. The old boat creaked and rocked as it pushed forward, sending ripples out before it as it cut through the water. The silhouettes of the trees grew darker as she drifted nearer, their shapes along the shore becoming more pronounced.

Alice took heart as she worked the oar and rowed toward land. Maybe it wasn't too late. Maybe she would find a way out of this after all.

The boat slid to a sudden halt.

Alice's stomach twisted with dread as she drew the oar back into the boat and sat motionless. Why had the boat stopped? She looked at the shoreline. It was only fifty yards away now, but the distance across the expanse seemed to stretch forever. She let the oar sink back into the water, scanning the dark depths nervously as she tried another cautious stroke. The paddle skipped and splashed through the water, but the boat still wouldn't budge. Dead in the water, she remained still and listened to the night, certain that something was about to happen.

Silence.

Alice shook all over as she bent her head over the side of the boat to peer into the water, searching for whatever had caught the hull and was holding it in place. All she found was a deep, murky blackness. The hull had to have run up against a rock.

Alice clutched the oar in her trembling hands and crawled over the bench to the prow of the boat. It swayed beneath her and she fought for balance as she lowered the oar into the water, searching for the rock. She couldn't tell how deep the river was. If it was shallow enough, a fallen tree could have snagged the boat.

The oar met nothing but deep water.

Alice kept her eyes fixed on the murky depths, expecting something to rush up at her at any second as she probed even deeper. Her hands slid to the very tip of the oar as she plunged it down, submerging it for its entire length. She still couldn't find the bottom. It lay somewhere beyond the reach of the seven-foot oar. She drew it back into the boat with a frustrated sigh.

Something wrenched it out of her hands.

Alice yelped as an unseen thing lurking in the watery depths ripped away the oar. Without thinking, she panicked and shot to her feet. The boat rocked perilously, and she lost her balance. She pitched to the side and fell in a heap onto the boat's bottom, her head narrowly missing one of the iron oarlocks.

For a long, tense moment she remained there, motionless, waiting with bated breath.

Nothing happened.

The boat steadied itself as Alice rose to her knees and peered into the water, waiting for whatever horror was down there to rush up and face her. Instead, the ripples rolling across the surface subsided. The night resumed its stillness.

Alice drew a breath, her heart pounding in her ears.

Something scratched at the hull of the boat.

Alice shrieked as something else raked at the hull—harder, angrier. The boat lurched with a sudden jolt that sent her reeling. She wobbled, struggling to maintain her balance as the boat rocked from side to side. Terrified, she looked toward the shore and gauged the distance. It would be a long, cold swim, but it might be her only choice.

Another jolt rocked the boat.

This time, the hull rolled dangerously on its side and the gunwale rose into the air. The rowboat was capsizing.

Alice had one last fearful look at the dark water before she splashed into its freezing current. The cold constricted her chest and stole the breath from her lungs as she plunged through the surface. Then she was kicking and flailing as she swam madly for shore. She was dimly aware of a terrible crashing sound behind her, like wood splintering and being torn asunder. Not looking back, she cut through the water with desperate abandon, waiting for when the hands would reach up to drag her down.

The shore drew nearer…

Ten yards…

Five yards…

Alice's feet found the shallow ground beneath her. Her heel scraped across a sharp rock, spilling blood into the icy water. She choked and gasped for air as she scrambled onto the grassy bank and collapsed to her hands and knees among the reeds and wildflowers. When she found the courage to look back over her shoulder, all that remained of the boat were bits of wreckage floating on the dark surface of the stream.

Exhausted and sputtering, Alice sank to rest on her side and took in her surroundings. She was on the edge of a lonely track of dirt that wound along the water's edge. Judging from the overgrown weeds and grass spouting from the muddy ruts, no one had used this road in a very long time.

Alice lay back and closed her eyes, willing her heart to calm its relentless pounding. When she opened her eyes again, she was looking at the sky.

The night was no longer black. It was a deep indigo blue.

Dawn was approaching.

Lying there, wet and shivering in the night, Alice knew she couldn't go on any longer. She didn't have it in her. It was too much—the cold, the pain, the fear, the loss—all of it was too much to bear. She would die out here. All hope of finding her daughter left her. She wouldn't even be able to save herself. She curled into a ball on the wet ground, wrapped her arms around her legs, and wept miserably.

"Abigail… I'm sorry… I didn't know…"

The echoes of her voice weren't the only ones that carried through the night.

Alice's tears froze on her cheeks as the angry shouts and cries of living people came to her from somewhere far in the distance. They were almost inaudible as they drifted on the breeze, but Alice recognized them at once. They were the sounds of a large crowd—the distinct voice of a mob.

Alice staggered to her knees and turned to where the old road vanished into darkness. A warm glow had risen on the horizon. There was a faint and flickering orange in the sky that silhouetted the trees and turned them into jagged rows of black teeth. A thick trail of smoke drifted into the air far beyond them, obscuring the moon.

Alice suddenly knew where she was. The stream had carried her from the lake and pushed her downstream into the North River—the same river that passed right by Salem on its way to the Atlantic.

Alice was somewhere on the outskirts of town, close

enough to walk, to hear its voices.

Salem was nearby. And somewhere in town, a fire was burning.

Chapter 40

A crowd gathered around the statue of Roger Conant on Salem Common. An enormous bonfire blazing on the open field crackled and sent embers sparkling into the air. It bathed the grim faces of the townspeople in the heavy shadows of its orange glow. There were perhaps a hundred of them, maybe more. They had come from all over: men and women drawn from the safety of their homes to witness their fears and anxieties coming to an end.

Before them was Sarah Bridges.

They had strung her to the scaffolding that still surrounded the giant monument to the town's founder. The thick rope of a pulley looped around her long, white neck was pulled taut in a makeshift noose. Her slender hands were bound behind her back with a leather thong cinched so tight it cut deep into her flesh. They stacked a giant pile of stones beneath her feet to support her and keep her from strangling… for now.

Magistrate Holm stood at the center of the throng. He gazed up at Sarah with eyes that were every bit as cold and hard as the stones piled beneath her feet. This was the woman who had defied his justice, who had tormented his townsfolk, who had sent her spirits to steal their children from their very beds. Now he had her at his mercy and the whole town would have the chance to make her pay for her crimes.

"Sarah Bridges," he intoned, his voice laden with wrath and fury, "known to Salem as the witch of Gallows Hill; cast out from this good town for your unholy ways. I give you this chance to confess and redeem your soul. What have you done with our children?"

An expectant hush fell over the onlookers.

Sarah said nothing. Instead, she stared past them into the raging bonfire. Her blue eyes glittered like chips of ice that somehow resisted even the warm glow of the flames.

"You'll torment this town no more!" Holm thundered. "Tell me now! Where are our children?"

Again, Sarah remained silent.

Holm stood glaring at her, the thick cords of his neck quivering with rage. Even now, the hateful woman continued to defy him, to embarrass him in front of his citizens.

"Remove a stone," he commanded.

A man stepped forward and laid his hands on one of the larger rocks stacked beneath Sarah's bare feet. Holm noted with some satisfaction that it was the same young father who had first come to them on the Common. He watched as the man hauled the stone from the pile and rolled it away with a dull *thud*. There was a hint of pleasure on the young man's face as he stepped back into the crowd and leveled his eyes at the woman teetering atop the remaining pile.

"I ask you again, Sarah Bridges. What have you done with our children?" Holm demanded.

When Sarah again refused to answer, the magistrate's blood rose to a boil in his veins. He felt an irresistible urge to strike her, to force her to look at him and feel the fear she'd subjected them all to. Instead, he nodded to the pile again.

Another man—one of Dennard's soldiers—advanced to remove the second stone. "That one's for Henry Maddock," he spat as Sarah's bare toes stretched and strained to maintain contact with the pile.

"What have you done with Ann Barstow?" Holm roared. His pale eyes blazed in the firelight and his voice shook with a fanatical tremor. "God damn you, woman! Where are the children? Where is Elizabeth Cole? Where is Joseph Meade?"

Just then, there was a low murmur and a slight commotion as the crowd parted. Alice spilled from their midst.

She was wet and shivering, wearing nothing but the filthy remains of her flannel nightgown. Her blond hair was a knotted tangle and her pale skin was bruised and bleeding in countless places. But what most caught Holm's eye was the horrific handprint stamped across her throat.

Alice emerged from the throng and gasped in horror at the sight of Sarah Bridges dangling from the scaffold. *This couldn't be possible!* She spun around, searching the crowd and recognizing dozens of faces. The Ingersolls, their servant girl, Sheriff Feake, Jonas's friend Pike; all stood mute, watching the grim proceedings.

Then Alice found another familiar face.

"Mr. Emmons!" Alice scrambled to where the old man stood at the center of the circle. "We must stop these men!"

"Mrs. Jacobs?" Benjamin's gaze fell on her as if he'd awakened from a dream. "Where have you been?"

"Giles Dicer is dead. Murdered, as was my husband. Please, we must stop these men! This woman has done nothing wrong. She may be the only chance our children have!"

The old man's face darkened into a grim frown. "Forgive me, Mrs. Jacobs," he said, lowering his eyes and shaking his gray head. "My daughter could not bear the loss of another child. I had no choice…"

Alice followed his gaze down to where her iron talisman sat in the old man's open palm.

It all became very clear. Alice's face tightened with a look of undisguised contempt as she snatched the talisman from Benjamin's grip and turned her back on him. She dashed to Sarah's side before anyone could stop her.

"Sarah, you must tell me what you know," she pleaded. "You had a mind to help me. I know you did. It's Gallows Hill, isn't it? *That's* where the children are; the last resting place of Rebecca Hale. That's where she took them. Please… tell me how to find Gallows Hill!"

"Madam, I advise you to step back," Magistrate Holm boomed from behind her. "This woman's night of terror has come to an end."

Alice whirled on him. "This woman may be the only person standing between my daughter and the grave!"

Holm's voice became a low and threatening growl. "Stand aside, I say."

Alice ignored him and turned to face the crowd. "It was the ghost of Rebecca Hale who stole your children! She has claimed them as her own, one for each of the seven that were taken from her a century ago. Sarah Bridges had no hand in any of this! This woman is innocent!"

"Who are *you* to say who is innocent?" Holm snarled. "For a year now, we have witnessed her awful deeds with our own eyes. *We* will decide her fate."

"And who are you to say she is guilty?" Alice cried. "I say she is innocent even though my own daughter has been taken!"

"Then you are deceived by her cunning! This woman *will* answer to our justice!" Holm spun around. "Sarah Bridges, I give you this last chance. Do not test my resolve, nor the limits of my mercy. Tell me now, what have you done with our children?"

Sarah remained silent, her frigid eyes lost in the blazing pyre. Then—very slowly—those eyes fell on the man who stood before her. She spoke to him for the first time in a low and hollow voice. "You will reap what you have sown."

A silence fell over them all. Holm glared at her, the heat of his rage rivaling that of the bonfire. His hand slashed through the air with one swift motion, and they hauled the last stone away.

Sarah's eyes flew to a hideous size and bulged from their sockets as her tenuous contact with the pile was broken. She choked and gasped, hanging by her neck and flailing at the end of the rope.

"*No!*" Alice lunged for her, but a powerful hand shot out to hold her back. She swung her elbow around hard and felt something fleshy squish and crack as it made contact. There was a muffled, pain-filled grunt, and then she was free.

She leapt to Sarah's side and wrapped her arms around the woman's waist in a vain attempt to lift her and keep her from strangling. But Sarah was too tall and Alice had too little strength left.

"Will no one help me release this woman?" Alice cried.

No one moved.

"Have you people no reason? If she dies, her secrets die with her!"

A choked gasp escaped Sarah's gaping mouth.

Alice looked up and found Sarah's icy blue eyes staring down at her. The woman's cold, slender hand found hers and tightened on it. "Please, Sarah…" Alice's pleas were low and soft as she realized there was no saving the poor woman. "For the sake of my daughter's life, tell me how to find Gallows Hill."

Sarah's lips twitched as if she meant to speak. Alice leaned closer and strained to hear two words carried by a tortured whisper. "The horse…"

Sarah's last breath passed through her lips. Her body ceased to writhe and went terribly still. An ugly silence fell upon the crowd as the woman's body hung by the rope fixed around her neck. No one moved until a series of sickening *cracks!* shot through the air as the vertebrae in Sarah's spine snapped apart one by one, pulled down by the dead weight of her lifeless corpse.

Alice let the woman's hand fall from hers. She rose and turned to the thunder-stricken bystanders. "Our children are lost. A century of horrors has taught you nothing. This town needs no curse to find its downfall."

Alice turned her back on the gruesome sight and pressed her way through the crowd to the bonfire. A glance at the ever-brightening sky revealed the sunrise was only an hour away, perhaps even less.

She had failed, and this was how it ended.

An abrupt shift in the breeze engulfed her in a cloud of fire smoke. Alice felt its acrid stench clinging to her, filling her nose, stinging her eyes. She winced and blinked and looked away.

Not thirty yards from her was a massive black stallion.

Alice blinked again. A young soldier stood next to the horse, gripping the reins and guarding it with a loaded musket. Alice recognized the animal immediately. It was the same one she had encountered in the Northern Woods—Jonas's stallion.

Holm and the soldiers must have captured the horse when they had gone to seize Sarah Bridges under the protection of her talisman. A flood of images filled Alice's mind as she gazed at the enormous animal. She remembered the ritual she had witnessed in Sarah's sacred grove; the strange markings the woman had painted in blood on the stallion's legs. She heard Sarah's last choked words echoing in her head: *The horse…*

The stallion was the key. It knew the way to Gallows Hill.

Alice knew what she had to do.

With a sudden burst of movement, she charged the unsuspecting guard.

Alice lowered her shoulder and aimed for the soft, exposed space where his stomach met his ribcage. Her attack was so sudden, so unexpected, she caught the soldier by surprise and sent him sprawling to the ground. He lay there winded, gasping and wheezing and trying to suck air into his lungs.

Alice was up on the horse's back in a flash. She heard an eruption of cries and shouts behind her. There was the roar of a rifle shot and then she was gone, charging through the deserted streets, racing the sunrise toward the edge of town.

Toward Gallows Hill.

Chapter 41

Magistrate Holm kept his sharp eyes on the woman as he spurred his thundering horse down the old Boston Road. Somewhere behind him, Captain Dennard and a private named Thripp struggled to keep up with Eclipse's blistering pace. They were falling behind, but Holm paid them no attention. A singular, all-encompassing sense of purpose possessed his mind. He has to stop the woman before she escaped.

It was now the blue hour before sunrise. Holm could see the dark and twisted shapes of apple trees flying by in the dusky light as he charged past the orchards. An early morning mist was just rising from the lonely fields. By now, it was obvious the woman headed for the Northern Woods. If she made it into their thick reaches, they might never find her again.

Holm couldn't let that happen. He had underestimated her back at the Common and she had taken him by surprise. He wouldn't allow himself to make that mistake again.

Holm squinted and gauged the distance to where Alice was

racing ahead of him. He'd been gaining on her since they had hit the open stretch of road, but she was still at least a hundred yards away. She would be at the crossroads within a few minutes. Holm could already see the distinct shape of the giant crucifix looming against the blue-black sky. He could never catch her before she reached the trees. She was too far ahead and her stallion was too powerful, too fast. He would have to do something else to stop her.

He unslung his musket from around his shoulder.

The horse charged along at breakneck speed while Holm waited for his shot. He cursed himself for not having seen the conspiracy earlier. He'd been confused and blinded by his experience in the Northern Woods, but now that the foul depths of the plot were laid bare, it all made sense to him. Sarah Bridges hadn't acted alone; she'd had help. This stranger begged for Bridges' life back at the Common. He should have known the woman was evil the moment he had seen the devil's mark branded across her throat.

Holm steadied himself in his saddle and raised his musket to his shoulder. He had only seconds to spare now. This was his only chance; if he didn't take the shot, he would lose her forever. Taking down a moving target from horseback was never easy, but Holm had done it before. He'd already made one woman pay for her crimes. It was time to punish the other.

He squeezed the trigger.

There was a roaring explosion of sparks and smoke, and the woman lurched in her saddle. Even in the dim blue light, Holm knew he'd hit his target.

The stallion vanished into the black mouth of the woods,

taking the woman's limp form with it. But Holm was no longer worried. He'd gotten what he had come for. If his shot hadn't been fatal, it soon would be. The only thing left was to drag the woman's body back with him.

With a surging sense of triumph, Holm snapped the reins and sped Eclipse past the crossroads toward the spot where the stallion had disappeared. It didn't matter that he no longer held the protective talisman. Now that Sarah Bridges was dead, her cursed guardians wouldn't be able to stop him. The narrow cleft of the old animal trail opened before him as he charged for it and thundered into the woods.

Holm's horse was suddenly dragged to a shuddering halt with a terror-stricken squeal and a furious pounding of hooves. The magistrate had no time to react. He pitched from his saddle, launched forward by the momentum of his blistering charge. He had the briefest sensation of weightlessness as he sailed through the air, somersaulting head over heels. Then a blinding pain exploded from everywhere at once as he smashed into the thick trunk of a massive hemlock.

There was nothing but white and a vague sense that something was terribly wrong. When Holm's thoughts returned, he had the strange impression he was looking back at the crossroads from a height that wasn't his own, as if he were somehow taller than he was supposed to be. He glanced down and saw his feet dangling above the ground. An instant passed in confusion as he wondered how it was possible.

Then he saw the bloody tree limb protruding from his stomach.

Holm became aware of a high-pitched squealing as he

hung impaled to the tree. His gaze fell to the ground in time to see his horse's head disappearing beneath the soil, dragged under by dozens of skeletal hands. The huge whites of the animal's eyes rolled with terror before they were gone and there was nothing.

Holm's gaze went up. Dennard and Thripp had halted at the crossroads and were gaping at him. He stretched a trembling hand out to them, imploring them for help. Neither man moved. Holm saw the terror in their faces. They would never cross the threshold of the cursed woods.

"Treasonous cowards," he spat with disgust. There was a liquid gurgle in his voice and a bubble of blood spewed from his mouth, along with his words. "I'll see you both shackled in the stocks when this is over."

Holm couldn't see the ghostly hands materializing from the darkness behind him.

He had enough time to wonder why the soldiers were backpedalling, their faces twisting with sheer terror. Then he felt the hands upon him—tearing at him—and his screams came loud and hard. One hand clamped on his face and yanked it to the side, digging in nails and ripping the flesh from the bone. Another grasped his wrist and wrenched his arm loose from its socket with a sickening *snap!* A warm rush coursed down his legs as they split his stomach open, spilling his insides to the ground at his feet.

Holm saw a fathomless darkness closing in. For the first time in many, many years, he no longer cared about the fate of his town.

Chapter 42

Alice could hear Holm's terrible screams resounding through the trees behind her. They didn't last for long. Within seconds, the echoes receded into the distance and the silence of the woods descended on her.

Somewhere in her hazy thoughts, she was aware that she was alone, clinging to the stallion as it sped along the murky paths. Holm's shot had caught her in the right shoulder, shattering the blade and splintering two ribs as the ball ripped through her. The impact had slammed her forward on the horse's back and her world had gone blank. She had no memory of anything else until the sound of the magistrate's shrieks had roused her from oblivion.

Now Alice sat slumped in the saddle, her right arm dangling at her side. It was all she could do to remain upright as the stallion plunged deeper into the heart of the woods.

The narrow trail twisted and turned through the dense forest. It joined something vaguely like an ancient road before diving back into the woods and melting into a vast labyrinth of tangled trails. The stallion seemed to move forward by instinct. It sensed every twist and turn without looking, as if it knew the precise number of strides until the next change in direction.

Alice was barely aware of her surroundings whipping by as she fought to maintain consciousness. There was a strange absence of pain. An occasional flash of agony would sometimes shoot from her shoulder whenever she was jolted by the horse's abrupt turns. Otherwise, there was only a dull, uncomfortable throb that she could somehow feel in her teeth. A crimson stain was spreading on her nightgown; there was too much blood oozing from the gaping wound.

Alice didn't know if she would survive it and she no longer cared. All she wanted now was to find Abigail before the sunrise, to see her daughter one more time and say her last goodbye. Even here, deep in the Northern Woods, she could see the moon had vanished below the horizon. Through the dense canopy of trees, she caught sight of the sky growing a lighter shade of blue with each passing minute. Soon the sun would rise and this nightmare would come to an end.

The stallion thundered through a shallow brook. From the corner of her eye, Alice glimpsed the green remains of an old bridge rotting in the forest. There was the steady rush of moving water somewhere to her right as the trail rose. The horse was charging up the steep incline of a rocky hill now.

Alice swayed in the saddle and clutched at the reins to steady herself. Ahead, an indigo swath of sky opened above a hollow in the trees. The stallion crested the rise, emerged from the woods, and came to a stop.

Alice found herself in a small, perfectly round grove. The skeletal remains of an immense oak tree rose at its center. It stood silhouetted against the morning sky like an unholy abomination, its dead limbs twisted and warped like giant talons stretching up from the pit of Hell. Alice shuddered at the sight of it and went cold all over.

She had seen this tree before in her visions. It was the old gallows.

And there before it stood a small girl in a white nightgown.

"Abigail!" Alice's cry rang across the hollow as she leaped from the stallion and rushed to take her daughter in her arms. "Oh God, Abby… Are you alright? Are you hurt?"

She fell to her knees and crushed Abigail to her breast, too overcome with emotion to notice the agony shooting from her devastated shoulder. "Where are the others? Are they safe?"

"They're here, Alice. They're all around you."

Alice clutched her daughter and glanced at her surroundings, wondering why she hadn't noticed before. Six long mounds of dirt radiated from the ancient gallows like the arms of a star. Alice saw them and knew them for what they were: graves.

Nearby, the gaping hole of a seventh grave lay waiting to be filled.

"I've found them, Alice."

A hot flood of tears spilled down Alice's cheeks as she wrapped Abigail tighter in her arms. "Abigail, I am your mother. Why do you call me Alice?"

"Why do you call me *Abigail*?"

Alice's blood turned to ice in her veins. This wasn't right. She had been too relieved to notice it before, but now she heard it clearly: there was something wrong with her daughter's voice. It was dry and hollow, like a whisper drifting through a keyhole in Hell's rusty gates.

Alice felt a horrible sickness in her gut as she released herself from the child's arms and pulled away, eyeing the girl warily. Something was wrong. Something was terribly, terribly wrong. This wasn't her daughter. It was something *else*.

"Why didn't you protect her, Alice?" the girl's hollow voice intoned. "Why didn't you believe? You could have taken her away from here, away from *us*."

The girl took a step toward her, gliding out from under the shadow of the gallows tree. Alice's stomach turned when she got her first good look at the child's face. It looked like Abigail, but her skin was ashen and cold. Livid stains ringed her dull gray eyes. It wasn't the face of a living girl; it was the face of a corpse.

"Stay away from me!" Alice recoiled and scrambled back across the ground.

The thing that was Abigail continued her steady advance. "Now you will suffer, Alice. Your daughter is in here, with us. And with the dawn, we must die again."

In that one terrible instant, Alice understood it all with horrifying clarity. This wasn't her daughter speaking; it was the wrathful spirits of Rebecca Hale and her dead children. "No! Please, spare my daughter!"

"It is too late."

"*Please!*" Alice fell to her knees. "Show the mercy that they denied you. If you must take life to satisfy your vengeance, then I beg you to take mine for my daughter's!"

"Your blood means nothing to us."

"Then what of the blood of my unborn child?" Alice cried.

The possessed child froze.

"The blood of my husband will not end with Abigail," Alice said. "I am with child. The blood of Judge Hathorne flows through the veins of the baby growing in my womb."

The girl's gray eyes narrowed with suspicion. "Impossible. You lie."

"Can you be so sure?" Alice felt cold and breathless as the last of her blood drained from her wound. She was dying, and if she had any hope of saving Abigail—of getting the spirits to release her daughter's body before the sun rose—she would have to do it now.

"All Hallows' Eve is drawing to an end. Dawn is nearly upon us and you've only minutes to discover the truth. Search my body, see if I am indeed with child, if Hathorne's blood will live on."

The ghastly child stood staring at her for a moment before her tiny face twisted with rage and she shrieked with an impossible voice. The awesome force of it sent a blast of wind across the hollow in all directions. Like the pressure-wave of an explosion, it knocked Alice to the ground. Sprawled in the dirt, she felt a terrible cold stealing over her and saw death's shadow sneaking into the corners of her eyes.

If only she could fight it off for just a few more seconds…

The child's hellish shriek reached unnatural proportions. She raised her head and a thick white mist burst from her gaping mouth, streaming into the sky and soaring into the air.

Alice had a vague impression of the mist merging into a swirling mass, coiling about itself, shaping itself into the sinister form of Rebecca Hale. The enormous apparition hovered in the air, staring down at her, its swirling eyes filled with hatred. The last of the mist poured from the girl's mouth and she suddenly went silent. Alice saw her daughter blink with bewilderment and glance around.

Released from the spirits' dreadful enchantment, Abigail's blue eyes fell on Alice and looked at her in confusion. Her face was flush and adorable, her voice weak and brittle but once more her own. "Mother?" she whispered.

Tears filled Alice's eyes. "Abigail… Carve a pumpkin for me."

The mist slammed into her.

Chapter 43

Something black and venomous coursed through Alice as the spectral mist invaded her body. She felt it moving everywhere, spreading out—her veins, her flesh, her eyes, her skin—scouring every part of her for the truth, for the baby growing inside of her. She tried to scream, but nothing came out when she opened her mouth. The spirits assaulted her thoughts and pushed images into her mind, horrible impressions remembered from a life that wasn't her own.

She was still standing at the center of the hollow, except now something was different. A noose hung from one of the oak's heavy limbs. She heard voices behind her and spun around.

Edgar Fisk was leading Rebecca Hale into the clearing.

Rebecca's cracked lips moved in quiet prayer as Fisk shoved her onward toward the gallows. The jailor stopped in his tracks. The condemned woman collapsed to the ground before him, weeping wretchedly.

"Why do we stop?" Sherriff Corwin demanded as he led a scrawny horse from the gloom of the trail. He kept his eyes on Rebecca and drew the nag to a halt beneath the hanging rope.

"She hath spoken the Lord's Prayer," Fisk replied.

"What of it?"

"Reverend Parris hath said that a witch cannot speak the words of the prayer without faltering. And yet—"

"This woman hath done just that." Corwin's bristling eyebrows came together as he looked down at the whimpering woman. Rebecca had just recited the Lord's Prayer flawlessly, something no witch could do.

"Why hath this witch yet been suffered to live?" A commanding voice boomed throughout the clearing.

The men whirled as a massive black stallion materialized from the mist—a horse very much like the one that had led Alice to Gallows Hill. Standing high in the stirrups was a severe man clad in black. A long cape curled from his shoulders as he emerged from the white of the fog like an ink stain rising to the surface of a fine piece of linen. His aging face was long and gaunt and hard as a millstone. His steel-gray hair swept back from a steep widow's peak like smoke blown from a pyre. He glared at the men with eyes as black and cheerless as a starless night as he rode across the clearing.

"Justice Hathorne." Corwin bowed his head.

The spirits roared with rage in Alice's mind as she watched, unseen. As they coursed through her body, exchanging thoughts and memories, she was now the ghost in their world. Her skin burned with their simmering fury as the imposing judge drew nearer.

"Sheriff Corwin, why do you delay your duties?" Hathorne's voice was so deep it seemed bottomless.

"She hath spoken the Lord's Prayer, your honor," Corwin explained with a nervous swallow. "She did it without fault. We heard it with our own ears." The sheriff chose his next words. "Surely the afflicted girls hath made some mistake. This woman cannot be—"

"Guilty?" Hathorne scowled. "Must I remind you that the Prince of Darkness is never more himself than when he appears as an angel of light?" The judge raked them with his blistering eyes. "This woman is guilty of witchcraft. You are both bound to execute your duties."

Hathorne's words carried a sense of absolute finality. Corwin's shoulders slumped with resignation and he nodded once. He motioned for Fisk with a grim frown.

Rebecca screamed as the big man hauled her from the dirt and tossed her onto the old horse's back. She teetered to one side and Corwin stepped forward to keep her from toppling over.

"Withdraw your aid, Sheriff," Hathorne instructed, surveying the scene from high in his saddle. "If the witch be strong enough to torment the children of Salem, then she be strong enough to hold her own."

Corwin did as he was told, leaving Rebecca swaying astride the pitiful horse. Fisk fetched a thick log to stand on and cinched the slipknot of the noose tight around her neck. He was about to drop a worn-out burlap sack over her head when Hathorne raised his bony hand.

"That will not be necessary, Mr. Fisk," the judge said. An icy look flickered across his rigid face. He reached into the folds of his heavy cloak and withdrew a small black bundle. "The woman lived as the devil's bride, so shall she remain in death." He passed the bundle to Fisk. "Let her forever mourn the loss of her immortal soul."

Fisk unraveled the bundle. In his gloved hands was a veil of black lace.

Alice watched with growing horror as the man laid the veil on Rebecca's head. The woman's green eyes focused into a beam of unbridled hate as she glared at Hathorne. Then the veil fell over her face and her eyes were lost forever.

Alice shuddered at the sight of the dreadful figure straddling the ancient horse. Rendered faceless by the awful veil, the shreds of her dress exposing her torn and bloody skin, the poor woman was an image dragged from a harrowing nightmare.

"Rebecca Hale, as High Judge of the tribunal, I give you this last chance to confess and give glory to God." Hathorne declared.

"I give glory to God, but not to gratify the devil," Rebecca's defiant voice flowed from beneath the veil.

"You deny signing your name to the devil's book?"

"If I am guilty of the black arts, then you, Judge Hathorne, may know as well as I."

Hathorne's eyes blazed with the blackest flames. "Then by your blood may you be absolved of your sins. And may God be merciful upon you!"

"If it is my blood you crave, then blood shall you drink until that of my children be repaid!" Rebecca's curse thundered from the depths of the black veil and echoed through the mist.

Fisk struck the old horse with a powerful swing and sent it charging. The noose snapped tight around Rebecca's throat and jerked her from the mare's back, hanging her from the heavy oak limb.

Alice tried to scream, but her voice collapsed in her throat. A sickening torrent swept up from the pit of her stomach as Rebecca's body twitched and convulsed with the last spasms of life.

The thrashing legs went terribly still.

An eerie silence descended on the clearing. In the dreadful aftermath that followed, the hangman's rope stretched and creaked as Rebecca's lifeless body swung from side to side, spinning in slow semi-circles above the leaf-strewn ground.

Judge Hathorne glowered at the veiled corpse dangling before him. "What a sad thing, to see this firebrand of Hell hanging there." With a frown, he spun his massive horse and charged from the clearing, leaving the other men behind. His cape billowed and whipped in the air as he vanished into the mist.

Alice looked on as the men fetched the miserable old horse and followed the judge's trail until they disappeared from sight.

Left alone in the gloom, Rebecca's body swung to a rest and hung motionless from the oak limb like the stone of a broken pendulum. The hollow went still until a shrill cry shattered the silence. A massive crow had perched on a branch in the upper reaches of the old oak. Others joined it, screeching hungrily as they swooped lower to investigate the grim fruit hanging from the gallows tree.

Alice's stomach turned, knowing what would come next, yet powerless to stop it. She watched with a rising sense of revulsion and waited for the inevitable feast to begin.

That was when the air came alive.

It began with the faintest stirring of the leaves. Alice caught them from the corner of her eye, first one, then another, quivering almost imperceptibly. Then the frayed edges of Rebecca's limp black dress trembled, the tattered linen fluttering as if touched by an unseen breath.

Alice felt the soft caress of a delicate breeze brush across her cheek. Another followed—stronger this time—scattering a handful of leaves across the clearing. She turned and what she saw took her breath away.

The mist was gathering itself all around her. It withdrew from the clearing like a wave pulling the surf back from the beach, and took shape on the outskirts, drawing itself together into a thick, roiling mass.

The gentle breezes strengthened, rising and intensifying like the harbingers of a violent storm. Rocked by the winds, the thick limbs of the gallows tree groaned and clattered.

Alice blinked and shielded her eyes as a sudden gust swept a heap of dirt and leaves across the clearing. She lowered her trembling hand and watched with growing dread as the mass of churning mist moved, slowly at first, then picking up speed as it revolved in long, steady loops around the clearing. It circled with the relentless patience of a predator, as if it were alive and had a mind of its own. With each steady revolution, it escalated and whipped itself into a dizzying, whirling fury.

The wind was howling now, picking up leaves and twigs and launching them into the swirling white mass spinning around the hollow.

Alice shielded her eyes from the flying debris as the raging whirlwind closed in on the clearing, growing angrier and more violent as it crept toward the lifeless figure hanging from the gallows tree. For a few seconds, Rebecca's corpse hung in the center of the howling vortex, untouched by the vicious winds, as if suspended in the eye of a churning white hurricane. Then her body came apart.

Rebecca's tattered dress disintegrated into tiny black pieces that whipped and flew away like ashes. Her pale flesh evaporated next, dissolving into twisting tendrils of smoke that twirled and spiraled high into the air before vanishing altogether. The whirlwind coiled its way up the woman's corpse, engulfing it, devouring it, absorbing it. The black veil disintegrated and whirled away like handfuls of black sand hurled into a tornado.

Battered by the blinding wind, Alice glimpsed emerald green eyes glaring back at her. She felt herself withering under Rebecca's baleful stare, overcome by the unfathomable hatred it carried. Seconds later, the face was gone. It evaporated into long coils of twisting smoke, obliterated forever as the terrible cyclone consumed the last of her remains.

In that instant, Rebecca and the mist became one.

An unexpected gust blasted Alice and sent her reeling. She staggered and strained through the tears streaming down her cheeks as she stared at the gallows tree in awe. It was barely visible now, just a vague and twisted shape immersed in the roaring whirlwind. Nothing remained of Rebecca's body. Only an empty noose hung from the oak limb. The frayed rope whipped and thrashed in the wind before it snapped loose and vanished into the vortex.

Suddenly, there was a vicious tightening in Alice's veins. She could feel her blood boiling with the fury of the spirits who coursed through it. *This is it*, she thought. *They've found the truth they were looking for. They've found my baby.*

Another violent blast knocked Alice from her feet and hurled her to the ground. She rolled to her knees, struggling to stand, but a mighty hand seemed to crush her back into the earth. She screamed, but whatever voice she had drowned in the deafening roar of the maelstrom.

An earsplitting *CRAAACK!* shot from the raging chaos, as if the world itself was being torn asunder. Alice stole a glance skyward in time to glimpse the giant oak tree splitting in two. Sprawled in the dirt, she shrank into a ball and shielded her head with her arms, praying that she had bought enough time. Sunrise was only moments away. All she needed was to keep the spirits inside her just a few minutes longer and Abigail would be safe.

With her face buried in the damp leaves, Alice wept as the world came crashing down around her.

Chapter 44

The impact of the mist slamming into her mother knocked Abigail to the ground. She rolled to her knees and screamed like only a child can, watching helplessly as Alice was engulfed in white. There was a concussive boom like the sharp blast of a cannon as the gallows tree cracked in two. Abigail looked up and saw one half of it swooping down to crush her.

Suddenly, there were firm hands sweeping her to safety.

"Don't look!"

Abigail's eyes shot up to find Jonas Hobbes standing over her. The sailor's left arm hung at his side as he buried her in his chest to shield her eyes. His shirt smelled of sweat and blood as Abigail dug her face into it, shutting her senses to the awful scene unfolding before them.

The swirling white vortex lifted Alice from her feet. Jonas squinted against the raging winds and watched as her inert body floated into the air with her back arched and eyes closed. She hung suspended for a moment with her limbs dangling and her mouth stretched open to a grotesque size.

Then she vanished into the white depths.

An instant later, it was over.

Alice was gone.

Jonas trembled in the dirt and pressed Abigail tighter against his body. The spectral mist twisted in the air and turned on the girl. Jonas sensed its terrible desire to claim the child, to drive itself back into her body. He shielded Abigail with his good arm as they scrambled backward.

The fog loomed over them in a murky cloud. It would surge at any second, striking with the blinding speed of a rattlesnake. The mist drew itself together, coalescing into the shifting, vaporous shapes of children. They coiled and writhed in the air, their ghastly voices filling the hollow, screaming with the unrestrained fury of a hundred years of torment.

Jonas cringed as the shrieks hollowed a chasm deep inside him and filled it with despair. Something gave way within him as all hope deserted him.

The mist reared up, ready to release its terrible wrath.

Jonas clutched Abigail tighter and closed his eyes, waiting for it all to come to a sudden end.

In that instant, the sun broke over the horizon.

A ray of light burst through the foliage and spilled across the hollow. Its ghostly beam danced with evanescence as it burned through the mist, evaporating it and sending it steaming away into nothingness. The hollow erupted with raging howls as the shapes of the children writhed in pain, seared by the daylight. The mist shrank into itself like a wounded animal as it soared into the air.

Shrieking…

Swirling…

Evaporating…

And then it was gone.

Silence descended on the hollow.

For long, long moments, there was nothing but an uneasy quiet as the sun inched above the treetops. Nothing moved. The forest, the leaves, the morning breeze—all stood frozen in a moment of perfect calm.

Abigail wept softly as she clung to Jonas. He cradled her in his arm, pressed his cheek to her head, and let her cry and cry and cry. Minutes passed until he had the sudden sensation that they were no longer alone. He became aware of a presence all around them, hovering over them.

There, bathed in sunlight, stood six other children.

His daughter was among them.

"Emily…" Jonas's voice trembled with tears as he folded his daughter into his arms with Abigail. "'Tis alright, little one. It's over."

Epilogue

"The sacrifice Alice Jacobs made twenty years ago has not been forgotten by the people of Salem," the schoolteacher said from the front of her class. "Nor would it be in vain. Invoked by a mother's loss, a mother's love had lifted the curse. In giving her own life to save her daughter's, Alice fulfilled the wish that was denied Rebecca Hale all those years ago and the woman's spirit could rest in peace."

The class of young boys waited, enthralled, as the teacher sipped from the glass of water she always kept on her desk during story time. She had been telling this story all her life. Now that she was nearing the end, she always felt a mixture of sadness and relief that it was nearly over.

"Jonas Hobbes raised Abigail as if she were his own child and the people of Salem learned to put their terrible past behind them. But every year, on All Hallows' Eve, they recall the events of that tragic night. Be it curled by the fireside or gathered among the glowing lanterns of the Harvest Moon Ball, the people of Salem whisper the tale of Alice Jacobs and the ghosts who haunted her."

The end of the teacher's story hung in the air as her students stared at her from their desks. Their eyes were wide and awestruck and their mouths hung open like gaping mouse holes as they gaped in the uncomfortable silence.

CLING! CLING!

The children jumped as a small bell chimed from somewhere beyond the classroom door.

"That will be all for today, class." The teacher chuckled as the school day ended. "Remember, tonight is All Hallows' Eve. Do not forget to leave a treat at your door to ward off evil spirits!"

The children smiled and sniggered among themselves as they gathered their books and filed from the classroom. The teacher watched them go and felt a brief flicker of guilt. Witches? Ghosts? Evil spirits? The boys were putting on brave faces now, but she wondered how many of them would ask their mothers to leave a light burning in their bedrooms when they went to sleep tonight.

Wrapping herself in her shawl and cloak, the young woman left the classroom behind, breezed down a short hallway, and stepped from the schoolhouse into the crisp autumn evening. Twilight had fallen on the cobblestone streets of Boston. Shriveled leaves swirled in the gutters as the schoolteacher made her way through the narrow lanes. Before long, the warm glow of oil lamps filled the windows of the houses that marked her neighborhood. The woman pulled her cloak tighter against the chilly wind as she mounted the steps to her own quaint cottage.

The schoolteacher lived alone. She had never married, although she was undeniably beautiful—striking enough to attract the guilty gawks of many of her students' fathers. She shut the door on the chilly breeze, shrugged off her cloak, and breathed the familiar scents of her home: apple cider, beeswax, cinnamon, spice cake.

Minutes later, the schoolteacher stood holding a lamp in the doorway to a small bedroom. Children's toys filled the shelves, a veritable library of fairy tales and an assortment of dolls of all shapes and sizes.

The woman's eyes fell on one particular doll. The bedroom glowed in the lamplight as she crossed the floor to study it. It was small and wooden and old.

Abigail's poppet.

Next to it stood a faded portrait sketch of the little girl herself. Alice's iron talisman hung from the corner of the old, worn frame. The schoolteacher gazed at both wistfully before turning away and heading downstairs to the parlor. She crossed the room to a large window overlooking the street, set the lamp on the windowsill, and pressed the wick of a stubby candle to its flame. The scent of beeswax rose to meet her, warm and honey-sweet, as the woman placed the candle at the bottom of a large, hollow pumpkin. Her eyes were soft and shining as she positioned the jack-o'-lantern in the window, where it glowed brightly in the falling darkness.

From behind the windowpane, Abigail stared out into the night and breathed a heartfelt whisper. "Come home, Mother."

Author's Note

Thank you, dear reader, for the generous gift of your time and attention. If you enjoyed this book and would like to see more, please consider taking a moment to leave a quick review on Amazon and/or Goodreads. A kind word from a reader like you is one of the best ways you can support independent authors and is very much appreciated.

Until next time, look under the bed, close the closet door, and whatever you do, don't turn around…

The *BOOK OF SHADOWS* series continues in *THE SUICIDE LAKE*

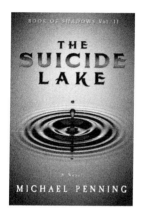

Chapter 1

Abigail Jacobs had only moments to spare before the man across the room shot the boy. How many seconds remained before he pulled the trigger? Ten? Five? Even fewer?

"Lower your pistol, Mr. Tunstall," she cautioned. "I assure you it will do no good."

Robert Tunstall didn't lower the pistol. Instead, he cocked the hammer and squeezed the trigger.

Abigail shouted and lunged for the flintlock, even as the eight-inch iron barrel erupted with a blinding flash and a deafening roar.

The lead bullet rocketed through the boy's forehead like a stone hurled through smoke. The peculiar child remained unscathed as he glared at Tunstall from the center of the fire-lit parlor.

"He... he's a ghost!" Tunstall exclaimed with a note of unhinged panic. Dressed in threadbare wool breeches and a shabby hemp tunic, the boy couldn't have been more than eight or nine. But what arrested Tunstall's attention—what filled his stomach with dread—were the boy's eyes. They were dull and lifeless and made Tunstall think of battlefields and funeral parlors when he saw them.

"Oh, Mr. Tunstall…" Abigail sighed. "I had sincerely hoped you wouldn't provoke it."

"Provoke it?" Tunstall's brown eyes were round and huge with fright as he waved his discharged pistol. "Provoke it to what?"

"Violence."

In a flash, the boy grabbed Tunstall by his exposed forearm. A freezing bolt of pain shot up to his shoulder and he let out a shriek. He sank to one knee and dropped the flintlock to the floor with a clatter. Another scream rose in his throat, but died when the apparition hauled him from his feet and hurled him across the room. Tunstall slammed into the parlor wall, shattering the gilded frame of an oil landscape and destroying a chestnut side-table as he crashed back down to the floor.

The boy's spirit swung around, his small eyes simmering with black malevolence. A low, animal snarl rumbled in his chest and evanescent wisps of mist trailed after him as he floated across the parlor.

Abigail dashed to Tunstall while he groaned and rolled to his knees. "Stay behind me!" she commanded.

The boy stretched out his skinny arms and reached for her, intent on snaring her in his freezing grip.

"Get away from it!" Tunstall cried, clutching at Abigail's sleeve to drag her away.

Abigail shrugged him off. With no time left to spare, she swung her fist and thrust a small iron amulet at the spirit. The boy slid to an abrupt halt at the sudden appearance of the rune-shaped charm. His mouth twisted and dropped open to an impossible size, like a snake unhinging its jaw to consume a larger prey. An ear-piercing wail burst from his gaping maw, carried on a blast of hot wind that smelled of a moldy grave. The floorboards trembled with the ferocity of the ghost's fury. Cracks appeared in the plaster walls.

Abigail remained firm, wielding the talisman and repelling the shrieking spirit. She felt a rush of exhilaration as the boy's figure came apart before her eyes, his ghostly body dissolving into swirling tendrils of white mist. The vaporous mass hung in the air for a moment, coiling and writhing like a serpent ready to strike. Abigail punched the talisman at it and the churning mist recoiled as if wounded before it surged across the parlor and shot up the darkened staircase.

An eerie silence descended. Nothing moved.

Abigail became conscious of the pounding of the blood in her veins as she hung the iron charm around her neck and let it dangle around the collar of her Spencer jacket. Her breathing came fast and hard in the uneasy stillness, and she could feel her muscles vibrating with an exquisite rush of adrenaline.

"How...? How can it be possible?" The bristling, salt-and-pepper tufts of Tunstall's sideburns puffed in and out on his cheeks and a line of sweat trickled from beneath his mass of waxed hair. His shirttail had come loose from his pantaloons and his sleeves were bunched to his elbows, exposing a skeletal handprint the ghost had left emblazoned like a tattoo on his forearm.

Abigail willed herself to maintain her patience. A man's first encounter with the undead was always harrowing, but most of her clients didn't have a loaded flintlock on hand when it happened. The pistol had appeared in Tunstall's hand so unexpectedly that Abigail cursed herself for having let it come to this. If she didn't find some way of getting the man to regain his wits, the consequences could be catastrophic for them both.

"The boy is here because we summoned him, Mr. Tunstall." Abigail's voice was smooth as honey. "You must believe me when I say there is nothing to be afraid of. This is why you engaged my services as a paranaturalist."

"But he—he couldn't be real! It can't be possible!"

"Please be silent," Abigail snapped. Her cool blue eyes remained fixed on the staircase where the sinister mist had retreated. She had bought them some time before the ghost returned, but not much. "'Tis possible because your house is haunted, just as you suspected. Have you ever heard of Venable's Home for Wayward Children, Mr. Tunstall?"

Tunstall's legs wobbled as he staggered to a wingback and sunk into the chair's plush cushion to examine his injured forearm. "Venable's? No, I… I can't say that I have."

Abigail frowned. "That is unfortunate, considering you have been living in it these past seven months. Sixty years ago, this house was an orphanage owned and operated by Mr. Phineas Venable and his wife Winifred. When Phineas died of cholera, Winifred found herself the legal caregiver for a house full of willful orphans. Apparently, the saintly burden was too much for her to bear. On a bitter January night, Winifred set fire to the orphanage with all the children locked inside. This house—*your* house—was built on the foundation of the ruined orphanage."

"How dreadful." Tunstall looked around the parlor as if something horrible was about to spring from the shadows at any moment. "Exactly how many children perished here?"

"Seventeen."

"Seventeen! There are seventeen of those… those *monsters* haunting my home? Dear God!"

There was a dull thump and a low moan from somewhere upstairs.

Abigail swung around. "Is there someone else in the house?"

The color drained from Tunstall's face. "I instructed my wife to remain in our bedchamber…"

Abigail's heart lurched. "I gave you explicit instructions to ensure the house was empty!"

"Well, I didn't bloody well expect to be raising the dead!"

"What exactly *did* you expect, Mr. Tunstall?"

"I don't know! Perhaps some kind of séance?"

Abigail snatched the pistol from the floor, turned her back on Tunstall, and hurried to a low chestnut table at the center of the room. There, something large and round lay concealed within a burlap sack. Abigail cast the sack aside and uncovered an unlit jack-o'-lantern.

Tunstall gave it a dumb look. "A pumpkin?"

Abigail threw him an irritated glance as she withdrew the melted stub of a tallow candle and went to the fireplace to light the wick. "A trap for the ghosts of the children haunting your home. Their last earthly memory was of the scorching pain and blinding light of flames. They are quite literally *afraid* of the light of the afterlife and so they remain here. With this, I intend to show them there is nothing to be frightened of."

The orange glow of the flames rising on the hearth turned Abigail's blond hair to molten amber as she placed the candle at the bottom of the hollow pumpkin and waited for the grinning visage of the jack-o'-lantern to come to life. "We must get your wife with us immediately. Without my protection, she is all too vulnerable."

Tunstall hustled after her as she marched across the room toward the staircase. "Vulnerable to what?" he demanded.

"Possession."

"Possession! What do you—"

Tunstall's voice failed him as he skidded to a halt and gazed up the stairs into the gloom.

Eleanor Tunstall stood on the second floor landing.

She was draped in a shapeless cotton nightgown and appeared as little more than a silhouette looming in the darkness. Her hair was loose and her head hung to one side at an awkward angle, like a marionette with cut strings.

Tunstall peered up at his wife's shadowy form. "Eleanor!" He beckoned her with a wave of his hand. "Eleanor, please come down here."

The shape didn't move.

A sickening feeling took root in Abigail's gut. She was already too late.

"Eleanor, darling…"

Eleanor's jaw dropped open and remained hanging wide as a voice slithered out from within. It wasn't Eleanor's voice; it was that of a very young girl intoning the singsong cadence of a nursery rhyme.

"What are little boys made of? What are little boys made of? Snakes and snails and puppy dogs' tails; such are little boys made of..."

Abigail stepped back from the foot of the stairs and laid a hand on Tunstall's arm. "We must protect the jack-o'-lantern at all costs. The candlewick is charmed; only I may extinguish it. But if the phantoms can somehow destroy the pumpkin..."

Abigail didn't tell him that if the pumpkin were destroyed, the ghosts of the dead children would tear them both limb from limb.

"What are little girls made of? What are little girls made of?" the chilling voice inside Eleanor chanted on. *"Sugar and spice and all things nice; such are little girls made of..."*

The thing that was Eleanor Tunstall hurtled down the staircase without warning. Her bare feet thundered on the wooden planks and she let loose a bloodcurdling scream as she lunged for her husband's throat. Her fingernails dug deep into Tunstall's flesh as they both toppled to the floor.

Abigail grabbed at the talisman slung around her neck, but Eleanor whirled on her and whipped out a clawed hand, ripping away the charm and sending it spinning into a dark corner. With Tunstall pinned beneath her, the possessed woman hissed and stuck her tongue out at Abigail like a grotesque parody of a child. In a flash, she sprang to her feet and launched herself, catching Abigail around the knees and sending them both pitching to the floor. Eleanor's mouth hung loose and wide as she clung to Abigail's ankles. A thick line of drool dripped from her lower lip while the child's voice inside her giggled and howled.

Abigail lost her grip on Tunstall's pistol as she fought to scramble away. Wild with fright, Tunstall wobbled to his feet and went for it. His eyes boggled and rolled in his head as he raised the barrel and cocked the hammer.

"No!" Abigail cried. "You'll kill your wife!"

But Tunstall was too terrified to hear.

Abigail swung around and punched Eleanor just as the pistol roared.

Tunstall's shot missed his reeling wife by inches and slammed into the parlor table, blasting off one of its thick wooden corners with a spray of chips and splinters. For one sickening moment, Abigail saw the jack-o'-lantern teeter onto its side and roll toward the shattered edge of the table. She dove across the floor without thinking. Her hand shot out just in time to get beneath the pumpkin and cushion its impact. Still illuminated by the charmed candle within, it bounced off her palm and tumbled away.

Eleanor pounced, slobbering and giggling and clawing at Abigail all at once. Abigail struggled to get free as she stretched for the jack-o'-lantern, straining to reach it. Her outstretched fingertips brushed against its waxy surface, but it remained maddeningly out of reach.

Somewhere behind her, Tunstall was reloading his pistol. His next shot wouldn't miss; he would murder his own wife.

Abigail summoned all of her strength to tear her leg from Eleanor's grip. She pistoned it back and caught Eleanor hard in the face with a kick that connected with a loud *crack!* The howling, laughing thing inside Eleanor barely reacted as the woman's jaw dislocated from her skull.

Still, there was just enough of a flinch to give her the time she needed.

Ripping herself free of Eleanor's grasp, she lunged across the floor and scooped up the grinning jack-o'-lantern. "Look! The light is harmless! You've nothing to fear!"

Eleanor came to an instant halt. She looked at the flickering light as if she was spellbound as she knelt on the floor.

"Come to it," Abigail coaxed. "Follow the light. Let it guide you from this house and its terrible memories…"

Eleanor didn't move.

Abigail's heart sank and went cold. It would not work. She had made a terrible, terrible mistake.

But just then, a thick white mist poured from Eleanor's sightless eyes. Released from the ghost's influence, the woman collapsed in a heap and Tunstall rushed to her.

Abigail ignored the man's sobs as the mist slithered through the air toward the pumpkin perched on her palm. The candle within flared unnaturally as the mist crawled through the jack-o'-lantern's eyes and mouth. A brilliant orange flame leaped from the pumpkin's lid.

Abigail winced and shielded her eyes.

Then it was over.

When Abigail opened her eyes, she found herself surrounded by a gathering of ghostly children of all ages and sizes. "Come… This light will not harm you."

One by one, each child turned to mist and went into the jack-o'-lantern with a blinding burst of flame. When the last of the children had vanished, Abigail rose to her feet. She reached into the jack-o'-lantern and murmured a strange, sibilant word before snuffing the candle with her fingertips. She then turned to where Robert Tunstall sat, cradling his unconscious wife in his arms.

"Now regarding my fee, Mr. Tunstall…"

READ *THE SUICIDE LAKE*

**She was innocent of witchcraft when they arrested her.
She was guilty when they hanged her.**

A Firebrand of Hell, a short story prequel to the best-selling
Book of Shadows series, is now available absolutely free!

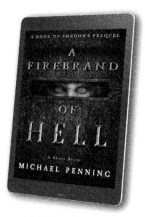

Set one hundred years before the events of *All Hallows Eve,*
find out what drove Rebecca Hale to sell her soul to the devil
on the eve of her hanging.

Visit www.michaelpenning.com to download your free copy!

BOOKS BY MICHAEL PENNING

Michael Penning is a bestselling author and award-winning screenwriter of horror and dark fiction. He has been obsessed with all things dark and spooky since before he could finish his own sack of trick-or-treat candy. When he's not coming up with creative ways to scare the hell out of people, he enjoys traveling, photography, and brewing beer. He lives in Montreal with his wife and daughter. For updates and free giveaways, visit www.michaelpenning.com and follow Michael on social media @michaelpenningauthor.

Printed in Great Britain
by Amazon